DISGUISING DEMONS

A DUSTY KENT MYSTERY

By
Brigid George

Published by Potoroo Press 2018
Nimmo Street, Middle Park
Victoria, Australia, 3206

Disguising Demons is Book #4 in the Dusty Kent Mysteries following *Murder in Murloo*, *A Devious Mind* and *Rippling Red*.

Please note: This book uses British English spelling. Readers who are used to American English might notice a difference in the spelling of some words. For example: centre (instead of center), colour (instead of color), realise (instead of realize), travelled (instead of traveled).

Print Edition

CHAPTER 1

I WAS SPRINTING across the sand, terrified. Dusty was convulsed with laughter. What had started out as a leisurely stroll along the beach had, for me, turned into a surreal experience.

Having arrived at Cape Tribulation early enough to avoid the groups of tourists, we were the only two people enjoying the broad stretch of soft white sand sheltered by the surrounding hills of the Cape. The silence was disturbed only by the whispered swishing of the ocean.

Renowned investigative journalist Dusty Kent and I were in Australia's Far North Queensland to look into the cold case murder of a Buddhist monk. I didn't know then that it would turn out to be the most disturbing case we had investigated.

All thoughts of work were put aside as we meandered along the water's edge watching the foamy wash of waves rippling into shore. Bathed in a sense of peace and warmed by the morning sunshine, I imagined myself on a deserted tropical island as my eyes scanned the ocean all the way to the horizon. People talk about the luck of the Irish; at that moment I knew it to be true. I was one lucky Irishman.

My illusions were abruptly shattered by an encounter of the prehistoric kind. Were you one of those people who had bad dreams about being attacked by a giant velociraptor after seeing *Jurassic Park*? That's exactly what happened to me. In real life!

A feathered velociraptor sauntered out of the palms and mangrove swamps bordering the beach. This huge bird with its long, bright blue neck and prehistoric crest that looked like a horned helmet ambled across the sand and headed straight towards us. I picked up the faint smell of damp feathers and compost. On top of its two scaly legs perched an ostrich-like body covered in glossy black plumage. I stopped walking. No; I froze in fright. My mouth was probably wide open as well. The tiny part of my brain that was still functioning told me this dinosaurian bird couldn't actually be a velociraptor. But what was it? A weird species of Australian emu? The red wattle flopping at its neck reminded me of the aggressive bush turkey I'd encountered in Byron Bay. That bird hadn't liked me either. When it was within a few feet of us, the creature straightened its body, extending its neck to its full height. Jaysis! It was six feet tall.

Dusty clutched my arm in fright, her nails digging into my flesh, and cried, "Shit!"

It was not often I heard Dusty swear but she echoed my sentiments exactly; an entirely appropriate response to the situation.

The avian dinosaur stopped and fixed its large brown eyes on me. Did I say large? Huge brown eyes! To say the beast had an intimidating stare would be an understatement. I could almost believe I'd travelled back in time and foolishly dropped into a world inhabited by giant birds. This was their leader come to dispose of the two human intruders. The creature's blue head darted from side to side as if listening to the emphatic thump of my heart.

"Keep walking!" hissed Dusty, relaxing her grip on my arm to pull me forward. Good advice. Why stand and wait to be attacked?

Without taking my eyes off the feathered dinosaur, I attempted a tentative step forward. The bird inclined its head slightly to one side as if curious about my ability to walk. Together, Dusty and I advanced several steps. Our new companion followed us. The thought of the silent predator behind me methodically placing one clawed foot after the other caused the back of my neck to prickle.

When I stupidly reminded myself Dusty and I were the only two humans on this beach with no mobile phone coverage, my body became so tense I could have been in rigor mortis.

"What is that thing? An ostrich?" For some completely irrational reason I was speaking out of the side of my mouth, lest the creature see my lips move.

"A cassowary. I think she likes you. It must be breeding season."

Dusty was trying to lighten the mood, unaware I was beyond humour.

"You sure it's not a prehistoric monster?"

Dusty dismissed my suggestion with a roll of her eyes. "Cassowaries live in the Queensland rainforests."

Cape Tribulation Beach was hardly a forest. Did that mean this one had come out of its natural habitat especially to 'greet' us?

"Is it a carnivore?"

Dusty chuckled. But I was serious.

Seeing the look on my face, she hastened to reassure me. "I think they eat fruit." She urged me forward again. "Let's keep walking. It might go away."

The bird jerked its head from side to side then pointed its beak toward my feet. What did that mean? Was it about to peck my toes off? I faltered, struggling to make my limbs obey the command I was sure my brain had issued. Dusty encouraged me with another tug of my arm. Gradually, we developed a smooth stride. The cassowary didn't go away; it kept pace with us.

"Tourists would pay top dollar to have such an up-close and personal encounter with a cassowary in the wild. Relax. Enjoy the experience." All right for her to say; she was walking with the ocean on one side, me on the other. I was next to Big Bird, basically acting as a shield.

"Achoo!" Dusty sneezed. The mood changed. The bird charged toward us. To be precise, it charged at me. It didn't appear to notice Dusty.

I ran. But the cassowary seemed to have the speed of a roadrunner. I glanced back briefly to see its long blue neck stretched forward like a racehorse at the finish line. Except *I* was the finish line. And it was gaining on me. Dusty was left standing on the beach while I tried to propel my body forward at high speed. In my mind, my long legs were spinning around so swiftly they looked like two wheels rotating in flawless synchronicity. In reality I probably looked like a lanky penguin trying to master stilts. It was either this or simply the sight of me being chased by a supersonic prehistoric bird that made Dusty burst into laughter. I failed to see anything funny; my thoughts were on survival.

I quickly realised I couldn't outrun my pursuer. An image of myself escaping by scaling the trunk of a tree flashed through my mind. Unfortunately, my path to the trees was blocked by Big Bird. My only chance of escape was in the ocean. I veered off to my left toward the sea. Do these creatures swim, I wondered. Will it follow me into the water? Somehow I managed to remove my sandals while still running, throwing them one at a time over my shoulder hoping to distract the cassowary.

I ran into the ocean in my knee length shorts and cotton shirt, splashing as much as I could while crisscrossing the shallow section in an effort to confuse the creature behind me. When the water was deep enough to give me some protection, I flung myself in, still splashing for all I was worth. For good measure I yelled at the top of my voice. At any moment I expected to see a dark shadow looming over me. I screwed my eyes shut. I didn't want to see death coming.

After a few minutes, realising I was still alive, I dared to open one eye.

At the water's edge, the bird was using its beak to poke at one of my sandals. Then, probably disappointed that the shoe wasn't edible, it seemed to lose interest. I yelled and splashed more loudly in case it was about to direct its attention to me and discover I *was* edible.

The bird turned its back on me, tucking its long head into its feathers, apparently preening itself, before wandering across the sand. I relaxed and stopped my desperate efforts to frighten the creature. When the cassowary reached the mangroves, I decided I was safe.

Then I remembered a lifeguard once warning me about splashing attracting sharks. It was too shallow for sharks here. Right? I stood up as gracefully as I could. That's what the lifeguard had said. *Move gracefully in the water. Noise and erratic movements are likely to attract sharks.* My heart was pounding so loudly sharks could probably pick it up with some sort of sonar ability. My eyes scanned the ocean for the telltale dorsal fin moving from side to side. Nothing. I let out the breath I'd been holding.

Then I remembered the crocodile warning signs we'd passed

along the road. A crocodile expert in Darwin had told us crocs can lurk below the surface of the water and suddenly leap out to attack its prey. It takes less than a second to be grabbed by a crocodile. It took *me* less than a second to get out of the water.

When I was well clear of the ocean, I stopped and looked back. Not a shark or crocodile in sight. Heaving a sigh of relief, I bent over, bracing myself with my hands on my knees to catch my breath.

I must have looked like an elongated drowned rat when, after retrieving my wet sandals, I strode back to Dusty. She erupted in a fresh peal of laughter.

CHAPTER 2

"ALTHOUGH HE DOESN'T know it yet, the monk meditating at the top of the hill will not live long enough to enjoy the warmth of the sun. Unseen in the small clearing, he sits in his yellow robes cross-legged on a straw mat with hands resting in his lap, his leather thongs side by side next to the mat.

"The day has begun the same as every other – with the silent arrival of the dawn and the peaceful retreat of the night. It's still dark. The birds have not yet started chattering to each other across the tall tree tops. Soon the sun will come up over the ocean. Each morning, its rays weave through the trees; their soft strokes brushing the robes of the monk. His fellow monks, in the buildings a little further down the hill on the other side, cannot see him. He is surrounded by bushland except for a narrow section of the cliff face in front of him. Here, a steep drop descends to a rocky ledge far below and beyond that, to the ocean. Though the morning light is soft on the tips of the leaves, the monk's mind is on another plane and he does not notice. Nor does he hear the whisper of the breeze."

Dusty paused for dramatic effect. With her wild auburn curls piled high on her head, she was dressed for the tropics in a white sleeveless top. Her smooth tanned legs were accentuated in a pair of cocoa coloured shorts. The hush of expectation fell between us before she continued. "Into this serene environment comes a dark shadow; the shadow of evil."

Dusty was briefing me for the case we were about to review, adding her own theatrical touches. I'd forgiven her for her display of mirth in light of my perceived life-threatening encounter the day before. Having worked with Dusty on several cases in the past two years, I was used to her sense of humour. In fact, the ability to see the funny side of almost anything was an Australian trait. I had learned early on that being able to laugh at myself was an important pre-requisite for earning the respect of Australians generally. It wasn't a difficult adjustment for me; we don't take ourselves too seriously in Ireland either.

"So he was murdered at dawn?"

"Pretty much. Based on his usual habits and forensic evidence, he was killed between four thirty and six in the morning."

The murder of the monk had not come under Dusty's purview in the usual way. She normally takes on a case in response to an invitation from family members of the victim. However, this time the invitation had been extended by one of the detectives originally assigned to investigate the murder.

Detective Sergeant Jake Feilberg, Dusty explained to me earlier, had been a trainee police officer the same time as she had. Dusty hadn't stuck it out at the Victorian Police Academy. Finding the discipline too oppressive, she'd turned to writing, discovering her niche in investigative journalism. Dusty relished the challenge of solving murder cases the police had been unable to close.

With a one hundred percent success rate, she soon established an impressive reputation. Jake had stayed in the police, establishing a notable reputation of his own within Victoria Police and later in Queensland. I didn't know it then, but the moment Dusty renewed her friendship with Jake Feilberg would be an uncomfortable one for me.

Leaning back in her chair cradling a fresh coconut, Dusty contin-ued. "The monk does not see the killer who sneaks up behind him, smashes his head in with a blunt object and pushes him over the edge of the precipice."

She paused to sip the coconut milk through the straw provided then looked at me, shaking her head in puzzlement. Her storytelling persona fell away. A wistful look crossed her face. "For almost fifteen years he's been living at Sunyarta Sanctuary, a forest community known locally as the monastery. He's quiet, respectful, committed to the community, and spends most of his time in the garden caring for the herbs, fruit trees and vegetables. He refuses to harm any creatures, even in the garden. If he sees a snail or a slug, he picks it up and relocates it. He volunteers to help in the township once a week by reading to residents of a retirement village. Except for when he had tasks to do on behalf of the monks, he didn't hang around the town after finishing his volunteer activities, preferring to go straight back to Sunyarta. Why would anyone want to brutally murder someone like that?"

It'd been a few weeks short of a year since Dusty and I had worked our last case in Darwin. This time we were in Port Douglas within breathing distance of the Coral Sea and about eighty kilometres south of Cape Tribulation Beach where we were yesterday. Port, as it is known to locals, is a coastal resort town home to around 3000 people situated adjacent the Great Barrier Reef and the Daintree Rainforest; both world heritage areas. Apart from what has been termed its 'seductive climate' of hot summers and warm winters, Port Douglas also lays claim to visits by famous people including, in 1996, United States President Bill Clinton and First Lady Hillary Clinton.

"And in a place like this," added Dusty. "It seems too tranquil for a vile act like murder."

Tranquil. Picturesque. Idyllic. Those were all words that could describe Port Douglas. We had begun our morning with a stroll along Four Mile Beach where the waves swished in to meet a sweeping shoreline of firm white sand lined with tall coconut palms. A friendly old local, a tall man with facial hair typical of Santa Claus, informed us Sir Charles Kingsford Smith had landed his plane on this very beach in 1932.

Since I'd arrived in Australia, I'd travelled much of the country on my Triumph Thunderbird motorbike and seen many impressive beaches. This was yet another one that took my breath away. The lazy atmosphere and uninterrupted views soon erased my nervousness about the possibility of another cassowary encounter.

The beach itself was completely free of buildings; just sand, sea and greenery. However, cafes and other businesses lined the esplanade. The cafe we'd chosen allowed glimpses of the ocean through the swaying palms.

"I agree," I said. "Murdered in a monastery in paradise seems gruesomely incongruous."

"Jake thinks the monk was murdered as an act of revenge against all the monks in the Sanctuary and he believes he knows who did it. That's why he's asked me to take the case on. He wants to make sure the killer pays for what he did. Jake was transferred off the case before he had a chance to gather the evidence he needed. Now the case is going cold." Dusty pointed to the forested headland in the distance which overlooked the town. "Sunyarta Sanctuary's up there."

I glanced up at the hill. Among the trees near the peak I caught sight of the rooftops of the Sanctuary buildings. "The monks must have a spectacular view. I bet the developers would like to get their hands on that land."

Dusty screwed up her face at the prospect of the hill cluttered with houses instead of blanketed with forest.

"Is there a precipice?"

Dusty responded to my question with a quizzical look.

"You said the monk was pushed over a precipice," I explained. "Doesn't look like a hillside with cliff edges; it appears completely covered in bush."

"Looks can be deceiving. According to the information Jake sent me, on one side of the summit there's a sheer drop from the top; a rocky cutting in the side of the hill. It's just in front of where the monk used to meditate. There's a clearing in the middle of dense bush where he liked to sit. The only access to it is off a walking track. Other than the path leading out of Sunyarta, the same path the monk would have used, the killer could get to that track two other ways. A public access road on the west side of the hill allows vehicles to reach the Sanctuary. Visitors can drive their cars along that road up to a certain point, park their vehicle and continue the rest of the way along the walking track."

"So the killer might have used the public access road?"

Dusty negated my suggestion with a toss of her head. "I think it would be too risky. A few houses have been built on land not owned by the monks lower down on that side of the hill. Driving up there early in the morning would definitely have attracted attention."

I wasn't ready to let go of my theory. "The killer might have dressed in black and walked up."

"Yep. Less chance of being detected that way. He could stick to the edge of the road and use the trees for cover. But he would have risked setting off remote lighting the residents almost certainly have installed around their properties."

"Right."

"He'd be more likely to use the bush track on the other side of the hill." Dusty pointed to the side of the hill closest to the beach. "There's more cover there and no residences." She cast a thoughtful glance in the direction of the Sanctuary buildings. "Unless the killer was a monk."

I could see that as a possibility. My mother used to say convents 'full of women with raging hormones and repressed emotions' were 'hotbeds of seething passions and spiteful jealousy'. A monastery full of men would be no different.

"Another monk could have even followed our victim out of the Sanctuary," I suggested.

"Possible. Whoever the killer was and whichever path he used, once he reached the top he'd have crept along the walking track…"

"Then snuck up behind the monk through the forested area surrounding the clearing."

Dusty nodded. "A killer who was able to walk quietly in the bush."

CHAPTER 3

G LANCING DOWN AT her notes, Dusty sighed. "The poor man had no family."

Her expression reflected empathy. She might have been thinking of the similarity to her own situation. Dusty has no siblings, her father passed away when she was fourteen. Her mother, who disappeared when Dusty was five years old, has been missing for thirty years. The turquoise sandals she was wearing today was in memory of her mother whose favourite colour was turquoise.

"It's been four months since the murder and with no family desperate to know why their loved one was killed, the case is only going to get colder."

"And forgotten?"

Dusty inclined her head in agreement, dipped her little finger into her coconut milk to scoop up some of the creamy liquid, licking her finger clean with unrestrained pleasure.

"What about the other monks? Don't they want to find out who murdered their fellow monk?"

"Apparently they've accepted it as a tragedy brought on by the forces of the universe. To dwell on the who and the why is not their way."

I couldn't help thinking that a callous attitude. "Extraordinary. What sort of monks are they?"

"Ah. An insightful question from Mr Maze Master." Dusty often gave me this title – playfully. She considers the inside of a computer and cyber space as a complex maze to people who are not 'maze masters' like me. My skills as an IT professional sometimes veer off course into, well, into areas where I really shouldn't venture. I'm not talking about serious hacking, at least not super serious. Just a little chiselling to get any information Dusty might need.

"They call themselves forest monks. They live a monastic, communal way of life in the forest and more or less follow the teachings of Buddha but don't belong to an established order. For them, care for the earthly environment and contributing to the lay community is as important as following the Buddhist philosophy. The land was donated to them for their monastery. Funds from donations are used for construction of buildings and maintenance. Apart from that, they are self-sufficient. They grow all their own food. Following a vegetarian diet means they don't need to keep poultry or animals. They don't go out begging. In fact, they often donate freshly baked bread and garden produce to the local charity centres. At the Sanctuary, they offer what they call peace therapy, for people needing time out from their lives."

"Peace therapy?"

"Yep. A place where troubled people can retreat for a week or a day or just a few hours. There's also a peace room where a monk listens to people who want to talk about their problems. They don't have to talk; they can just sit."

"And the Sanctuary doesn't charge for this?"

"Nope. No-one is required to pay them although they accept donations if offered."

"Right."

Dusty grinned at me. The grin broadened until she threw back her head and laughed. Had I somehow or other made a joke or committed a faux pas? That would not come as a surprise. I'd often done so in the past due to my ignorance of Australian colloquial expressions. Noticing my embarrassment, Dusty explained her mirth.

"Sorry. It just suddenly felt good to have you back." My embarrassment morphed from discomfort to contentment. "I've decided you're the best research assistant I've ever had."

I relaxed and inhaled the sandy, salty outdoor smell mixed with the aroma of freshly brewed coffee.

"Here's to you, Sean O'Kelly." Dusty picked up her coconut shell, tilting it towards me.

"Have you had many research assistants, then?" As far as I knew she'd only had one other assistant; an Indian student who taught her how to cook Indian food.

"It doesn't matter how many I've had. You're still the best. The tallest too."

Compared to Dusty, who was only five foot two, I was noticeably tall at six foot.

Two young children in bathers raced past our table executing a giddy circuit around the dining area giggling and calling to each other. Their parents, smiling indulgently, followed at a more leisurely pace. Our table was at the edge of the general dining section, slightly separate from the other tables. Dusty had chosen it for that reason. In fact, we'd moved the table further away than it was originally positioned to reduce the risk of others overhearing our discussion of the case. When the children's parents, a tanned couple in their late twenties, had passed by, Dusty resumed talking.

"Anyway, back to our case. I haven't seen the police files yet so I don't know everything. Jake mentioned a couple of unusual things about the murder. Things which haven't been released to the public."

"Nor to Dusty Kent."

"Not yet. In time all will be revealed." Her eyes sparkled. "For now, I'll share what I do know." Turning to a page in her notebook, she scanned it quickly. Dusty had not acquired the habit of using electronic media to the extent I had, preferring to carry a paper notebook in her handbag. She nodded as if her notes had confirmed what she'd already been thinking and leant back in her chair.

"The dead monk was discovered by one of the other monks who saw his yellow robe caught on a shrub about halfway down the cliff. The monk's body was lying at the bottom of the ravine; naked except for a pair of underpants. Police believe the killer stripped him of his robe before pushing him over the edge."

"A strange thing to do. Strip him of his robe, I mean."

"Very strange. It was probably meant as some sort of statement."

"Right. You mean a protest against monks?"

"That's the theory. Their community is on a significant piece of land. Some locals resent the fact the monks acquired this prime piece of real estate, which is probably worth several million dollars, for zilch."

"Jaysis! Millions of dollars? How'd they manage to get it for free?"

"For one thing, the land was bought for under its value. It had been in the Mulligan family for generations. Jim Mulligan and his wife Fiona owned it as well as several businesses in the area. They planned to develop the hill with residential and tourist accommodation. Unfortunately, the family ended up heavily in debt. Jim Mulligan didn't know how to handle money. He spent more than he should. The Mulligans had a lavish lifestyle; an opulent mansion in Brisbane as well as the family home here in Port, a 33 metre luxury yacht complete with helipad and a private jet. In 2000, Jim Mulligan had pretty much lost the family fortune and was facing bankruptcy. It was too much for him; he took his own life. His widow and adult son Mike tried to fight the bankruptcy but it was too late. Everything the family owned was sold and the money went towards paying the family's debts. An overseas buyer bought the hill land and later donated it to the forest monks."

"Right. I can see how the locals might have their noses out of joint but that was years ago."

"Yep. The Sanctuary started out as a handful of Burmese monks who had arrived in the 1970s when Port was a sleepy little fishing village with a couple of hundred residents. The monks established their community in a couple of wooden shacks on a small forested block some distance away from the town centre. Then they got Mulligan's land."

"Surely animosity toward the monks has simmered down by now."

"To a certain extent. However, the flames are regularly fanned by Jim Mulligan's son, Mike. His mother never recovered from the double tragedy of losing her husband and the family home. She fell ill and died three years later. Mike never got over losing his parents and his inheritance. You can imagine how he felt when the monks acquired the property free of charge; a property that had been home to generations of his family. All his anger was directed at the monks."

"Making him a suspect for the murder?"

"The police's number one suspect. Their only suspect. Talking of the police; here comes Jake now."

CHAPTER 4

S TRIDING CONFIDENTLY TOWARD our table and smiling broadly, was a man close to my height wearing a wide brimmed bush hat known locally as an Akubra. For a brief moment I visualised him astride a stallion, reins in his hands, thundering across the red earth of Australia's outback.

Dusty jumped up to greet him. She had only taken a few steps toward Jake when they both stopped and simply looked into each other's eyes.

I instantly recognised what was happening. This was one of those occasions when time stops for the people involved. Their suspended moment lasted long enough for me to start feeling as though my presence was an intrusion. Knowing they were both oblivious to anything and anyone outside their personal euphoria did not alleviate my discomfort.

I knew then that Jake was the reason Dusty had never been able to commit to a relationship. She had once told me she tended to ignore the strong men she was attracted to and choose men who were weak which eventually resulted in her losing respect for them. That was the conclusion she'd drawn as to why she had 'given up on love affairs'. Although she probably believed that to be the reason, I now realised she was fooling herself. I had no doubt this ruggedly handsome detective was the reason Dusty Kent, at age thirty three, had never made the commitment to a long-term intimate relationship.

During one discussion, I'd advised her to open her heart to a strong man since that was the sort of male companion she believed she needed. Naturally, I was thinking of myself when I made the suggestion. What I didn't know was that Dusty had already lost her heart to a man who met her criteria. Jake's advancement in the police force was evidence enough he had strength of character. His appearance and body language confirmed it. Although it was probably subconscious, I was sure Dusty compared every man she met to Jake Feilberg and found them wanting.

I was momentarily swamped by a sense of loss. I didn't stand a chance against Jake. I had to put aside my foolish fantasies of telling Dusty how I felt about her. The very thought of doing it had caused my heart to quicken and my hands to shake. Nevertheless, I had determined to follow through during this trip to Port Douglas. I'd held back for so long. The time had come for me to know if I stood any chance at all with this audacious, unpredictable, irritating and frustratingly captivating woman. Now I knew. In that instant I made a decision.

The standstill moment between Jake and Dusty passed and they came together in an embrace. I noticed Jake held Dusty's hand when they separated, as though he wanted to keep her close. He turned toward me, his smile spreading to his deep blue eyes. Although he greeted me warmly, I sensed he'd instantly dismissed me as no competition for Dusty's affections. That irked me. I straightened my body and inflated my chest. A fleeting smile in Jake's eyes simultaneously acknowledged my posturing and its futility. Despite this, I couldn't help but like him.

When he held out her chair, Dusty smiled up at Jake in thanks, her cheeks tinged with pink. Feeling awkwardly redundant, I decided it was a good time to order coffee. After Dusty indicated she was content with her coconut milk, I took Jake's order and headed to the counter.

When I came back, Dusty and Jake were absorbed in an animated conversation peppered with laughter, their heads almost touching. I announced my return with a noisy scraping of my chair before sitting down.

"So," said Jake, leaning away from Dusty and assuming a business-like manner. He tilted his hat back from his forehead revealing strands of chestnut coloured hair. "Thanks for agreeing to take on this case." He spoke in a slow drawl, sharpened almost imperceptibly by the severity of an experienced police officer.

"Just so you know." He glanced at each of us in turn. "Apart from a couple of people on my team, no-one in Queensland Police knows I've asked you to investigate the monk's murder. Naturally, I'll acknowledge your work if..." Jake paused and grinned at Dusty... "*when* you get a result." He pulled on the lobe of his left ear. "But I don't want my superiors to find out just yet."

"No worries," said Dusty. "We'll be discreet about your involvement."

Jake turned to me. "I was taken off the case and transferred to another big homicide. I can still work on the monk's murder. I just don't have time."

He was probably sincere about his expressed reason for inviting Dusty to take on the case, but I wondered if the thought of seeing her again had been a contributing factor. I also suspected Dusty's acceptance, despite having several other cases on her waiting list, was due to a similar motivation.

Jake raised his hands in a gesture of helplessness. "I wish I did have time to work on it. It seems wrong to me – the poor monk dying a lonely death at the bottom of a ravine and then his murder going unsolved. We weren't even able to locate his next of kin. It was like he'd been abandoned." Jake lowered his eyes and cleared his throat. The tough Queensland detective seemed abashed that he'd exposed his softer side. I felt sure he would never have revealed such feelings to his police colleagues.

He looked up, smiling sheepishly. "To be honest with you, I felt *I* had abandoned him when I left his case. Especially as I was sure I knew who the killer was." The sharp edge returned to his voice as he uttered the last sentence.

Dusty's hand reached out toward Jake's in an expression of empathy. "You had no control over the circumstances, Jake. You have to do what the bosses tell you."

Jake inclined his head toward her, smiling his thanks. "I know. But still. Ah... I dunno." He sighed in resignation. "The monk had no-one else in his corner. The other monks were fond of him and expressed sadness at his passing but they viewed his murder as a tragic fact of life, no different to an unfortunate accident or a heart attack. As far as I'm concerned, murder is different."

"Murder means someone thinks they have the right to take another human being's life," said Dusty.

"Yup. I know that's always made you angry, Dus." Dusty cast a sideways glance at me at Jake's use of what was clearly an intimate nickname. Jake didn't seem to notice; the name was obviously so familiar to him from their past association he hadn't given a thought to whether its use was still appropriate. "The arrogance behind the act of murder. That's always bothered you, hasn't it?"

Dusty pressed her lips together in a determined line as she nodded her agreement.

Jake took out his phone. "I keep my notes on this thing," he said as he tapped the screen and opened the folder he wanted. "I'll give you more details on the murder of Brody Johnson – that's the monk's name."

"Brody Johnson? Didn't I read something in the notes you sent me about another name?" said Dusty, idly watching a waitress serving drinks at a nearby table.

"Yup. He was known locally by his monk name."

Dusty raised her eyebrows. Jake enlightened her.

"When someone enters Sunyarta they choose what is known as a monk name; a name that reflects who they are or something significant about them. Johnson chose Ram."

Dusty challenged his pronunciation.

"Isn't it pronounced Rarm?"

Jake shook his head. "Johnson insisted his name was Ram not Rarm."

"Unusual name. Ram. A male sheep." She turned to me and grinned. "Or something to do with computers."

I was surprised Dusty had made the connection. Although random-access memory was the first thing I had thought of, Dusty was the last person I would expect to make the association with computer technology.

"Was he like, a computer nerd?" I asked. "I mean before becoming a monk."

"Don't know much about him before he became a monk." Jake swiped his phone's screen to scan through his notes. "Born in Melbourne in 1969–"

"What date?" Dusty interrupted. "What date was he born?" She gleamed with triumph. "Bet he's Aries the ram."

Jake looked appraisingly at Dusty and pointed his finger in her direction to acknowledge her idea.

"You could be right. Unfortunately, we don't have those details."

Jake explained that the only background the monks insist on is name plus year and place of birth. Novices are asked to arrive with nothing except the clothes they are wearing. Keys, wallets, credit cards etc are not brought into the Sanctuary. Ram had joined Sunyarta just after the monks had been given the land on the hill and was the first non-Burmese to join.

"So, Ram might have been living here in Port Douglas when he entered the Sanctuary," said Dusty.

"We didn't get to the point of digging too far into his history," said Jake. "If we'd had longer to work the case, we would have done an extensive background check. As it was, we only looked into his background as a monk. My focus during the investigation was naturally on his current life and the local scene. We interviewed all the monks. Ram seemed to be well-liked. Certainly no indication any of them wished him harm."

The waitress arrived with the drinks I'd ordered. We smiled our thanks and she responded with a cheery "Enjoy!"

CHAPTER 5

JAKE WENT ON to explain that the police had established Ram's movements in the twenty-four hour period leading up to his death. The day before he died had been his regular day for volunteering at the retirement home called Alexandra Village.

"The monks said he was uncharacteristically agitated when he returned."

"Because…?" Dusty raised her eyebrows.

"He wouldn't tell anyone what was wrong. Just went straight out to the garden and stayed there till after sundown. One of the other monks found him sitting on the ground in a vegetable patch as if he'd slipped into a reverie and hadn't noticed the time passing."

"Something happened at the retirement village to upset him?" suggested Dusty.

"Nup. Not there. On his way home. Moose Mulligan attacked him. Moose has always hated the monks. Calls them bludgers – among other things. Blames them for taking his family's land. That day he took his anger out on Ram."

Dusty interrupted. "Moose?"

"Mike Mulligan's been called Moose as far back as I can remember."

"You being a local boy an' all."

Jake responded to Dusty's mocking with a good-natured grin before turning to me. "I was born in Port. Grew up here."

That surprised me. "I thought you trained with the Victorian police."

Jake explained that his family moved to Victoria when he was in secondary college. On leaving school he had entered the police service there and later transferred to Queensland Police.

"I couldn't wait to leave the Arctic state and come back to the sunshine," he said with a teasing glance at Dusty.

"Arctic state!" Dusty defended her home state indignantly.

Satisfied at eliciting the reaction he'd anticipated, Jake grinned and changed the subject. "Back to Mulligan." He glanced down at his notes. "The day before Ram died, Moose's red truck was parked in Macrossan Street near Rocky's Cafe. Ram was walking along the footpath. When he drew level with Moose's truck, he stopped to adjust one of his sandals, using the vehicle for support. Mulligan came out of a shop just up the street. The sight of Ram leaning on his truck got Moose all riled up. He rushed at the monk waving his arms about like an agitated gorilla. Apparently, Ram turned around awkwardly, lost his balance and fell over."

"Let me guess," said Dusty. "Moose Mulligan just drove off and left the monk lying on the footpath."

Jake nodded. "Rocky came to the monk's rescue. He was sitting out the front of his cafe playing the guitar which he often does when business is quiet. He helped Ram to one of the cafe's outdoor tables and gave him a glass of water."

"Was that the first time Moose had attacked Ram?" asked Dusty.

Jake shook his head. "He'd already had a go at the monk a few weeks before the Macrossan Street incident. He was convinced Ram had dobbed him in to the police."

"For doing what?"

"Moose has a few acres not far out of town; land that wasn't part of the fire sale to pay the family's debts. His grandfather gave it to him as a twenty-first birthday present. It's quite secluded, hard to access and surrounded by National Park forest so Moose came up with an idea for a lucrative business enterprise."

"Growing marijuana?"

"You got it, Dus. He'd established a thriving illegal marijuana plantation. When someone reported it, Moose reckoned he knew who it was. Ram. For Mulligan this was the last straw. The way he saw it, first the monks took his family land then they took away his only remaining source of income. One day just after he got out of jail, Moose bailed Ram up in the street. He was basically behaving like a feral adolescent screaming his head off, yelling, 'How dare you! How dare you!' Witnesses say he was throwing around the famous expletive starting with F as if it was a new word he'd just discovered."

Dusty grinned and turned to me. "See what a gentleman Jake is. He's protecting my sensitive ears."

"I haven't forgotten." Jake gave Dusty a warm glance. "You always hated people using that word."

"A legacy from my nan. I probably should get over it. Thanks anyway."

"You'd better brace yourself when you interview Moose Mulligan; he's not the type to spare anyone's feelings."

Dusty shrugged. "How did Ram react when Mulligan let loose at him?"

"Didn't say a word. Just moved away. Which made Moose even angrier. He was spoiling for a fight and didn't get one. Called the monk a yellow-bellied dingo who didn't have the balls to stand up for himself."

"Why did he think it was Ram who'd reported him?"

"He says he saw one of the flower pots – his term for the monks – in the National Park not far from where it backs onto his piece of land. I doubt it was really one of the monks he saw, probably glimpsed a tourist in a yellow dress or something. A few days later, he saw Ram going into the police station here in town. Just a couple of days after that, the drug squad swooped on his pot plantation. So of course the idiot jumped to the wrong conclusion."

"Ram didn't go into the police station to report the marijuana?"

"Nah. He just had some minor document he needed to get officially witnessed. The tip-off re the marijuana plantation was an anonymous phone call."

"Flower pots?" I was curious about Mulligan's nickname for the monks.

"Yup. No one else calls them that. Only Mulligan and his cronies. It's just Moose being malicious; a reference to the colour of their robes which was chosen to match the wild hibiscus that grows in this area. Moose probably thinks he's being clever because flower and pot are both words sometimes used to refer to marijuana."

We paused as an elderly couple, both dressed for the warm weather in shorts and cotton shirts, shuffled past our table. A little unsteady on his feet, the gentleman was aided by a walking stick.

I picked up an English accent when the woman addressed the man, presumably her husband. "What would you like to have to drink, ducks?"

Dusty smiled after them. "I'm tempted to go and help them." Jake and I both started to get up. "But that would be incredibly patronising." I exchanged a bashful look with Jake as we both sat back down.

Dusty was right; it would seem condescending given the couple, although undoubtedly octogenarians, possibly older, were not in need of assistance. However, I understood Dusty's desire to reach out to them. She was probably thinking of her grandmother who had cared for her after her mother disappeared. I was certainly thinking of my grandparents back in Castlerea, both of whom were on the twilight side of eighty.

Dusty returned to our discussion. "Where was Mulligan at the time of the murder?"

"Claims he was in bed – said he always sleeps late. Sneered at the suggestion he'd be up 'at the crack of a sparrow's fart' as he put it."

"So no alibi. I'm guessing you haven't got him on CCTV near the Sanctuary?"

Jake's eyes twinkled. "This is not the big city, Dus. No CCTV on the hill."

"Was there any DNA evidence on the body?"

"Zero."

"How would Mulligan have known Ram would be on top of the hill at dawn?"

"Members of the public are free to come and go as they please at Sunyarta. He could have gone up there, wandered around and asked a few questions to get the information he needed. He might not have even had to do that. Ram's meditation routine seemed to be fairly well known, partly because the particular platform he used was in such a stunning location."

Dusty nodded thoughtfully. "That means anyone in Port Douglas could have known where to find Ram at dawn."

"True. But Moose is the only person I know of who had a motive to harm him."

Jake's phone beeped. He grinned apologetically as he checked the caller ID.

"A message from my sergeant. I've left the team in charge of a case in Cairns while I'm here. 'Scuse me a sec." Jake read the text and typed out a quick response. "Sorry." He placed the phone on the table. "Hopefully we won't be interrupted again."

Dusty waved away his apology.

"By the way," added Jake. "I've asked Rocky, the cafe owner I mentioned earlier, to give you any help he can – local knowledge, that sort of thing."

Dusty frowned. "Somehow I can't picture someone called Rocky as a cafe owner. I can't shake this image of a tough bikie with overdeveloped muscles and knuckle dusters."

Jake threw back his head and laughed. "Rocky's got a good physique but no knuckle dusters and he doesn't look a bit like a bikie. Actually, he's a bit of a softie. You know what he does? He has this exchange thing where customers can put money in a jar for an extra cup of coffee. The money pays for a free cappuccino for a homeless person or anyone who can't afford to buy a coffee."

"Interesting. Maybe he's been homeless himself at some stage. It seems to happen to almost everyone these days."

"True." Jake reached out and, grinning mischievously, tapped Dusty lightly on the scalp. "Touch wood, it doesn't happen to any of us."

Dusty gave him a mock scowl. Jake was clearly aware of Dusty's love of superstitions.

Watching the way they interacted with each other reinforced the decision I'd made earlier. I would make a call as soon as I had a private moment.

"Anyway, Rocky's a mate. We were in primary school together but his family moved to Melbourne years before mine did. We lost touch until he came back to Port a couple of years ago." He took a last sip of his coffee. "There's just a few more things I wanted to go over with you and, as I mentioned in my email, you'll be interested in a couple of things which haven't been released to the public."

A shrill telephone ring interrupted us. The screen on Jake's phone lit up. "Sorry." He looked at the screen briefly. "It's my sergeant again. I'd better take the call."

He pushed his chair back and stood up. His call finished before he had time to move away from the table. He turned back to us. "Sorry. Gotta go." Leaning over, he touched Dusty lightly on the arm. That simple act of familiarity carried Jake's confident assumption about Dusty's feelings for him. To my mind, it also revealed a level of hubris, something I'd observed in other men in their attitudes toward women. Growing up in a house full of girls had taught me not to take anything for granted where women were concerned.

As he hurried away, he called over his shoulder. "I'll call you."

Dusty looked after him for a moment. "Let's take a short walk." She pointed toward the hill.

As we left the cafe, I noticed the elderly couple had chosen a table on the edge of the dining area where they could both face the beach. 'Ducks' was enjoying a large cold drink, possibly ginger beer. His wife, with a slightly unsteady hand, was pouring hot tea from a teapot into a bright blue cup with a matching saucer.

CHAPTER 6

D USTY'S SHORT WALK turned out to be a steep climb to the top of the hill where the Sanctuary was situated. Thankfully, the ascent was made easier by a cemented surface. Fitted handrails and had the added bonus of views of the Coral Sea. However, the quality of the trail deteriorated into a rough bush track about a third of the way up. Dusty seemed in her element and charged ahead passing several other walkers and leaving me trailing behind.

"No one would have seen the killer creeping up here before dawn that morning." She had paused at the halfway point to allow me to catch up. "By the way, before you surfaced this morning I was gathering information from the lady on the desk."

I knew from the gleam in Dusty's eye she'd been waiting for the right moment to share the intelligence she'd gleaned. I arranged my face in my best listening expression. Dusty cast a furtive glance around, beckoning me closer before continuing in a low voice.

"She told me another monk from Sunyarta died in mysterious circumstances. According to her, it was an accident which might not have been an accident." Dusty nodded with satisfaction when she saw she'd roused my curiosity. "I don't think the police looked into it for a possible connection to Ram's death."

On the other hand, I thought, the police might have dismissed it as local gossip and malicious muckraking. Sunyarta, being a community of people who did things differently from the norm, would be a prime target for fanciful speculation by bored locals looking for an injection of excitement in their lives.

"Was it recent enough to be connected to Ram's murder?"

Dusty shrugged. "A few years ago. Could be a connection though.

You know me, Sean; leave no stone unturned."

Dusty gazed out at the ocean, clearly enjoying the ambience of our rest area. I took the opportunity to ask about her mother's case. She had lived most of her life wondering what had happened to her beloved mother who had disappeared without a trace. Just last year, there'd been a breakthrough when a police informant identified the place where Anna Kent was buried. It'd come as a shock to Dusty at first. She'd finally had to let go of the hope her mother might one day return. Dusty's friend, Senior Sergeant Ken Nagle, now had a team of detectives working on it.

"Thanks for asking, Sean. I'll fill you in later." She turned to give me one of her brilliant smiles. "Over a G & T."

The rest of the walk took us through more dense bushland and tall trees. At the top we passed through the un-gated entrance to Sunyarta and approached the Sanctuary along a neat stone pathway. Both sides of the path were lined with colourful plants growing in tangled harmony and spilling over the edges of rocks. The path widened as we continued downhill towards a cluster of timber buildings elevated from the ground by floor stumps to encourage natural air conditioning through the circulation of cool air from the ground.

Dusty looked back towards the top of the hill. "A monk could have easily made it up to Ram's meditation spot from these grounds without being seen. Even though the bush here is not as dense as at the top, it's thick enough to provide good cover. A monk intent on murder could have used the trees for concealment and not even had to go on the path."

"A monk in yellow robes?"

Dusty gave me a scornful look. "Don't you think a monk with murder on his mind might have found a way to procure some dark clothing to wear?"

"Right. Just what I was thinking."

She returned my grin with one of her own then pointed to the right. "Talking of yellow."

Creating a striking border around a pond were trees whose large, heart-shaped leaves complemented vivid yellow flowers with deep red centres, their heads dipping toward the water.

"Reminds me of the story of Narcissus; the colour of the flowers and the way they way they seem to be looking at their own reflections in the pond."

"Long ago when the people of this land lived in nature…" The soft male voice startled us.

We spun round to see a man of advanced years with a shaven head dressed in a robe matching the colours of the flowers on the tree. Brown skin, wrinkled with age, silver hair and wisps of grey beard in the centre of his chin combined with his Asian features to suggest he might have been one of Sunyarta Sanctuary's original Burmese monks. He was not much taller than Dusty so that I felt I was towering over both of them.

The monk continued speaking calmly without acknowledging us or our surprise. "There was a beautiful dark-eyed princess who loved the flowers of the hibiscus trees growing along the river where her people lived. Each day in the late afternoon she swam in the river."

Dusty and I both gasped in horror. A tourist brochure at Four Mile Resort where we were staying warned visitors that the river, assuming he meant the Daintree River, was home to hundreds of crocodiles. On our recent trip to Darwin, we'd been educated by Australia's leading crocodile authority on the dangers of crocs lurking in the water. Surely people whose ancestors had lived on the land for thousands of years understood the risk.

Unperturbed, the monk continued the story. "When she emerged from the water, the princess liked to pick fresh flowers to wear in her hair. One day she did not return from her swim. The men of her tribe searched the river. Alas, no trace of the girl was ever found. From that day, the yellow hibiscus flowers began to darken every afternoon. At four o'clock, the time the princess used to go to swim, the flowers dropped from the trees like carmine tears. To this day, the yellow blooms fall from the wild hibiscus trees at the same time each afternoon."

"Serious?" Dusty's tone expressed her awe. "The flowers all drop from the trees at four o'clock every day?"

The monk's calm smile indicated his wonderment at this phenomenon had long since morphed into ready acceptance of the miracles of nature. "They say the flowers look down into the water all day long in search of the beautiful hibiscus princess."

To my surprise I detected a soft glistening in Dusty's eyes.

"I don't know of any other princess, or queen, or any other woman who has been honoured with a more exquisite tribute."

This was not the time to remind Dusty that it was just a story someone had invented, possibly created by Aboriginal people to explain the dropping of flowers at a certain time each day. There was no opportunity for further discussion anyway for we were dramatically interrupted.

CHAPTER 7

A WOMAN IN her mid to late forties, jeans and red T-shirt moulded on her trim, athletic body, marched purposefully along the path towards us. Blonde hair, short and thick, fell forward over her forehead. It might have been her thick dark eyebrows and her flushed cheeks combined with the forest backdrop that caused me to momentarily imagine her as a woman of the wilderness. As she closed in on us, that impression was reinforced by the fierceness in her violet eyes. She came to an abrupt halt in front of Dusty. Feet apart. Lips in a tight line.

The woman's chest heaved, from anger rather than exertion. I judged her to be fit enough to easily run up the bush track Dusty and I had just ascended. She pointed an accusing finger at Dusty. "I know who you are!" Dusty responded with a questioning look. "Doesn't take long for word to get around in a small town like this. You're investigating the death of that monk." She jerked her head in the general area of where Ram had been meditating the morning he was killed. "No-one investigated my son's death. It's not right!"

Her nostrils flared. Freckles that peppered the bridge of her nose stood out like flecks of burnt embers in white ash.

"No one cared about him. But these monks… Oh, yes! Let's bring in the famous Dusty Kent. Waste time and money and pull out all stops to find out how *he* died. But a young man who had his whole life ahead of him? Oh, no! No-one cares about that. My beautiful boy died up here too. Doesn't that tell you something? Oh, but monks are so holy." She snorted in derision. "Evil more like it. One of these so-called monks is evil. These monks…" She jabbed a finger in the direction of the Sanctuary buildings. "They ought to be held accountable." As the woman's anger started to subside, her eyes welled with tears. "They were supposed to be looking after my boy."

Her attention was diverted when she noticed our companion for the first time. Rage flared in her eyes again. One hand tightened around the set of car keys she was carrying and clenched into a fist.

"You!"

The angry woman jabbed an accusing finger at the elderly monk. "You were supposed to protect my son."

The monk bowed his head. The woman stood glaring an accusation at him. Time passed in slow seconds. I was about to step in front of the elderly monk to block a potential attack when Dusty broke the silence.

"I'm so sorry." Realising the woman's rage sprang from a deep grief, she offered her condolences with warmth and sincerity.

The woman shook her head vigorously. "No! No! No!" I wasn't sure if she was rejecting Dusty's expression of sympathy or the fact of her son being dead. Tears rolled down her cheeks. She turned sharply and headed back the way she'd come, one hand up to her face wiping away the tears.

Dusty took my arm, urging me forward. "Try to calm her down before she gets behind the wheel."

I hurried after the woman, my long strides closing the distance between us. By the time she emerged from the bushland into the cleared area where her car was parked, I was almost level with her.

"Excuse me." I kept my voice low, aiming for a gentle tone.

She spun round, a look of startled fear flashing into her eyes momentarily.

"I'm sorry." I kept my expression serious hoping my eyes reflected kindness. "I didn't mean to startle you."

Her features relaxed slightly. Despite the tear-smudged mascara, I noted how attractive she was. Her eyes remained on me as she took a step away. Realising that, given her heightened emotions, she might perceive me as intimidating, I also took a step back. I doubt she had taken much notice of me during her earlier outburst. Now, however, I saw recognition glimmer in her eyes. This was the time for my so-called disarming smile. Unfortunately, it didn't have the effect I was after.

"What do you want?" The question catapulted from her mouth like a whip cracking. The next sound was the familiar beep of car locks being released when she pressed the remote key. I noticed the image of a pair of paw footprints at the bottom of the car's rear window and wondered about their significance.

"I only wanted to make sure you were okay." I allowed my Irish brogue to deepen, knowing it sometimes had the power to charm.

Alas, she didn't appear to be charmed. However, I noticed a faintly discernible change in her demeanour.

"I'm not all right, if you really must know." Still defensive. But her delivery was now more of a thud – like a whip which had failed to crack. Her shoulders slumped. I concluded her angry energy was now spent. She turned and started to walk toward the driver side of her car.

"Would you like to tell me about your son?"

Her back straightened. She hesitated. Her eyes, when she turned to look at me, reflected suspicion. She wanted to talk about her son but she was wary of my motives.

"I'm close to my mother. I have seven sisters, but I'm her only son. She's back in Ireland and constantly worries about me being thousands of miles away in a strange country." The grieving mother in front of me must have picked up on my sincerity for her expression softened. I could see she was feeling empathy for my mother. She came back around the car to prop herself up against the rear, leaning forward slightly, cradling her car keys in both hands.

"Your poor mother. She must worry about you." Her tone had mellowed.

I joined her in leaning against the back of the car, feeling a pang of conscience that I hadn't been in touch with my mother recently.

"What is your son's name?"

"Josh. Joshua really. Everyone called him Josh. He was a beautiful person; gentle, artistic. An artist." She looked up at me smiling proudly. "Josh loved to paint. He had real talent. And dreams."

She gazed out at the ocean and the mountains beyond. The view from this hill would be an inspiration for any artist. "He had such dreams." An anguished whisper.

Time to put into use the listening skills I had developed during my short stint as a barman when I first arrived in Australia.

"Did he come up here to paint?"

"He was staying here."

She pointed in the direction of the Sanctuary. Did she mean her son had become a monk? If so, he could be the other monk Dusty had mentioned who'd died in mysterious circumstances.

"Josh had…health issues. Caused by drugs. I thought… We both thought…a rest here where it was peaceful, beautiful surroundings, close to nature. He loved nature." She glanced at me. "We weren't being reckless by throwing away his medication and putting all our faith in nature. I don't mean that. He brought his medication with him. I just thought it would be a good starting point. I hoped being in a place like this might help him reconnect with the things which were once important to him – nature, painting. He'd lost all that. Couldn't see the beauty around him anymore."

I didn't want to risk arousing her grief again by asking her what happened. My mission was to calm her down before she started driving. I suggested Dusty would be interested in talking to her about her son. Her response was a sceptical stare.

"The police refused to investigate his death. Refused! Because he had a drug problem he's dismissed as just another junkie who took his own life. I know someone gave him the heroin which killed him." Her eyes locked with mine, challenging me to question her last statement. "I know! I just know."

I decided not to point out to her that even if someone did give her son the drugs, his death would still be a suicide. Unless someone forced the drug into him. Or tampered with it.

"If someone else was responsible for your son's death, the same person could have killed the monk, Ram."

Surprise flickered in her eyes. I could see she hadn't considered that possibility before.

"Yes." She nodded thoughtfully. "One of those monks is evil, or crazy, or both. People like that don't have to have a logical reason to kill. He might even be getting ready to bump off someone else as we speak."

She retrieved her business card from the car and handed it to me. "Thank you." This was accompanied by a tilt of the head and lowered eyes. It was the same sort of expression of appreciation I'd received behind the bar. It combined embarrassment at sharing a confidence with a stranger with gratitude for having been listened to.

As her red Toyota hatchback disappeared down the hill, my phone beeped. A text from Dusty informing me she and the monk were on their way to the meditation spot where Ram had met his death. The angry woman's words flashed into my mind: *He might even be getting ready to bump off someone else as we speak.* Jaysis! Concern for Dusty sent me racing back the way I'd come.

CHAPTER 8

TO MY RELIEF Dusty looked completely at ease as she chatted with the elderly monk. I cursed myself for allowing my imagination to get the better of me. There was nothing sinister about the monk. And yet... No. It was just my foolish fancy.

Brittle twigs snapped and leaves crackled underfoot as we followed the monk along a rough path in the bush. A startled bird fluttered its wings and flew to another tree. Dusty yanked her head clear of overhanging branches, frantically sweeping her hair in response to the light touch of a falling leaf, as though afraid spiders were dropping from the trees. This thirty-three-year-old Dusty bore little resemblance to the young girl who spent much of her childhood racing through the Australian bush with her many cousins chasing lizards and snakes.

We emerged into a small clearing where the ocean was visible through the trees: Ram's meditation spot.

The monk pointed to a slatted wooden platform raised slightly from the ground. "Ashin Ram sat here. Every morning he was in this place."

I could have covered the distance between the platform and the edge of the precipice in one stride. Rolling the unconscious monk's body over the side would have been easy for the killer. An eerie sense of foreboding gripped me when the monk stood next to Dusty who was near the edge. I moved quickly to her side, taking her arm to steer her back to safety.

Dusty looked up at me with a quizzical expression. "I wasn't thinking of jumping."

The monk observed us with an enigmatic smile. I had the uncomfortable feeling he knew what I'd been thinking and was amused by it. What did that mean? Was he entertained by the idea that I'd discovered his evil intention and could do nothing about it? Or was he amused that I should harbour such thoughts about an inoffensive, peace-loving monk? I felt my face warm with a flush of embarrassment. That's exactly what he was: inoffensive and peace-loving and probably wise about the workings of the human mind. What was the matter with me?

Dusty seemed oblivious to my moment of discomfort. She was focused on taking in as much as possible about the murder scene.

"What a spectacular place to greet each new day. So he came up here along the path leading from the Sanctuary, then through the bush as we just did?" Dusty looked back the way we'd come, visualising Ram arriving.

Our companion nodded. "The path through the bush was used often at that time, you understand. It was easier to walk. Now it is rough again; no-one treads here anymore."

Dusty grinned ruefully as she bent down to remove a stray leaf which had become caught in the strap of her sandal before resuming her imagined scenario of Ram's last day on the hill. Last day on Earth.

"When he got here to the clearing, he unrolled his straw mat, laid it out on the slats, slipped off his thongs and placed them beside the platform. Then he sat cross-legged on the mat, facing the ocean."

The elderly monk moved his head several times in agreement.

"How long did Ram usually sit here?"

"Perhaps one hour, perhaps two hours."

Dusty's eyebrows arched in surprise. I struggled to imagine her attempting to sit still, let alone quietly, for that length of time.

"So at some point during Ram's peaceful meditation his killer crept quietly along this path and..."

With a quick glance at the monk, Dusty refrained from articulating in his presence the details of what had happened to Ram. The monk moved his head slightly as if to acknowledge her thoughtfulness.

Dusty looked back at the narrow track leading to the clearing.

"When this bush track was well-trodden, would it have been easy for someone to walk along it without making a noise?" Dusty nodded vigorously as if suddenly receiving the answer to her own question. "Yes! I remember when I was a kid playing games in the bush with my cousins. We used to kinda lift our weight off our feet while we were walking. That way, if you were careful not to tread on twigs and break them, you could move silently through the bush, even when there was no track." She looked up at me with shining eyes. "I'd almost forgotten that."

"The murderer might not have been someone with bush skills," I reminded her.

"True. But it's more of an instinct than a skill. Anyone with a strong desire not to be heard would probably walk that way intuitively."

Maybe the reminder of what had happened in this spot was too much for the elderly monk. He rose and turned to leave. Dusty forestalled him with a question.

"Have you been at Sunyarta for long?"

The monk's gentle smile suggested the answer to her question was self evident.

"So you must have been here when the other monk died; the one who had the accident a few years ago."

Only the merest flicker in his eyes revealed his surprise.

"He died here in this spot too, didn't he?" Dusty must have read something in the monk's face which prompted this stab in the dark. It was the sort of thing I'd observed her do on previous occasions. She was usually right on target.

"Come." An invitation cast over his shoulder as he started back through the trees. A short distance along the track, the monk paused. "Our brother died here." He followed the line of a tree trunk with his eyes. "It was a sad accident."

He continued walking. Behind his back, Dusty looked at me with raised eyebrows.

CHAPTER 9

O N LEAVING SUNYARTA Sanctuary, Dusty and I walked downhill
along the visitor access road. On the lower level of our descent,
we passed driveways leading to luxury multi-storey homes and
glamorous holiday apartments. Elegant palms with bright pink trunks
stood sentinel at some driveway entrances.

Dusty had been correct earlier when she said it would have been
too risky for the murderer to make his approach along this route.
With traffic virtually non-existent so early in the morning, any car
spotted perhaps from an upstairs window would have stood out like a
sore thumb.

"A bit of a dark horse, wasn't he?" Dusty was referring to the
elderly monk.

He had taken us on a tour of the Sanctuary refraining from telling
us his name until the end. The tour included the peace room: a simple
building which was long, spacious and empty of furniture. The edges
of the shining wooden floor were lined with neat stacks of meditation
mats and floor-to-ceiling glass doors were folded back to create an
alfresco feel. Our guide explained that 'lay people' from the town
came to sit in the peace room.

"They find it helpful when they are troubled," he said.

The last area on the guided tour was a contrast. The building's
architecture had a strong Asian influence and gave the appearance of
being an ancient Buddhist temple. However, inside was a modern
office complete with computers, desks, a printer, and shelves overflow-
ing with books, documents and stationery. One end of the office had
been converted into a reception area with a coffee table, a drinking
fountain and several modern lounge chairs arranged in a semi circle.

Dusty and I each accepted a glass of chilled water before sitting down opposite our guide.

The monk bowed slightly. "I am Saya."

Dusty was unable to hide her surprise. "You are the senior monk here at Sunyarta?" Jake had told us the senior monk's name was Saya.

He smiled and nodded. "You have come to see me?" He held his plastic cup in front of him with both hands, resting it on his knees. Watching him, I found it difficult to figure him out. I had the impression he was playing a game with us, almost as if he knew who we were and why we were there. He understood the power of keeping knowledge to himself and possessed a natural restraint that allowed him to do so without effort. Was he hiding something? Or was he merely wise?

Dusty barely had time to introduce herself and explain why we were there when a young monk interrupted us, appearing tentatively at the open doorway and hovering there with his eyes downcast after a quick glance at Saya.

"Ah." Saya turned to us as the young monk respectfully withdrew having silently delivered his message. Saya had to leave to 'attend to some appointments' but invited us to return another day.

"Why do you think Saya waited till the end of our tour to introduce himself?" said Dusty after we left the office.

I'd also been wondering about that. Those thoughts led me to contemplate what might lie beneath Saya's benign exterior. Could he be hiding a sociopathic personality? A murderous heart? Maybe my earlier imaginings were not so ridiculous after all.

"Saya seems to be a bit of an odd fish all round," I said. "He appears open, welcoming and willing to help us. At the same time, he's pretty good at keeping things to himself. He wasn't forthcoming about the other monk who died. And isn't it strange he didn't say anything about the recent suicide? Surely it would be a natural thing to do after the boy's mother had made such a dramatic entrance and flung accusations at him? There's more to that monk than meets the eye in my opinion."

Dusty glanced at me curiously. "So that's where your thoughts are going. Interesting."

It also occurred to me Dusty had missed the opportunity to question Saya about the suicide but I kept my mouth shut on that subject.

The sound of children's voices signalled our arrival at a large park overlooking the ocean. A young woman jogged past us. Looking after her, Dusty abruptly grabbed my arm.

"The angry woman. Did you find out anything about her before she left?"

I retrieved the woman's business card from my shirt pocket and handed it to Dusty.

She scanned the details on the card. "Kellie Edwards. Portpaws Veterinary Clinic."

I told her what Kellie had said about her son Josh. Dusty nodded thoughtfully.

"We'll go and see Kellie Edwards. She can tell me her theories about how her son died. I have to interview her anyway. She blames the monks for her son's death; perhaps she hated the monks enough to kill one of them."

Somehow, I thought as we walked through the park back toward the town centre, I can't see Kellie Edwards taking kindly to being interviewed as a suspect in Ram's murder.

"Her son's name was Josh. Correct?" Dusty took a last look at Kellie's card before putting it in her bag.

"Joshua actually, but he was known as Josh."

"Joshua? Now that's interesting." She didn't elaborate on why she found the boy's name of interest, returning instead to the dead monk's name. "What about Ram? Isn't the ram a symbol of sacrifice in some religions? Christianity, for instance?"

She looked at me as though I might be some sort of authority on the Christian religion probably on the assumption all Irish people are die-hard Catholics. In truth, I'd spent very little time in a church since my school days. All the same, her question was an easy one to answer.

"Yes. Abraham offered a ram as a sacrifice to God in place of his son."

"*Very* interesting." After that Dusty fell into a preoccupied silence, eventually coming out of her reverie to suggest lunch.

CHAPTER 10

LATER THAT DAY, Dusty received a text message from Jake telling her he'd had to go to Cairns, a city around sixty eight kilometres south, and wouldn't be back until after eight in the evening. He would finish briefing us about the murder at his accommodation in Davidson Street.

I suggested Dusty go and meet Jake on her own but she insisted I accompany her. I wondered why. Was she nervous about being alone with him? I didn't doubt strong chemistry, for want of a better word, was pulling them together. Was Dusty afraid to act on it? Did she want to find out if Jake was free to act on it before she got too close?

"It's important for you to be there, Sean," she said. "You need to hear what Jake has to say about the case."

I didn't raise any objections.

"Can't work on an empty stomach. Something my nan used to say," announced Dusty as we headed out to have our evening meal before the planned meeting at nine o'clock.

Fortified with a generous dinner at an excellent restaurant we strolled along Macrossan Street enjoying the balmy evening. Blurred conversations, bursts of laughter from diners, the clattering of cutlery against plates and the clinking of glasses followed us.

"Not bad, Jake," said Dusty when he ushered us into his first floor apartment at the boutique hotel where he was staying. "Queensland Police pay for this?"

"Not likely. I use my accommodation allowance but it doesn't cover the full tariff. Still, it makes it affordable – for a couple of days, anyway."

"So you want me to wrap this case up in a couple of days?"

Jake grinned. "I don't doubt you could do that but it won't be necessary. I'm only here to get you started. Then I'll go back to Cairns." I fancied I saw a passing shadow of disappointment in Dusty's eyes.

"I'll keep in touch of course. Plus, Cairns is only an hour or so away so we can meet up whenever we want." I had the feeling Jake wasn't referring only to meeting up for the case. "Righto. Let's get to it. The sooner we finish the sooner we can adjourn to the balcony for a drink."

"You mentioned some things about Ram's death which haven't been released to the public," said Dusty as we settled around the table in the living area. "What are we talking about?"

"His thongs, for example."

"His thongs? In the notes you sent me I read that he took them off to meditate and placed them neatly beside the mat he was sitting on."

Jake nodded. "Correct. One of them was still there, apparently undisturbed. It would make sense for both thongs to still be there."

"Possibly knocked over the edge during the struggle?"

"If there was a struggle, it wasn't violent because the monk's meditation mat, although it had slipped off the platform, was still on top of the cliff. I think the monk was taken by surprise and immobilised before he knew what was happening. We searched the area thoroughly for the missing thong thinking it might have gone over the cliff. Found no trace. Can't see it being taken by an animal – hardly any animals can get to the cliff face, certainly not the sort of animals capable of picking up a thong and carrying it away. It's not likely to have made it all the way to the ocean – too many obstructions on the way down."

"An animal could have taken it from the top of the cliff," suggested Dusty.

"Unusual for an animal to take one thong and leave the other one neatly in place," said Jake. "Besides, we found no animal tracks near the platform. No. It looks like the killer took it."

"A trophy?"

"Possible. Especially if the killing was a protest against the monks."

"Any idea why the killer stripped the monk of his robe?"

"We haven't solved that riddle. It's possible the robe just came off during the process of pushing the body over the edge." Jake went on to offer an explanation which could have fitted with Moose Mulligan being the murderer. "Or it could be some sort of message; for instance, a message of contempt for monks."

Dusty acknowledged the possibility with a nod. "What other information was not released to the public?"

"Only one other thing really, but I believe it's significant. It's the reason I think the stripping of Ram's body might have been a message of contempt."

"I'm all ears."

Jake lowered his voice, perhaps conscious the sliding doors to the balcony were open. "The blow on the head wasn't the only injury Ram suffered. It's what killed him but he'd also received a kick elsewhere on his body."

"Elsewhere?"

"His testicles."

I winced. "I hope the poor man was already dead when he was kicked."

Jake acknowledged my reaction with a conspiratorial grin indicating he also understood the imagined pain of such an attack. "We think so. I believe the kick in the groin was a statement by the killer – you don't have the balls to be a real man – that kind of thing. Exactly the sort of message Moose Mulligan might want to send about the monks."

Dusty's brow furrowed. "Another thing I was wondering about. The killer didn't really go to any lengths to hide the body, did he?"

"Didn't look that way. Almost looked like he was advertising it. The bright yellow of the monk's robe in the bush was certain to be spotted sooner rather than later."

"As if he wanted the body to be found – because he was making a point." Dusty scribbled in her notebook. "In which case the killer was probably someone with a grudge against Ram or the Sunyarta monks in general. And he was confident he wouldn't be caught."

Jake spread out his hands as if to acknowledge an obvious conclusion. "Exactly. Mulligan fits the bill. He has the right kind of ego to convince himself he could get away with murder. In fact, that's one of the reasons he was so angry about being caught with the marijuana plantation. In his conceited mind, he was sure he was smart enough to hide his illegal activities from the police. Therefore, to his way of thinking, the only way authorities could have found out was if someone grassed him up."

I made a suggestion of my own, possibly influenced by the attitude of dissidents back home in Ireland.

"Or he felt the point he wanted to make was worth getting caught for. He might feel making a point about the monks having property which, in his eyes, rightfully belonged to his family was worth going to jail over."

Jake nodded thoughtfully. "You could be right there, mate. It wouldn't surprise me if Mulligan saw it as a badge of honour to avenge his family by committing murder."

Dusty shook her head in disgust. "He chose this particular monk to be the scapegoat because of his mistaken belief Ram had turned him in to the police. Is it possible Ram met his horrible, lonely death because of one man's stupid assumptions?" Her hand shot up quickly. "Don't answer that! I know only too well people commit murder for the most bizarre reasons." Dusty looked directly at Jake. "We can't afford to get stuck on only one suspect, Jake."

His eyes held hers for a brief moment. I wondered if he might have taken Dusty's comment as a criticism of the police investigation.

However, he smiled, raising his hand to acknowledge her point. "The thing is, there wasn't anyone else with a motive, Dus."

"You might have found someone if you'd had enough time on the case to dig deeper."

"Yup. That's where you come in. You have time and I know you'll be meticulous and conscientious."

"And," Dusty flashed a grin at me, "I have a research assistant who can dig deeper than Howard Carter."

Shortly after that, Jake finished the briefing. Dusty's body language during the meeting told me any reservations or fears she might have had concerning her feelings, or renewed feelings, for Jake had gradually dissipated. By the time Jake suggested we adjourn to the balcony, I knew Dusty would not be returning to her apartment that evening. It was time for me to go. Besides, I had something I had to do. I politely took my leave but was stopped at the door by a cryptic comment from Dusty.

"Keep your eyes out for a woman with short dark hair wearing a pair of beige pants and a black sleeveless top." She laughed at my nonplussed expression. "I'm surprised you didn't notice her following us when we left the restaurant."

I couldn't read the look that crossed Jake's face. Concern? Alarm? Dusty, on the other hand, was being playful.

"If she's still out there and sees you come out on your own who knows what might happen."

Jake joined in the good-natured ribbing. "Could be your lucky night, mate." He winked as I pulled the door shut.

CHAPTER 11

OUTSIDE, I CAST a glance along the street. A couple of family groups, two men about my age speaking what sounded like a Scandinavian language and an Indian lady wearing a summer shawl decorated with glittering butterflies laughingly relating something to her female companions were the only other pedestrians in sight. No sign of the woman Dusty had described.

The only thing unusual I came across was when I rounded a corner in one of the smaller streets and saw the name *Ellen* chalked in white on the footpath. It was not a casual scrawl; more like pavement calligraphy. The name had been carefully penned in old-fashioned flowing script as though the writer wanted to show his devotion to the mysterious Ellen. I wondered if someone had recently lost a loved one by that name.

Apart from the curious message, the walk back to Four Mile Resort was uneventful. Dusty's stalker did not materialise. She had presumably invented the story about the dark haired woman in beige slacks in a fit of high spirits. I was under no illusions as to what had caused her ebullience. My noble inclination to feel happy for her was overshadowed by a dull pain.

Back at my apartment, I took some cans of Guinness out onto the balcony. As I drank, I wallowed in a sense of loss. A stupid reaction. I'd lost something I never really had. Seems fierce stupid to be grieving over a fantasy. One more Guinness and I pulled myself together. It was time to act on the decision I'd made this morning. Taking out my phone, I pressed on the familiar face in the contacts list, punched the call sign and waited for Ingrid to answer.

After working on the last case with Dusty in Darwin, I'd spent some time in Kakadu National Park, camping and riding around on my motorbike. I'd been there on a previous occasion and felt a sort of affinity with the place. Its wilderness, wide open spaces and ancient rocks created a natural environment totally foreign to me yet I felt at home.

While I was there, a television crew filming for an outdoor show for a commercial network in Victoria turned up. Ingrid was the show's presenter. Too beautiful to ignore with long blonde hair and a fresh smile, she looked especially fetching wearing an Akubra hat to protect her face from the sun. I wasn't surprised to learn she'd once been a model and an actress attracting bit parts in various feature films and television shows.

At five foot eleven, Ingrid was one of the few women I could look in the eye without stooping. For some reason, she took a liking to me. It might have been my so-called disarming smile or my 'lilting Irish accent'. She had a slight accent herself, having been born in New Zealand. We discovered more common ground when Ingrid mentioned she'd spent some of her childhood years in East Gippsland. I'd become acquainted with the area when I first worked on a case there with Dusty.

Ingrid had recently broken up with her long-time boyfriend. That might have made her receptive to my attentions as much as the things we had in common. Whatever the reason, chemistry ignited between us. When Ingrid returned to Melbourne with the rest of the crew, I followed.

Since our last case, I'd signed a deal with Dusty's publisher Poppins Press for my humble chronicles to be published as companion books to Dusty's journalistic exploration of her cases. It's a good deal financially. I get royalties and a generous retainer which means I can go for long stretches without seeking work if I want to. However, the retainer does mean I need to be willing to drop everything and join Dusty when she takes on a new case. That's what happened on this occasion.

When Dusty's email instructing me to go to Port Douglas arrived, I was jolted into the realisation that in the months since we'd last worked together, I'd become settled. I wasn't sure it was a good thing.

Although reluctant to leave Ingrid, I'd left Melbourne looking forward to being on the move again and working with Dusty once more.

Now things were different. Seeing Jake and Dusty together had been a reality check. Pushing the empty can of Guinness aside, I checked the time in Western Australia where Ingrid was currently on location filming an episode of her show. Just after nine o'clock in the evening. Perfect.

"Hello darling." It wasn't until I heard her soft breathy voice on the line that it occurred to me in an unexpected flash of insight she might not say yes. My throat felt dry.

"Hello." Despite what Dusty calls my 'Blarney stone accent', I'm not really into sweet words. I hesitated, not sure how to continue. Nervousness was beginning to take control so I rushed to the point. "Er. I want to ask you something."

"Anything your heart desires, darling Irishman." I heard the smile in her voice. She didn't realise the question I wanted to ask was a serious one.

I asked her. She did say yes.

The next morning I woke in the surreal knowledge I was now engaged to Ingrid Olsen: a stunning thirty-year-old Australian ex-model. This was the real deal; the first step to marriage, children and all that goes with that. My mother would be right chuffed – to use one of her expressions.

I wondered how to tell Dusty. She didn't need to know just yet anyway; not until the engagement was made official. How would I give her the news? I could just send her an invitation to the engagement party when the time comes. Cowardly? Then I realised I was having bizarre thoughts. Why should I not tell Dusty?

Breakfast was a strong cup of coffee. Tired from a sleepless night and a little hung over, food was not attractive to my stomach. Taking long, slow slurps of the coffee to allow its medicinal properties to take effect, I mulled over some information I'd picked up last night at the pool table. I was sure Dusty would be interested.

To clear my head, I set off for a walk along the beach. A few people were already there – some lounging in deck chairs, some wading in the shallows. Kicking off my thongs, I carried them loosely in one hand, allowing the waves to wash over my feet as I walked along the shore. Seduced by the sapphire-blue sea and clear skies, I went further than I intended.

On the way back, I encountered the octogenarian couple from yesterday. The woman wished me a sweet good morning. The smile accompanying the greeting illuminated her face and radiated to her clear brown eyes. She must once have been quite a beauty. I wondered if Ingrid and I would one day reach our twilight years together.

As if to bring me back to the present, my phone in the back pocket of my shorts vibrated, delivering a text message from Dusty telling me Jake had arranged for us to meet Rocky at his cafe today.

CHAPTER 12

R OCKY'S CAFE, OR La Cucina di Rocco to give it its official name according to the sign across the door, was one of those quirky places with its own individual character. On the right side of the open doorway propped up against the wall the cafe shared with the quaint old house next door, was a stainless-steel man's bicycle. I wasn't sure if it was meant to be part of the decor or the means of a ready getaway for a chef whose meals hadn't pleased the patrons.

Several outdoor tables near the entrance were distinctive for their lack of uniformity. Tables were different shapes; chairs were multi coloured. The jumbled mishmash created a fun, inviting atmosphere.

The theme of colour and diversity continued inside. Handwritten notes, in a variety of writing styles and sealed with some sort of clear finish covered the interior walls in a haphazard fashion. Some messages were single words; others were short phrases. Large overhead fans provided a natural coolness rather than the iciness of air conditioning.

As soon as we entered, we were greeted by a smiling young man whose facial features indicated he had Down syndrome.

"Hello. My name is Nathan." An expression of eager helpfulness brightened his face. "I will take you to your table." Starting toward the back of the cafe, he grinned over his shoulder at us. "You're Dusty." He looked up at me. "You're Sean."

The mystery of how he knew who we were was soon solved when Nathan led us to a table in a corner at the back of the cafe. Jake was already there and must have told Nathan our names.

A mouth watering antipasto platter had already been placed in the middle of the table. My stomach, now fully recovered from the excess

Guinness I had devoured the evening before, quivered with excitement. Jake rose to greet me with a handshake. Nathan made a discreet departure. The look that passed between Jake and Dusty told me all I needed to know.

"Rocky's busy in the kitchen. He'll come out and join us shortly," Jake told us.

"Rocco," said Dusty, referring to the sign above the door. "Is that how he came to be called Rocky?"

"Yup. His full name is Angelo Rocco Tibaldi."

Dusty smiled. "I like Angelo." I could see her earlier superficial prejudice against the man because of his nickname had evaporated. "Is he Italian?"

"Rocky's as Aussie as Vegemite sandwiches but his family is Italian. His grandparents migrated to Australia just after the war." Jake lowered his voice. "Unfortunately, Rocky's parents were killed in a traffic accident." Jake shook his head. "Bloody maniac drunk at the wheel. The other driver, I mean. Rocky would have been around eighteen or nineteen at the time."

"How awful." Dusty's sympathy for Rocky was immediate and sincere.

"Tragic. Even now, Rocky's not comfortable talking about his parents."

When we were seated, Jake said, "I also had a word with Carmen, a well-known local. She knows everything there is to know about Port Douglas."

Dusty raised her eyebrows. "Another old school friend?"

Jake laughed. "She's almost ninety years old." I wondered if Carmen might be one of the residents in the retirement home where Ram had volunteered. "As a matter of fact, I invited her to join us for lunch."

A little unusual. Although I suppose there's no reason why a retirement home resident couldn't go out to lunch. The hospice probably has a community van or some sort of taxi service for them.

My thoughts were interrupted by the arrival at our table of a man in his thirties with short dark hair, a fine physique evident under his firm fitting T-shirt and casual black jeans.

"Rocky!" Jake half rose to shake the cafe owner's hand.

"Hey, buddy," said his friend, returning the handshake warmly.

I saw immediately why Rocky was well-liked in the community. His round brown eyes gleamed with sincerity and his smile radiated goodwill. He had an easy way about him; one of those people who would feel comfortable anywhere. The sort of person others gravitated to. I sensed he took this for granted, assuming it was normal for everyone to possess this sort of social poise. An earring in one ear, a double tiger's eye bracelet and an elaborate tattoo on his right wrist might have been a reminder his cordiality was backed up by an individual spirit and physical strength.

"I know you by reputation," he said to Dusty. "A cold case warrior. You do good work. So many murderers get away scot free."

"Until I come along." Dusty was never one for false modesty.

Rocky's reaction was an indulgent smile.

"If I can give you any help at all while you're in Port, just ask." He reached for one of his business cards from a pile loosely arranged in a small dish on the counter and handed it to Dusty.

"Thank you." Dusty placed the card in her bag.

"You're staying at Four Mile Resort?"

"How did you know?"

Rocky grinned. "It's where the rich and famous usually stay."

Dusty ignored his good-natured teasing. "I gather the opening of the Resort in 1988 was cause for great excitement in Port Douglas."

Rocky shrugged. "Wouldn't know. I wasn't here then." Dusty gave him a sharp look. Rocky quickly explained. "What I mean is, I was here – but I was only a kid."

"Me too," said Jake. He stretched up to high five with Rocky. "You going to join us, mate?"

Rocky shook his head. "I'll join you later, if that's all right." He flashed Dusty a smile that gave him a boyish look; a smile more disarming, I was sure, than mine. Jake's eyes rested on Dusty for a split second as if he was assessing the impact of Rocky's charm. I knew her well enough to know she had warmed to Rocky, yet I fancied she was not captivated. A part of her was holding back; the suspicious investigator in her doubts everyone on first meeting.

"Have you been to interview Jake's prime suspect yet?" Although the table next to us was empty, Rocky kept his voice low. Dusty arched her eyebrows and glanced at Jake.

"No secrets in a place like this, Dus. The whole town knows we focused our investigation on Moose Mulligan. Some of them hated us for it."

"Because he's a local? They don't believe one of their own could be a murderer?"

"You got it in one, Dus."

"Even though he has a criminal record and is known to be a drug dealer?" I said.

Jake nodded. "Most people around here wouldn't see selling marijuana as serious drug dealing. Besides, the Mulligans have been a respected local family for generations. Local people sympathise with Moose because of what happened to his family. They make allowances for him."

Rocky, who stood facing the front of the cafe with a hand resting on the back of one of the vacant chairs at our table, uttered an exclamation of pleasure.

"Here comes my favourite neighbour."

CHAPTER 13

ROCKY STOPPED NATHAN'S advance toward the front of the restaurant with a light shake of his head and hurried to greet the new arrival. Nathan's happy smile remained on his face as he watched Rocky gallantly ushering in... Well, ushering in an explosion of colour. That's the best way I can describe my first vision of Rocky's neighbour. This was evidently the well-known local Jake had mentioned earlier and clearly not a retirement home resident as I had supposed.

"Did you say she was nearly *ninety*?" Dusty hissed at Jake.

"Shh! She's not aware I know her real age."

This exotic woman looked like a well preserved sixty-five-year-old. The curves of her body, accentuated in a clinging red dress, would have been the envy of any young woman. A colourful turban style headdress sporting an elaborate display of feathers, beads and ribbons extended her height by six to eight inches.

Like a queen attended by a royal escort, she draped a hand over Rocky's arm, pausing just inside the door as though an appreciative audience waited. This was a woman who commanded attention with a presence that went beyond her outlandish clothes. She carried herself with model-like poise and at first glance I had thought her to be taller than she actually was. As she walked slowly toward us, hips swaying, I realised the turban and her platform shoes had given the illusion of height. In fact, she was probably even shorter than Dusty, possibly only around five foot.

Multiple bracelets jingled as she held out her arms in welcome to Jake. He quickly rose from his seat and accepted one of the outstretched hands, bringing it up to his lips and brushing it with a soft kiss. I shared Dusty's surprise, indicated by her raised eyebrows. The gesture seemed out of character for this down-to-earth Queensland cop.

"Daa...rling." Our 'royal' guest drawled the word out in her husky voice. "How wonderful to see you." I guessed her accent to be South American but could easily be wrong. I don't have a good ear for foreign accents.

Jake turned toward us. "This is Carmen Miranda."

I was momentarily taken aback. Was that her real name or was she actually pretending to be Carmen Miranda? I could see a resemblance to the 1940s singer known as the 'Brazilian Bombshell' famous for wearing fruit hats. When I was a kid I often snuggled up next to my mother while my sisters slept, to watch old movies. In one of those movies, which we viewed many times, I saw Carmen Miranda. In my memory she is glittering in red but that must have been my imagination because it would surely have been a black and white movie. This lady was glittering in red, but who was she?

When I rose from my chair to greet her, the difference in our heights was immediately evident. Carmen stepped back, tilted her head and looked up at me.

"Darling, you are a tree. A tree most handsome."

She held toward me the hand Jake had brushed with his lips, fingers gracefully drooping toward the floor. I obliged by awkwardly aiming my lips at the extended hand but falling short of the mark. How is a tree supposed to kiss the hand of a dowager? Although Dusty wasn't in my line of sight at that moment, I was sure she was suppressing a chuckle.

"This young lady most radiant is Miss Dusty Kent. Yes?"

Dusty, who was wearing a knee length, crisp white shirt and turquoise sandals, stayed seated but smiled warmly in greeting. Jake quickly moved to pull out a chair for Carmen as Rocky slipped away in the direction of the kitchen.

"You are famous, Miss Kent."

Dusty laughed. "As famous as Carmen Miranda. Please call me Dusty."

"Certainly we must call each other by the first names, isn't it?"

On closer inspection, I saw that artfully applied makeup account-ed to some extent for Carmen's appearance belying her age. However there was a vitality about her that assisted the impression of youthful-ness. The effervescent octogenarian charmed and entertained us all during lunch. The antipasto was followed by several excellent Italian dishes including the fettuccine carbonara I ordered.

When Dusty asked Carmen about her name, the irrepressible local celebrity seemed to be under the misapprehension she really was Carmen Miranda. There was no sense that she was playing a part. Maybe she had inhabited the role of Carmen Miranda for so long that, for her, the persona had morphed into reality. She cheerfully informed us she'd faked her death in 1955 to escape the publicity and came to Australia to live a quiet life and had been living in 'Port' ever since.

"They have not tracked me down; the photographers, the auto-graph hounds." Her broad smile revealed perfect teeth, possibly whitened with cosmetic assistance. "Here, in this place most beautiful, I am left in peace."

I didn't like to point out to her that if she really were Carmen Miranda she would be 107, which I'd established by discreetly holding my phone under the table and doing a quick internet search for Carmen Miranda's birth date. It occurred to me that Rocky's neighbour was just as savvy as her namesake. By being outlandish she had ensured that she would always command attention and, even in old age, never be overlooked.

Jake interacted with Carmen respectfully, as though he had ac-cepted her for who she said she was in the same way that Rocky seemed to have done.

Dusty turned to Carmen. "You live close by?"

"It is my house next door."

I was glad I hadn't voiced my earlier speculation Carmen might be a resident of a retirement home.

"Once this was my house also." She swept an arm in a wide arc to encompass the cafe. "My house, it was too big for me. So the builder he chop it in half." Carmen's bracelets jangled as she made a chopping motion with her hand. "He build the cafe; he make the apartment up the stairs." She pointed toward the ceiling. "That is where Rocky lives. He is two times my neighbour, isn't it?"

Dusty smiled. "A neighbour with a business next door and a neighbour who lives next door."

Carmen bestowed an appreciative glance on Dusty. "You must come to my house any day, you and your handsome Irish tree." She angled a flirtatious glance at me.

When Nathan had cleared away our plates earlier, he hadn't asked us if we wanted coffee. I understood why when Rocky returned, carrying a silver tray of cocktails. Each highball glass contained a pale lemon liquid and ice, and was decorated with small slices of tropical fruits on a long cocktail pick with a paper parasol perched on the rim.

"This is a speciality of the house." He placed the cocktails one after the other on the table. "In fact, it is the only cocktail we serve here."

Dusty, who had a penchant for espresso martinis, eyed the colourful concoction. "It looks delicious. What is it called?"

Carmen's eyes widened in surprise. "Darling, you do not know?"

"This cocktail is called the Carmen Miranda." Rocky rolled a hand in Carmen's direction as if presenting her for the first time. "It was created in honour of my best landlady."

"He is a cheeky boy." Carmen's wide smile reflected her pleasure. "But it is true what he says. You are drinking the cocktail the world created for me." Rocky sat at the remaining vacant chair at our table. Carmen raised her glass to Dusty. "I drink to the famous detective, she will help Jake… How do you say? Crack the case."

Carmen's use of the vernacular expression brought a smile to the lips of all of us at the table. We followed her example and raised our glasses.

"She's already hot on the trail of the killer, Carmen," said Rocky.

Dusty protested. "I wouldn't say that. I have a lot more work to do before I narrow it down to one suspect."

Jake glanced at Rocky. "I told you she'd have her own ideas."

"I just need more choices, Jake. You know what I'm like. I can't choose the first dress I see when I go into a boutique. I have to have a good look at everything in the shop first."

Jake grinned. "And then go back and choose the first dress you saw."

We all laughed, Dusty included.

"We drink to the cracking of the case." Carmen tilted her glass toward Dusty before downing her cocktail in one swig.

"It's non-alcoholic," said Rocky, seeing the look on our faces. "Almost, anyway. Just a drop of rum with a mixture of tropical fruit juices, bitters and soda water."

With the drinking of the toast over, Dusty turned to business.

"A question for the locals." This was directed at Rocky and Carmen. "What can you tell me about Kellie Edwards, the local vet?"

CHAPTER 14

"**M**ISS KELLIE, SHE work very hard but her son… Ah, she should not have such a burden." Carmen clicked her tongue in disapproval and glanced at Jake. "You know this sad story, darling?" Jake nodded. "Dah. Such a story."

"Josh was a drug addict," explained Rocky. "Took an overdose while he was with the monks. Weird that. Two deaths at Sunyarta Sanctuary happening exactly a year apart."

"You mean the monk was murdered on the anniversary of Joshua Edwards' death?"

"Yeah," said Rocky. "Strange coincidence, isn't it?"

Dusty raised an eyebrow at Jake. He shook his head. "I didn't realise that."

Carmen pushed her chair back. "Now I must go to fetch Sylvia and Eric." She rested a hand, sparkling with rings, on Dusty's arm. "When you want information for your investigation, you must come to Carmen. I know everybody, everybody knows me. Isn't it?"

Placing the drinks tray on the counter, Rocky offered his arm to Carmen as she stood up. She blew us each a kiss and turned to Jake.

"Do not leave without the visit to Carmen, my good friend."

"I wouldn't dare." Jake laughed.

Rocky escorted Carmen to the door where she turned to offer us an aristocratic farewell wave.

Dusty took the opportunity to ask Jake the obvious question.

"Does she really believe she's Carmen Miranda?"

"Yup. She's never been anyone else. At least, not here in Port. She wasn't born here. No-one really knows when she arrived, probably in the sixties. Port was a pretty quirky town back then with a lot of wacky people; wacky in a good way."

I was watching Rocky. He'd remained just outside the cafe door talking to a smartly dressed woman in her late twenties. His expression was serious, hers was earnest, her body language tense. At a guess, I'd say she was asking Rocky for something he wasn't willing to agree to. I interrupted the conversation Dusty and Jake were engrossed in.

"Is she your mysterious stalker; the woman you saw following us last night?" I indicated the girl with Rocky.

Dusty looked up. "Nope. Not tall enough."

The girl shook her head at Rocky before storming off along the street. Rocky returned to our table, erasing his troubled look with a smile when he reached us.

"Rocky," said Dusty. "There's something I want to ask you."

I thought I saw a guarded look flash into Rocky's eyes. I wondered if he was bracing himself against a possible question about the young woman he'd been talking to. However, that was not what was on Dusty's mind.

"Who are Sylvia and Eric?"

When Rocky looked blank, Dusty reminded him of what Carmen had said.

"I have no idea." He shook his head and shrugged his puzzlement. Almost immediately his eyes shone with understanding. "She's looking after two small dogs for a friend. That must be their names."

"There she is!"

Dusty, Jake and I had just emerged from Rocky's after saying our goodbyes. Dusty was pointing at a cafe on the other side of the street. Several of its outdoor tables were occupied but I didn't know who she was pointing at.

"Who, Dus?" Jake looked mystified.

"The stalker." Dusty called over her shoulder as she stepped off the footpath to cross the road. She adroitly dodged the oncoming vehicles to reach the other side. Jake and I caught up and followed her into the cafe which was lined with shelves of books inside.

"She came in here." Dusty scanned the faces of the people at the tables.

A determined look on her face, she strode into the next section of the shop searching for her prey at the tables hidden among the carousels of books and greeting cards. I wasn't sure if we were in a bookshop that sold coffee or a cafe that sold books. The mix of the two created a cluttered environment ideal for concealing yourself. Dusty's mysterious woman must have done just that, then doubled back to exit the cafe without being seen because we failed to find her despite a thorough search of the premises.

"You sure it was the same woman, Dus?"

"Yep. It's her all right. She was watching Rocky's Cafe. I saw her through the windows as we were walking out. That's when she bolted, when she spotted me looking at her."

Jake jerked his head in my direction. "She's probably got a weakness for tall Irishmen."

Dusty turned to me. "Did you see her last night?"

"I did not. I thought you were like, just having a lend of me."

She grinned. "Maybe I was a little. But she did follow us along Macrossan Street after we left the restaurant."

Thinking about last night reminded me I was now an engaged man but this was not the right time to tell Dusty.

"Whoever she is, sooner or later she'll have to explain herself." Dusty's nostrils flared. "I don't like being followed round like that."

CHAPTER 15

J AKE ACCOMPANIED US part of the way to where Dusty's car was parked, filling us in on what he knew about Kellie Edwards' son as we walked.

Joshua Edwards experienced violent episodes, as a result of drug induced schizophrenia. Worried he was a danger to himself and others, his mother encouraged him to go to the Sanctuary, hoping he would find some peace there. During his stay, Saya offered him guidance and a listening ear; encouraging Josh to talk without passing judgement. Ram invited the boy to work in the garden.

The tranquillity of the Sanctuary and the ready acceptance by the monks seemed to be exactly what Josh needed. He began to show signs of getting better. So much so that he decided to stop his medication – against the advice of his mother and the monks. One morning, not long after he ceased taking the prescribed medicine, Josh was found dead from an overdose.

When we told Jake about our encounter with Kellie at Sunyarta, he was not surprised she'd been so angry.

"She believes the monks should have taken better care of her son. Because she trusted them, she felt the monks had let her down. Worse than that, she believes they caused his death by supplying him with the drug that killed him."

Jake's tone suggested he had little patience with Kellie's grievances. While he did have a sensitive side as suggested by his sympathy for Ram in his lonely death, he was a man used to dealing with tough situations where decisions had to be made without the interference of emotions.

"You didn't take her seriously?" Dusty queried.

"We found absolutely no evidence of foul play and no reason to think anyone would want to kill her son."

"Maybe he owed money to his drug supplier."

"Moose Mulligan, for example," I suggested.

"Josh Edwards didn't get his heroin from Mulligan. I spoke to his drug supplier. Josh didn't owe him money and, as far as the supplier knew, the boy had been clean for two years."

"If you know the creep is a dealer, why don't you arrest him? Get him off the streets." Dusty's lips tightened into a hard line; her anger stirred by the thought of a drug dealer escaping the law rather than aimed at Jake.

"I know he's a dealer and he knows I know. But he's smart. We haven't been able to get the evidence we need to make a case against him."

I admit to being naive about this sort of thing. How could the police stand by and let a drug dealer carry on his business? My shock must have shown on my face because Jake reassured me.

"Don't worry. We'll arrest him one day. When that happens, he'll be off the streets for a long time." A determined glint in his eye and the set of his mouth left me in no doubt of his serous intention.

"And with your help," Jake looked at Dusty, his expression softening, "the same thing will happen to Moose Mulligan."

"No problem. If he's the killer, I'll hand him over to you with pleasure before I leave Port." Dusty always had unshakeable confidence in her ability to track down her prey. "Anyway, back to Josh," she added. "Can we assume he didn't smuggle drugs into Sunyarta when he first went there?"

"He wasn't permitted to take any belongings in with him and he had to undergo a thorough body search by a doctor before the monks accepted him."

"So you don't know where he got his last heroin hit from?"

"No. Someone has delivered it to him somehow. He probably asked a friend to help him out."

"Unless there *is* a crazy monk at Sunyarta as Kellie Edwards suggested."

Jake rolled his eyes. "She's clutching at straws. Users who are newly clean don't need the same amount of the drug to get high as when they were regular users. They don't know how much heroin to give themselves. They inject what used to be a normal dose, which is now an overdose and end up killing themselves. That's what I think happened to Joshua Edwards."

After parting from Jake, Dusty and I drove to Portpaws Veterinary Clinic; a single storey building painted a soft muted green that was almost grey, similar to the colour of the continent's desert flora. Someone once told me during my travels around Australia that the grey-green leaves on plants such as spinifex grass and desert peas reflect sunlight, thus enabling the plants to keep cool. The bullnose verandahs were also a feature designed to help keep the interior of the building cool.

A faint antiseptic smell greeted us when we stepped inside. White walls and slate floors added to the clinical atmosphere.

Kellie Edwards, wearing a white coat over her clothes, greeted us cordially. When she saw me, her face creased into a smile, spawning dimples in her cheeks. Her expression became serious again as she ushered us into a small office. She pushed a bang of her blonde hair back from her forehead and sat down behind the only desk in the room, gesturing us toward the two vacant chairs in front of it.

"As I told you on the phone, I have a short break at the moment," she said.

The anger and resentment toward Dusty was not evident today. However, she was not entirely friendly either. Once again I was struck by her compelling face and the strong personality it conveyed. Her un-plucked eyebrows added strength and sensuality to her face as well as accentuating her violet eyes. Rather than emotionally volatile as she had been that day at Sunyarta, today she conveyed the impression of vibrant energy simmering behind a reticent manner – an air of restrained vitality coiled and ready to ignite.

She glanced at the clock on the wall. "I have a cassowary chick with a bung leg coming in for treatment in half an hour."

"A cassowary?" Dusty's eyes met mine. "You mean cassowaries

are kept as pets?"

In my mind's eye I could see the six foot tall creature we had met on the beach. "Aren't they rather large to be pets?" My question drew a smirk from Dusty. I knew she was recalling our 'amusing' encounter with Big Bird.

"Oh yes, they're big. An adult southern cassowary would be almost as tall as you."

"*As* tall as me," I asserted with conviction.

Dusty struggled to keep a straight face.

"They have an appetite to match their size," Kellie continued. "They can easily kill people too. The cassowary is the world's most dangerous bird."

Dusty's face paled. "I didn't realise that."

I saw her apology in her eyes. She understood now that the situation on the beach could have been a deadly calamity. Vindication for me; I had been absolutely right to take the creature's attack seriously.

"Plus they can run fast," I suggested.

Kellie gave me a probing look so I briefly recounted my experience at Cape Tribulation Beach.

She nodded her understanding. "The cassowaries at Cape Trib are used to people. The sneeze might have startled it, but it was probably just curious – might even have been playing with you. If the bird had been aggressive, you would not have come away unscathed, believe me."

Dusty shot me a look as if to say: *See, it was just a bit of fun, after all.*

Kellie smiled at me. "The chick coming in today isn't a pet. Someone found it dangling in a tree. Its leg was tangled and it was distressed. I'll do what I can for it then transfer it to a refuge until it can be released into the wild again."

Kellie sat back with her hands in her lap, looking expectantly at Dusty. Although she obviously enjoyed talking about her work, she would not allow herself to be distracted. It was time for Dusty to state her business.

CHAPTER 16

"MY SINCERE CONDOLENCES on the loss of your son." The genuine empathy Dusty felt for families who lost loved ones was evident in her voice, causing Kellie's face to soften a little. "I am very, very sorry you suffered such a devastating tragedy."

Dusty paused briefly to allow the moment to settle before continuing.

"I'm interested in the possibility you raised yesterday about one of the monks being a murderer."

Kellie's jaw tightened. "I don't believe Josh took his own life. Not for one second."

"You think someone injected an overdose of heroin into his veins?"

"I know they did."

"What makes you think it was one of the monks?"

Kellie raised her hand in a gesture of exasperation. "Who else?"

"Isn't it possible Josh managed to contact his supplier for heroin then accidentally injected too much?"

A brief glimmer of doubt in Kellie's eyes acknowledged that Dusty had raised a valid point.

"I don't believe that's what happened." Kellie really meant that she didn't want to believe her son had weakened and returned to using. She wanted to remember him as a brave young man who'd fought his addiction and won.

Dusty turned the conversation to the murder she had come to Port Douglas to investigate.

"As you know, I'm looking into the death of Ram, the monk who was killed in February."

Kellie's eyes narrowed. "I'm sorry the monk died the way he did but his death is insignificant to me compared to the loss of my son."

A flash of anger seared through me at her lack of compassion for Ram. He'd never done anyone any harm and gave his time and energy willingly to help others. The man deserved some sympathy yet no-one seemed to be mourning him. It didn't seem right. My indignation loosened my tongue.

"Do you really think it's right to blame the monks at Sunyarta for your son's death?"

Those violet eyes flashed and locked with mine. "He was in their care."

The unfairness of this detonated the next words from my mouth. "You've never lost a patient in your care?"

"Hardly the same situation," snapped Kellie. "Some things are out of my control."

I could have pointed out to her the same thing applied to the monks who offered a peaceful sanctuary to her son. How could they force him to take his medication? How could they have stopped Josh from taking his own life?

Dusty, noticing I was still bristling, put a stop to any further indiscretions on my part with a question.

"Kellie, I believe the day Ram died was the first anniversary of your son's death. I hope you understand why I feel that is significant and why I need to ask you where you were on the morning of Wednesday February 19th."

"Unbelievable! You're trying to turn me into a murder suspect."

Dusty remained calm in the face of Kellie's hostile stare. "Eliminating innocent people is the first step in getting to the actual killer. If you help me with the investigation into the monk's death, it could help me also find out how your son really died. If the person who murdered the monk is the same person who killed your son or supplied your son with drugs, I will find out."

Kellie relaxed with a heavy sigh. "Very well. If you must know, I went for my usual morning jog and then…" She lowered her eyes. "Then I closed the clinic and lost the day in a bottle of vodka." Shame crossed her face. "I'll never do that again." She must have realised trying to find peace through an 'injection' of alcohol was not so different from what her son had been doing with heroin, even if her drug of choice was less dangerous.

I was becoming restless, anxious for the interview to end before the cassowary arrived. However, Dusty had more questions.

"Did you have contact with Ram in the days before his death? Did you speak to him, or see him in town?"

"I did not."

"Did you go anywhere near Sunyarta Sanctuary the morning he died?"

"Of course not!" Kellie ran her fingers through the bang of hair that fell forward over her forehead, pushing it back momentarily.

Her defiant denial sounded sincere to me but I noticed a tell-tale gleam flash into Dusty's eyes. When she was like this I sometimes compared her to a cat – a bright-eyed cat that had clocked a mouse. It's the way she looks when she has detected, not a mouse, but a lie. I waited for her to pounce. She looked straight at Kellie, holding her gaze.

"Are you sure?"

Kellie didn't flinch, maintaining eye contact with a cold stare. Without saying a word, she stood up, walked over to the door of the office and ushered us out.

A van pulling into the driveway as we stepped outside probably had an avian passenger in the back. I didn't hang around to find out.

"Don't you want to see how cute a cassowary chick is?" Dusty called after me as I headed to the safety of the car.

"There's a reason why that so-called bird has the word 'wary' in its name," I said, sliding into the driver's seat.

Later, when I started to apologise for losing my cool with Kellie, Dusty stopped me with a raised hand.

"No worries. Doesn't hurt to get interviewees rattled. You never know what they might let slip."

"She did let her guard down at some point, didn't she? The Dusty Kent lie detector picked up something during the interview. Right?"

"What an astute observer you are. Yep. I think she *was* near Sunyarta on the morning of the murder. I'm sure you noticed the slight change in her voice and the way her eyes darted toward the door when I asked her if she'd been at the Sanctuary."

I hadn't noticed either of those things but I nodded sagely.

"I wonder why she lied about that," added Dusty.

CHAPTER 17

TWO DAYS AFTER our visit to the veterinary clinic we returned to Sunyarta. This time, instead of walking up the hill, we took Dusty's car which she'd again given me the honour of driving. Before going into the Sanctuary grounds when we reached the top, Dusty paused to take in the panoramic views of the Coral Sea.

"By the way, if you were wondering why I didn't ask Saya about Joshua Edwards yesterday…" I tried to look innocent. "It's because I wanted an excuse to come back here and poke around a bit. I'm not convinced everything is as it seems at this monastery. Three unnatural deaths in the last few years. Two took place at the same spot exactly a year apart. Too many coincidences add up to…"

"Evil?" I suggested, as we entered the grounds and started along the path.

Dusty suddenly grabbed my arm, gripped it tightly and pointed upward.

"Look!"

My eyes followed the direction of her finger but I could see only the trees.

"What am I looking at?"

"A crow. On the tree branch up there."

By the time I'd focused my eyes on the spot she was indicating, the bird had taken flight. All I saw was a glimpse of black wings.

I couldn't understand why Dusty seemed agitated. "Was it a special crow?"

"Yes! Do you remember the other day when we first came here, and we stopped about halfway up to take in the views? I saw a crow in the trees then."

My blank expression must have revealed my lack of comprehension. Dusty rolled her eyes, throwing her hands up in frustration. "That means the crow has been in this area for a few days. It's an omen, isn't it?" This was a good time to keep my mouth shut. Dusty shivered. "A single crow hanging around an area is a sign evil is present."

Dusty's illogical belief in superstitions was something that always surprised me. I responded with carefully chosen words.

"Right. Makes sense since a murder was committed here."

"That was months ago. The crow is not telling us evil happened in the past. It's telling us evil is here now."

"I suppose that could mean the murderer lives here."

Dusty nodded, her expression serious. "Or it could be telling us another murder is imminent."

I thought it might be a good idea to dilute the power of the superstition.

"Unless it's not a single crow hanging around. It could be like, a couple of different crows paying a polite visit to the Sanctuary." Dusty gave me a withering look and marched toward the main buildings.

The yellow robes of the monks strolling along the paths added a touch of brilliance to the natural surroundings. The monks showed no sense of haste as they went about their daily routine.

"Monks' uniforms have come a long way since the olden days," said Dusty.

"You mean brown robes with hoods worn by Christian monks?"

Dusty nodded. "Dreary. Must have been depressing to wear boring brown every day. The only good thing about them was giving us the word cappuccino."

"How so?"

"Cappuccino comes from the brown colour of the robes of the Capuchin order of monks. At least that's what I read somewhere." She grinned and added, "Maybe there's a delicious yellow Sunyarta spritz named after the robes of the monks here."

"Right. Sunyarta spritz. I like it."

From somewhere in the distance came the sound of someone

sweeping a stone surface with a straw broom. The sound gradually became more distinct as we approached the main building. There, we saw a young monk sweeping away leaves from the path that led to the entrance.

"Ram's missing sandal could be a clue, couldn't it?" said Dusty with a glance at the monk's leather thongs.

"You mean, find the sandal, find the murderer?"

"Maybe. If the murderer took it, then it was almost certainly taken as a trophy. What sort of person would be likely to do that?"

She gave me a troubled look and I realised what she meant.

"Right. A person who kills from some sort of psychotic motivation might want to keep a memento of the deed. Is that what you're thinking?"

Dusty nodded. I suspected her superstition about black crows had influenced her. Now she was concerned the murderer was a monk about to strike again.

Saya, who'd been expecting our visit, met us at the door of the main building and escorted us to the back area to sit under an open verandah surrounded by trees. Morning sunshine filtered through the leaves.

"You are seeking answers." It was a matter-of-fact statement with the barest hint that he considered Dusty's search for answers a futile endeavour.

"Before I seek my answers, Saya, there's something I need to tell you. Well, to warn you about really."

As diplomatically as she could, Dusty raised the possibility one of the monks at Sunyarta might be a killer. Saya's face remained impassive even as Dusty suggested he and the other monks be on the alert for danger.

"We are a peaceful community," was all he said.

Dusty, who didn't share my suspicions about Saya, persisted. "If you think of anything at all, even the smallest thing out of the ordinary in the behaviour of any of the monks here, please contact me immediately."

Saya smiled and inclined his head. Dusty's eyes met mine. I read the beseeching message there: *Please don't let another murder happen here.*

Realising there wasn't much more she could do to convince Saya, Dusty began the interview by asking about Josh Edwards. Sadness crossed the elderly monk's face.

"The boy struggled. His heart and mind could not meet in peace." Saya gazed at the natural stone floor.

"Did you or the other monks have any inkling Josh would take his own life?"

Saya didn't answer directly. He explained Josh had been in the guest accommodation with a live-in mentor who stayed with him during the day as well as sleeping there. Sometimes Ram was his mentor, sometimes one of the other monks. He went on to explain they were concerned when Josh stopped his medication so Ram visited his mother to let her know. However, when Kellie came to talk to him, Josh would not see her.

"I spent many hours with Joshua. Often we sat together in silence. Sometimes Joshua talked. I listened. After he stopped his medication he talked only a little. He became restless."

"How did he get the heroin he overdosed on?"

"We do not have drugs here." Saya gazed up at the tree canopy, seeming to examine the leaves gently swaying like green marionettes. "It is not pleasant for me to talk of these things. For many years we have lived here in harmony. We have cared for the environment. We tried to help the lay community and we have welcomed all to Sunyarta. Talk of death and drugs brings a sour note to our place of peace."

Dusty was quick to reassure him. "Oh, no. What you've established here is an exquisite example of living with nature."

It seemed natural, after that, for us all to slip into silence and absorb the presence of the trees, the sprinkles of sunshine and the blue of the sky.

CHAPTER 18

SAYA EVENTUALLY BROKE the quietude. "You wish to ask about Ashin Ram?" Without waiting for Dusty to respond Saya gathered his robes and stood up. "Ashin Ram became a good gardener but his true gift lay elsewhere. Come. I will show you."

We followed Saya inside, our footsteps echoing in the long hall as we continued to his office. He stood behind a long desk on the opposite side of the room, extending his arm from under his robe to point to four paintings along the wall behind the desk.

"Ashin Ram was an artist."

"He painted these?" Dusty peered at the corners of the paintings where an artist's signature might be found.

Saya's smile was all knowing. "His name he painted on the back."

Dusty nodded, looking in admiration at the row of paintings. "They're good." All of the paintings depicted ocean scenes. Dusty studied the one at the end: a dramatic image of waves breaking up against rocks. Something piqued her interest. She moved even closer to examine a section of one of the rocks.

"I think there's something written in this rock crevice. It's hard to see because the writing is almost the same colour as the rocks." She examined it again. "It looks like...Port...Port something."

"Port Douglas," I suggested. "Is this one of the local beaches, Saya?"

Saya arched his eyebrows, causing his forehead to crinkle. After a moment's thought, he shook his head. "I think it is a place of Ashin Ram's childhood."

"It's not Port Douglas." A note of excitement in Dusty's voice. "It's Portsea. Look!"

I looked at where her finger was pointing. The writing, done with a brush, was well obscured. Most people standing back to view the picture would not have noticed it or if they had would have taken it for a mark on the rock.

"Portsea?" Saya repeated the word as though hearing it for the first time.

"Yep. Portsea is a famous place in Victoria with some dangerous beaches. In fact, one of our prime ministers disappeared there in the 1960s." Dusty turned her attention to the other paintings. "The one in the middle is…" She paused thoughtfully, unsure how to describe it.

Saya nodded his understanding. "Not like a picture painted by a monk." That's exactly what I'd been thinking. So had Dusty, apparently, because she nodded vigorously. Nothing in Saya's expression suggested he was judging us for stereotyping monks. He'd probably had years of experience in dealing with the ignorance of the lay person.

The passionate energy and dynamic colours in the painting contrasted with the perception of stillness I associated with people living a life of meditation. The canvas was completely filled by an unusual looking tree, branches extending on either side all the way along the trunk, heavy with dark green leaves. Underneath the tree and entwined in its coiled, twisted roots was what looked like an ancient coffin with a bright green lid.

"I guess it's symbolic in some way." Dusty put her head to one side, her eyes still on the painting. "Maybe it's about the regeneration of nature. Or incarnation. After death comes new life." She looked across at the monk for confirmation of her theory.

"It is a good suggestion that you make, that it is symbolic."

"Did Ram tell you what it represents?"

Saya shook his head. "It does not matter what the artist wished to symbolise. It matters only what we see."

Not convinced, Dusty persevered. "You have looked at it every day here in the office. What do you think it means?"

"Each day the meaning is different." Then, as if the painting had released something within him, Saya began to talk about Ram while still staring at the dead monk's extraordinary artwork. "Before he went to volunteer in the town I did not know he was an artist. It was only then, after he found some peace within, that our brother began to paint. He was not a beginner. You can see his work is of high quality."

"So you think something happened to Ram before he came here, something which made him withdraw and protect himself from his fellow human beings?"

Saya sighed. "That is what I think. Ashin Ram was wounded when he came here."

"It sounds like he was betrayed by someone, or even by society in general."

"Perhaps betrayed by himself." Saya bowed his head.

"Betrayed by himself? Oh, you mean he did something he was later ashamed of."

"It is possible. He did not speak of it. I only know what I saw in his eyes. His spirit was damaged. It was his spirit I thought of when I asked him to take care of the garden."

I could understand the symbolism in that. Plants suggest renewal. On a practical level, working so close to nature was likely to have a therapeutic effect.

"Ashin Ram knew nothing of gardening," continued Saya. "At first, he pulled out weeds which were really herbs. No matter." Saya's lips curled up in an indulgent smile.

"Did gardening help Ram?"

"After some time, it began to soothe his spirit, I think. Ashin Ram did not like to go out of Sunyarta but after some years I encouraged him to go into the town."

"Because you knew he had something to give?"

Saya turned to look at Dusty. Reading his eyes, she answered her own question. "No. Because going out would help Ram?"

Saya nodded.

"Who went into town to volunteer at the retirement home before Ram?"

A brief passing shadow in his eyes was the only hint Dusty's question had thrown Saya off guard.

"A different monk." His voice remained calm yet I sensed wariness in his manner. Was he feeling defensive because he had something to hide or because he considered Dusty's questioning had crossed the line into the Sanctuary's private business.

"Why did that monk stop going?" Dusty was never one to back down because of someone's sensitivities. In fact, she viewed any discomfort on the part of her interviewees as a green light to go full steam ahead.

Saya bowed his head. "He could not continue his good work."

Once again I had the sense there was much he could have told us but chose not to. Why did he feel it necessary to be so secretive?

"What was that monk's name, Saya?"

Dusty had told me earlier she had a hunch Ram had taken over the volunteer duties of the monk who had been killed several years earlier.

The old monk inclined his head. "His name was Ashin Khin."

"Ashin Khin. Do all the monks use the title 'Ashin'?"

Saya dismissed the choice of title with a wave of his hand. "It is just our way. We use it here. It is not necessary for lay people to use it."

Dusty nodded thoughtfully. "By the way, do you have a photograph of Ram?"

Saya shook his head.

"What did he look like?"

Saya smiled. "A middle-aged man with a shaven head wearing yellow robes."

Dusty laughed and didn't press him further. Instead, she asked his permission to use her phone camera to snap Ram's paintings.

I took one last look at the painting with the casket. Was it something to do with sacrifice? The tree with its sideways branches might represent a cross. A life had been surrendered to a tree rather than on the cross. But whose life? Did Ram have a premonition his life would be sacrificed? I brushed away my fanciful thoughts. If the painting had any symbolic meaning at all, it could simply reflect Ram giving his life to nature here at the Sanctuary.

At the doorway, Dusty turned to ask Saya what I call an ambush question. She often used this tactic of waiting until after she'd wrapped up the interview and said goodbye before asking a question to catch the interviewee off guard.

"Did you see Ram the morning he died?" Her tone was offhand, as if her query was of no particular interest.

Saya answered without hesitation, his face impassive.

"I saw him."

"Where?"

"He was on his way to meditation. He walked past the office." Saya pointed to the desk and computer. "I came here that morning before first light." He gestured at the window behind the desk in the main office area. "It was still dark outside, a few minutes after four, but I saw Ashin Ram."

"Was he alone?"

Saya responded with a slight raise of the eyebrows. "Of course."

Clearly, the idea of Ram doing his morning meditation with another monk was incongruous.

"Did you see anyone else on the path that morning?"

The monk shook his head. I got the feeling if he'd seen one of the other monks he would not have told Dusty. Or the police.

CHAPTER 19

A NEGLECTED WHITE house with a cast-iron roof surrounded by overgrown lawn stood behind a chain wire fence. Just as we pulled up outside, a dusty red truck hurtled into the driveway, coming to a noisy halt in the carport. A tattooed grizzly bear swung himself out of the cabin while balancing a can of beer and a lit cigarette in one hand. Prolifically tattooed arms bulged out of a well-worn black T-shirt. More tattoos decorated the skin on his chest. He scowled in our direction. The scowl deepened when we entered the property though a rusted old gate which gave the impression of being permanently open.

"Who the bloody hell are you?" This came out as an intimidating growl.

If Mulligan didn't like our answer to his question, his next words would surely be: *Get off my property!*

Blue-grey eyes glared out at us from a round face accentuated by close cropped hair and a receding hairline. His neck was so short his double chin almost sat on his chest.

"I'm Dusty Kent."

The sound of Dusty's voice set a dog barking. It was the bay of a large dog. Chains rattled. Dusty and I had been walking along a cement path towards Mulligan. Now we stopped and looked cautiously in the direction the barking had come from. The dog appeared to be under the house. The underfloor space, created by raising the house on stumps, was high enough to allow the average adult to enter without bending over. Through the slats of timber around it I could see a black Rottweiler with brown face markings. Thankfully, the gap between the slats was too narrow for the dog to squeeze through.

However, a gate under the steps leading up into the house appeared to be open. I hoped the rattle of chains meant the dog was tethered.

Moose Mulligan, without taking his eyes off us, dropped his cigarette butt on the cement floor of the carport. He extinguished it under the sole of his thong with a decisive twist of the foot. A line of tattoos ran from his feet and along his beefy calves to the frayed hem of the grubby pair of shorts he was wearing.

"We called you several times and left a message." That was true. Dusty had asked me to use her phone to call his number while she was driving. When I didn't get an answer, I had texted him to let him know we were on the way.

Dusty took a few more tentative steps forward. Mulligan brought his can to his lips and gulped down what was left of the beer. The dog remained under the house, its muzzle pressed up against the timber slats.

Mulligan's silent stare indicated this was the point at which he might order us off his property and threaten to set his dog on us. Dusty was keen to avoid this.

"I'm writing a book about the murder of the monk at Sunyarta Sanctuary." By presenting herself as an author rather than an investigator, Dusty was hoping to distance herself from the police and thus avoid stirring Moose's antipathy. "I know the police had you down as a suspect. I wondered if you wanted to tell my readers your side of the story."

Mulligan narrowed his eyes, squinting suspiciously at Dusty. I knew he was deciding whether to welcome or banish us. The Rottweiler made its opinion clear with a deep, threatening growl. Moose Mulligan crushed his empty beer can in one hand and threw it over his shoulder into the tray of his truck. One last squint before his body relaxed. He turned in the direction of the growling dog and bellowed. "Down, Butch!"

His tone changed only slightly when he addressed Dusty. "I've heard of you."

He didn't strike me as the kind of bloke who would spend a lot of time reading. On the other hand, one of Dusty's books had been made into a television mini-series. I could imagine Mulligan watching true crime shows with the intention of learning as much as he could to avoid being caught.

Dusty introduced me.

"Wanna beer?" A gruff offer directed at me but extended to Dusty by an enquiring glance.

Dusty, who didn't usually drink beer, accepted enthusiastically. She probably realised Moose Mulligan wouldn't have a wide range of beverages on offer.

Mulligan directed us around to the back of the property and dis-appeared inside to get the beers. Behind the house, well-used chairs waited for us at a plastic table shaded by the overhanging branches of a jacaranda tree growing in the next door property. Parrots, hidden in its lacy purple canopy, whistled to each other. A terracotta plant saucer in the middle of the table was full of old cigarette butts. Dusty used a pen from her bag to nudge the make-shift ashtray to the other side of the table, screwing up her nose at the smell.

Mulligan tramped down the back steps of the house carrying an armful of cold cans of beer. He gave Dusty a surprised look of approval when she cracked open her can with an expert pull, watched the froth bubble out and spill over the rim and raised it to her lips. Mulligan sat back in his chair which only just managed to accommo-date his bulk. The animosity that had been steaming from him earlier had now evaporated, making him slightly less intimidating. He pulled a battered packet of cigarettes from the pocket of his shorts, offering it round. Dusty and I declined.

"Lung cancer in a packet, eh?" He pulled out a crumpled ciga-rette, grinned and shrugged. "What the hell, you only live once." He poked around in the saucer of cigarette butts until he found a small lighter. Once the tobacco was burning and he had enjoyed a long drag, Dusty judged the time right to open the conversation.

"The police say you hold a grudge against the monks because they're occupying land that used to belong to your family."

"Too bloody right I do. That land was in my family for years. For generations. Then some rich foreigner bought it and gave it to that lot of flower pots. Gave it to them! Land we'd worked on all our lives. And they just walk onto it and do what they like with it." Dusty was not about to point out that the monks were not at fault. Moose wanted to tell us how he'd been wronged. Our role was to listen.

"You still own some land though, don't you?" said Dusty.

Moose snorted. "A piddlin' few acres."

"But big enough for a marijuana plantation?"

"About all it's good for. I was doin' all right with the pot, too. Until the friggin' cops got their hands on it. After some friggin' lowlife dobbed me in. That land was makin' money for me till that happened. Now look at me." He gestured at his house. "I can hardly keep this place upright."

"You believe Ram, the dead monk, was the person who reported you?"

"It had to be one of them and he was the one crawling off to the cops."

"What did he say when you accused him?"

"He didn't say nothin'! Just cowered like a frightened dog and slunk away with his tail between his legs. Bloody pansy."

To Moose, a pansy was probably any man who preferred peace to fighting but monks who have the audacity to wear robes instead of trousers would rank even lower in his estimation.

"That convinced you he was guilty?"

"Convinced me he was a bloody wimp. Just the sort who'd go sneaking off to the cops."

"The police told you it wasn't him, didn't they? They received an anonymous tip off. Ram had legitimate business at the police station that day. It had nothing to do with your pot plantation."

"Police! Ha! Lyin' lotta wankers they are."

A long shrill birdcall rang out followed by an angry burst of barking from Butch. Moose twisted his body around and yelled at the dog.

"Down, boy!" He turned back to us, gesturing at the overhanging tree. "It's the bloody whipbird that sets Butch off. Doesn't mind the parrots but can't stand that bird's darn shrieking."

When the bird rendered a second long, drawn out call finishing with what sounded like a whip-crack, Butch detonated another burst of ferocious barks. Moose finished his beer, squashed the can with one hand and aimed it at the tree. A smirk of satisfaction crossed his face at the sound of wings fluttering as the frightened whipbird quickly departed.

Dusty's face was impassive but her anger at Moose's childish response to the bird's song was reflected in her next question.

"Is that your normal reaction when something annoys you, Moose?" His eyes narrowed in a threatening squint challenging her to elaborate. Dusty obliged. "Did you make the monk 'go away' because he annoyed you?"

Moose picked up another can of beer, opening it with a decisive click of the ring tab. I wondered if he was showing contempt toward Dusty's questions or playing for time. Dusty wasn't about to give him too much time.

"What about the day before Ram was murdered? Did you see him in Macrossan Street?"

"I didn't touch him!" I had to take my hat off to Dusty. The anger in Moose's voice suggested she'd managed to unsettle him.

"You spoke to the monk that day, didn't you?"

Moose rolled his eyes as though to acknowledge he'd been caught out.

"I told him to get away from my truck. That's all. Made me bloody mad seeing him walking along with that superior look on his face."

He threw his head back, tilted the can and poured beer into his open mouth. I wondered if Dusty too was thinking that this tattooed hulk, whose anger could be sparked by the mundane act of walking past his truck, had enough bottled up resentment to make him as volatile as a powder keg.

Whatever she thought of him it didn't show in her expression or her tone of voice as she pressed him further. "The monk made you so angry that you stewed on it all day and all night. The next day, you got up early in the morning and went to the Sanctuary."

Mulligan had told the police he was nowhere near Sunyarta on the morning of the murder but Dusty spoke with such quiet conviction Moose must have thought she knew otherwise. He wasn't to know she was simply throwing out a speculation to see how he'd react. His reaction was not the incensed, indignant denial I expected.

His hand tightened around the beer can but he maintained his self control. "I did not kill the bloody monk." He emphasised each word, his eyes flashing his anger as he spoke.

Dusty was ready to reel him in. "You were at the Sanctuary, weren't you?"

"Hell! Look, I just went up there to check the place out."

"Check the place out?" Dusty's tone was wreathed in scepticism. She wasn't going to let him get away with that. "Early in the morning?" Moose definitely did not give the impression of being an early riser.

"So I couldn't sleep." His stare challenged her to contradict him.

Dusty refrained from voicing her disbelief. Instead, knowing Moose was ready to justify his reason for being at Sunyarta Sanctuary that morning, she returned his stare with an attentive expression to encourage him to continue.

"Shit!" He was annoyed at the realisation he'd gone too far and would now have to explain. "So I was going to throw a few rocks around, break a couple of windows, smash up a few things. That's all. I couldn't have done anything even if I wanted to." Moose took a final swig, wiped his mouth with his bare arm and squashed the empty beer can with one crunch.

Dusty raised her eyebrows. "What do you mean?"

Moose aimed his flattened can at a nearby hole in the ground where it landed with a metallic clink on top of other discarded cans. "Someone else was there. All right?"

Pushing her empty can aside, Dusty leant forward. "Someone else? Who?"

"I dunno who it was. Even if I did…"

"You're not a grass." Dusty finished his sentence. "What time were you there?"

"Middle of the bloody night! Four thirty. Five o'clock. Something like that."

"If you have nothing to hide, why did you lie to the police? You told them you were nowhere near Sunyarta the morning the murder took place."

"None of their business."

"But you're telling me."

"Yeah, well. None of your business either. But you're good. You always get the killer you're after. So I reckon I might as well help you. Once the real killer is caught, at least the cops'll have to get off my back. Maybe I'll even sue them for harassment."

As we walked along the path back to the gate a short time later, Dusty couldn't keep the smile from her face.

"Are you smiling at the thought of Moose suing the police or because you picked up on a clue?"

"Both."

"Did you believe that stuff about wanting the real killer caught?"

"I think that could be Moose's devious way of trying to convince me he's innocent."

Butch discharged one final barrage of canine profanity as we passed his enclosure.

CHAPTER 20

"NOW THAT MOOSE has admitted to being at Sunyarta on the morning of the murder," said Dusty during our drive back to town, "I might be able to get him to take that admission a step closer to a murder confession."

"Right. He might have dug a hole he can't get out of."

"Exactly. For the time being though, I'll let him think he's in the clear. Talking about digging, you'd better see what you can dig up on our tattooed beer drinker in cyber space. With a bit of luck, we could find someone with a grudge against him who might be willing to 'help us with our enquiries'."

"Sounds like a long shot. But I'll do my best."

"The thing is, Sean, I think he only admitted being on the hill that morning to cover his tracks before I found out myself. Don't you find that interesting? Why would he think I might find out?"

"You think he told someone?"

"Yep! He's the sort that'd be itching to boast about murdering the monk. Word may have got around. There just might be someone who wouldn't talk to the police but who would be willing to point *us* in the right direction. Now that he's admitted being there, all we need is a piece of evidence linking him to the murder." Dusty's eyes were bright with the anticipation of success. "Do your best Mr Maze Master; he's the only real suspect we've got so far. Apart from the possibility of a crazed monk."

Dusty smiled and waved in response to enthusiastic tooting from a passing motorist who pointed at the FJ Holden approvingly. Dusty's car often attracted attention from other drivers excited at seeing the iconic 1955 model on the road.

I considered telling Dusty about Ingrid. However, when I realised I hadn't passed on some pertinent information I had uncovered, I decided that would be an easier topic of conversation.

"By the way, I picked up some information at the pool table the other night."

After Ingrid had wished me a loving goodnight that evening, a stupid, irrational shaft of fear at the thought of how my life would change after marriage sent me racing out the door to the car park where my Triumph Thunderbird, which had been trucked up to Port Douglas, was waiting. I had headed out along the open road, revelling in the sense of freedom being on the Thunderbird always gave me. When I had ridden long enough to settle my attack of nerves, I pulled up outside a bar where I'd noticed a pool table earlier and played a few games with a couple of locals.

"Do tell," said Dusty with a wide grin.

"Seems Rocky's a bit of a ladies' man but was engaged to be married until recently."

"He broke her heart, didn't he?"

"He did. His fiancé was devastated when he called off the engagement."

Dusty nodded knowingly. "I told you. He comes across as charming in a sweet and gentle way but underneath he's just another insensitive male."

I was about to protest that not all men are insensitive when I saw the corners of her mouth curl up in a smile. I ignored her teasing.

"Anyway, it was what I learnt about his fiancé that I really wanted to tell you."

Dusty put her head to one side and raised a curious eyebrow. "I'm all ears."

"Right. Her name's Beth. She's a part-time chef at Rocky's Cafe. One of my fellow pool players just happened to mention he saw her talking to Ram."

"Interesting. When was this?"

"The last time Ram was in town. The day he had the run-in with Moose."

"That means she had contact with Ram in the vital twenty four hours leading up to his death. I'll need to interview Rocky's ex." Dusty's eyes flicked to the rear vision mirror. It wasn't the first time she'd done that during this short drive.

"Are we being followed?" I started to turn my head to look at the cars behind us. Dusty stopped me with a sharp command.

"Don't look round!" I stared at her in surprise. "She's following us again. I noticed her silver Toyota following us to the vet's the other day. And guess what? A silver Toyota was parked near Sunyarta the first day we went there. I saw it when we were walking back down the hill. I reckon this woman has been tracking us since we arrived in Port Douglas."

"Every second car in Australia is a silver Toyota," I reminded her.

"True. But they're not all driven by the same woman with short dark hair." Dusty gave me a triumphant look.

I risked a glance in the passenger side mirror and saw a silver car behind us, some distance back. I couldn't see the driver clearly.

"That car doesn't look like it's following us."

"She's dropped back a bit now. Probably realised staying close behind me would look suspicious." The scepticism must have shown on my face because Dusty uttered an indignant protest. "Don't you dare suggest I'm imagining things!"

I raised my hand in surrender.

"Anyway, back to Beth," said Dusty. "Where can we find her?"

"She still works a couple of days a week for Rocky. She also does volunteer work at Sunyarta – helps them out on their open days when they have a lot of visitors."

"She won't be hard to find, then."

A few minutes later we were back in the town centre with the silver car still behind us. Dusty pulled over into a parking bay and grabbed a pen from her bag.

"I'll get the rego number as she goes past."

The silver Toyota passed us and continued along the street. The dark haired woman behind the wheel was focused on the road ahead and didn't look in our direction.

"Quick!" Dusty was writing the car's registration number on her hand. "Get out and see where she goes. Only don't make it obvious you're watching her."

I scrambled out of the car as quickly as I could. Using a street tree as a shield, I watched the Toyota through the leaves as it continued along the road before eventually turning left.

Dusty leant across the front seats to speak to me. "Where did she go?"

"Turned left at the end of the street. Probably just a local resident going about normal daily business. She didn't seem interested in us when she drove past."

"Would you turn to look at someone if you were following them and didn't want them to know?"

"Right. Good point."

Dusty held up her palm with the registration number written on it. "Here's another job for you, Mr Maze Master. See if you can find out who owns this car. It's a Queensland rego so she could be a local, but I don't think she's just going about her normal daily business."

I snapped a photo of Dusty's palm with my phone.

"If she was following us…" We were inside a small cafe at a back table which offered some privacy when Dusty posed this question. I'd brought my laptop from the car and had started searching the internet while we waited for our coffees.

Dusty glared at me, nostrils flaring. "If?"

The use of 'if' was probably what is known as a Freudian slip because it had crossed my mind Dusty was being overly suspicious. I attempted to minimise the damage.

"I just wondered whether she could be your everyday local busybody wanting to know what the famous Dusty Kent is up to in her little town."

By the time we'd finished our coffees that theory was very much in doubt. Dusty's suspicions seemed to be valid. I looked up from the computer screen to pass on what I'd discovered.

"Access to the details of this registration number is restricted," I said. Dusty's eyes widened. "It could be risky for me to venture into that particular restricted area, but I can give it a go."

Dusty shook her head. "No. Leave it for now. I have a couple of other jobs I want you to do. Firstly, see what you can find out about Ashin Khin, the monk who had the 'sad accident' in the same spot where Ram was killed. Secondly…" She lowered her voice as a waiter whisked by balancing steaming cups of coffee on a tray. "See if you can connect Ram to Portsea. Was there an artist called Brody Johnson living there?" Her face was glowing with the excitement of the chase. "I really believe the key to finding this murderer lies in Ram's past. His painting has given us a place to start."

CHAPTER 21

"**G**OOD NEWS!" I said to Dusty on Monday morning. "I can tell you everything you want to know about the mysterious death of Ashin Khin."

Hours in front of the computer over the weekend had yielded mixed results but I had at least managed to ascertain how that particular monk had died.

Dusty and I were reclining in a pair of deck chairs in the grounds of Four Mile Resort with tall palms gently swaying behind us. Dusty had wrapped her bikini clad body in a sarong after her morning swim. She peered expectantly at me over the top of her sunglasses which she'd slipped along her nose.

"Khin was killed in the spring of 2013 when a falling tree branch fell on him and pinned him to the ground. Paramedics tried to revive him but he died at the scene. The coroner ruled the death a tragic accident. No suggestion of foul play. An arborist was called in to examine the tree and found no signs it was diseased and no indication the tree had been tampered with in any way."

Dusty removed her sunglasses, holding them in one hand while she considered what I'd said.

"Did they say what sort of tree it was?"

"That wasn't mentioned."

"It might have been a gum tree. They have this neat trick of suddenly dropping branches to save themselves from dying – especially during dry weather when they can't get enough water to sustain the whole tree."

"Sounds like a dangerous neat trick."

Dusty nodded. "Yep. There's no warning except a loud cracking sound. By that time there's no chance of getting out of the way if you happen to be in the path of the falling branch. Still, I shouldn't think branch dropping is a regular occurrence in this area, with all the rain they get. The poor monk was just unlucky." Dusty sighed. "Shame that line of enquiry turned out to be a dead end."

Dusty had thought Khin's death might link to Ram's murder therefore strengthening the theory that one of the monks was our killer.

"We're not making much progress in this case, Sean. We're back to Moose Mulligan and we haven't got anything on him."

Unfortunately, I hadn't yet been able to find anyone willing to talk to us about Moose.

"What about Kellie Edwards?" I thought it might cheer Dusty up to consider another suspect. "She hated the monks and she lied about being at Sunyarta on the morning of the murder."

"The thing is, Sean, I think we're looking for a male murderer because of the kick in the testicles. I mean, I can see a woman kicking a man in the testicles if he was attacking her or trying to rape her. But Ram's murder was a different situation."

"Right. So you don't think Kellie Edwards would have done it?"

"I didn't say that. I can see her murdering Ram. But why kick him in the groin?"

"She wanted him to feel excruciating pain."

Dusty gave me an appraising look. "Good point. I wasn't thinking of it that way." After a moment's reflection, she continued. "Okay. She kicks him in the testicles because she wants him to suffer. She strips him of his robe because it's a symbol of the monks she despises. But there's the missing sandal. Do you see Kellie Edwards as the sort of person who would take Ram's thong as a trophy?"

I thought about that for a moment. "No. Because she hates them so much she wouldn't want to keep anything at all connected to the monks."

"I agree." Putting her sunglasses back on, Dusty reclined in her chair. "If you call that good news, I hate to think what the bad news might be."

"The bad news is I haven't been able to find anything suggesting Brody Johnson might have lived in Portsea."

"Keep trying. See if you can make contact with artists living in the area. They might know something. Also, try to track down his birth records. You might need to use your highly developed hacking... I mean IT skills... for that."

"I'll get right on it, Boss."

Dusty gave me a mock salute. "There could be something in his past to give us a clue as to why someone would want to hurt him. There certainly doesn't seem to be anything since he became a monk."

"Unless we're looking for a fellow monk who is a psychopath."

I was thinking of Saya.

"Yep. A mild mannered monk hiding a raging beast inside. That's the point really. We all walk around disguising the beasts in our personalities. Luckily, most of us don't have the sort of inner demons which make us murderers. If only there was some way of telling which of us does. We don't know if someone is a psychopath – they usually look just like the rest of us. I hate to say this, but the only way to confirm our theory of a psychopathic monk would be if he kills again at the Sanctuary." Dusty paused briefly in reflection. "If Ram was killed by a fellow monk, why now? Unless our psychopath is a new recruit, he's had years to kill Ram. Did something happen last February or around that time to cause the monk to commit murder?"

"Good point. Worth checking out."

"The same point applies to anyone else. What triggered the desire to kill Ram five months ago? Moose's trigger could have been the altercation with Ram the day before he died. Kellie's trigger could have been the anniversary of her son's death. That's why the victim's last twenty four hours is so important; that's when the reason for the murder usually happens."

Later, I filled Dusty in on what I had done so far to track down the birth records of Brody Johnson. Saya had told us Ram was born in 1969 in Melbourne. With that information I had already tried to track down the monk's birth records, employing my 'highly developed

IT skills' to access the data bases and cover my tracks. Should I be caught, I risked deportation back to Ireland; the last thing I wanted. However, thinking about getting caught is foolish; it can lead to a lapse of concentration, resulting in mistakes. So I had put that out of my head.

Trying different spellings of both Brody and Johnson and searching within a five year range on either side of 1969 yielded nothing. Then I considered the possibility he might have been lying about his place of birth. Maybe he hadn't been born in Victoria. I did the same extensive search in all the other Australian regions. Still no trace of his birth records. Johnson being a common name made the task more difficult. Also, Brody might not have been his birth name. It might have been a name he acquired during his lifetime. Therefore, he could be any one of thousands of other Johnsons.

"Ram might have been born overseas," I suggested.

"Would that be hard to check?"

"I could probably search Australian Government records of incoming passengers and citizenship records; that sort of thing. It would be extremely time consuming though."

"Let's not go down that track unless we have to. I don't want your time taken up with that when I have other jobs for you to do. Besides, the other possibility is that Johnson wasn't even Ram's real name. He might have given a false name to escape a dark past."

Judging by the anticipation in her voice, I concluded that this scenario appealed to her. Dusty loved unearthing secrets. Her brow furrowed as her excitement began to recede. "The trouble is, if he's not Brody Johnson, how do we find out his real identity?" Her eyes appealed to me, like a child hoping to convince a parent to hand over a treat.

"Right," I said, acknowledging it was a job for someone with my skills. "But I need something to start with. Even a maze master can't find a needle in a haystack."

"Ah. And here I was thinking you were a magician." Dusty flashed me her familiar cheeky grin. Her face became serious again as she pondered the problem. "We don't even have a photo of Ram."

Her expression brightened as another idea caught her imagination. "I know Jake said there was no CCTV on the hill but Ram might have been snapped on camera when he was in Port Douglas. Maybe at Alexandra Village where he volunteered."

"He's been dead for almost five months. I doubt they'd still have the footage."

"Of course. You're right."

She swung her legs over the side of the recliner and sat up, gazing thoughtfully at her bare feet. Bright turquoise nail polish decorated her toe nails.

Abruptly coming out of her reverie, Dusty slapped the side of her head with the heel of her hand.

"Nincompoop! That's what I am. Why didn't I think of it before? The police will have his DNA. I could ask Jake to run it through the data base." Her brow furrowed again. "That would take too much time. Besides, Jake can probably only access the Queensland data base. If Ram's DNA is on record for any reason, it's most likely to be with Victoria Police if that's his home state. On the other hand, it could be in any state in Australia." She shrugged and started tapping out a message on her phone. "It's worth a try though. I'll ask him."

Jake responded almost immediately with a text informing her that the police had a sample of Ram's DNA. However, it had not been released for testing as this required permission from the deceased person's next of kin. They had been unable to locate any family of Ram.

"So there goes my brilliant idea." Dusty grimaced ruefully.

She stood and began pacing up and down along the edge of the pool. After a few moments she turned, eyes shining. "All is not lost. I have another brilliant idea. You," she jabbed her index finger at me for emphasis, "might still be able to find out if he changed his identity. What if Ram altered his name the same time he entered Sunyarta Sanctuary? If he was running from something or someone, it stands to reason his change of name and move to Queensland happened at the same time. That would give you a starting point; the date he entered Sunyarta."

I tapped on my computer keyboard, searching for change of name in Australia. "Could be a problem," I said as I read the pertinent information. "If you don't need your new name on legal documents like your driver's licence, passport, that sort of thing, you can change your name without having to register it."

Disappointment crossed Dusty's face. "He wouldn't have needed those sorts of legal documents living as a monk."

"Right. He could have changed his name to Brody Johnson and left all his legal documents in his original name. I'll check it out just the same. We might get lucky."

"Good thinking. It's also possible Brody Johnson was just the name he used as an artist. You know, like authors use pen names. If you can't find a name change, go back to his art. After all, he left a clue there. Keep searching for artists who lived, worked or painted in Portsea." Dusty held up both hands with her fingers crossed for luck. "Check out all the artists from Portsea, even if the names don't match."

Dusty had gone out to meet Jake, lorikeets were partying loudly in the trees outside and the day was drawing to a close by the time I'd found the information we needed. Dusty was going to be shocked to learn who Ram really was.

CHAPTER 22

DUSTY'S FACE WAS ashen. "Are you serious?"

The morning breeze wafted in through the open balcony doors of Dusty's apartment as I explained how I'd followed the Portsea lead and eventually struck gold. I sent a photo of Ram's paintings to an artist who had lived in the area all his life. In return, he emailed me a snap of a painting which had been part of a series of ocean scenes hanging in a Portsea cafe. The particular picture he sent me was almost identical to one of the paintings hanging at Sunyarta. The ones in the cafe had been done by a local resident called Paul Walker, a talented amateur artist.

Walker's paintings were removed from the cafe display after Paul Walker, who was a primary school teacher, had been accused of sexual abuse of three of his students.

Dusty shook her head in disbelief. "Are you sure Paul Walker and Ram are one and the same?"

"The artist in Portsea is confident both paintings were done by the same person. Not only that, Paul Walker's year of birth is the same as Ram's."

Dusty swallowed. "No. This can't be true."

I understood how she felt. Even though I hadn't known Ram personally, everything we'd learned about the man had caused me to like him.

"Sean, you say he was accused. Is it possible the girls were just being spiteful; trying to get back at their teacher for not giving them a good mark or something like that?"

"I doubt it. The girls were in their late teens by the time they made the accusations."

"I see what you mean. They're not likely to hold a grudge about a bad mark in primary school for so long."

"Paul Walker's lawyer claimed the girls' motivation was financial. Not long before the girls made their accusations, Walker had come into a considerable amount of money. His case was strengthened by the fact he had an alibi. At the time one of the girls said he was in her tent abusing her, he was seen at the other end of the campsite with another staff member, watching the antics of a ringtail possum in one of the trees. He could not have been in the girl's tent at the time she claimed."

"So it *was* a false accusation?"

"That was the defence. However, the girls' accounts of what happened to them were seen as credible. Their lawyer pointed out that the girl had made a mistake about the time. It was dark and she was in shock. Walker didn't have an alibi for the time the other two girls were being abused."

"Was he convicted?"

I shook my head. "The case against him fell apart when one of the girls decided not to testify."

"Sounds fishy to me, Sean. Surely if she were a genuine victim she would want to do everything she possibly could to nail her abuser."

I have no doubt that would have been the way Dusty would react. She would fight with fierce determination to the very end. It was difficult for her to understand that someone else might react differently.

"I imagine a teenage girl could find it traumatic to stand up in a court of law and relate what happened," I suggested. "The general consensus was that the girls were telling the truth. Those who witnessed their testimony had no doubt they'd been raped by their teacher. One newspaper report hinted that even Walker's lawyer had doubts about his innocence."

"I see. Public opinion would have been enough to finish Walker's career as a teacher."

"Right. So he moved interstate and became a monk."

"That's assuming Ram *is* Paul Walker. We need to be absolutely sure before we proceed any further, Sean. I don't want any hint of paedophilia to be associated with Ram if he isn't Walker. It would be so unfair." Dusty gazed thoughtfully into the distance. "I can ask Jake to see if the police can locate Paul Walker's family and get a DNA sample for comparison. But it'd be a lot quicker if we could get a photo of Walker to see if the monks can identify him as Ram." Catching the smirk on my face, she paused. "What are you looking so smug about? Don't tell me you've already got a photo of him."

I swivelled the laptop around so she could see the image on the screen; the only photo of Walker I'd been able to find.

Dusty studied the image for a few thoughtful moments. "Hard to believe that's the face of a paedophile." She sighed. "Jake should be able to get the police sketch artist to change this photo. You know, age Walker's face and shave his head."

The photo was soon on its way to Jake's email address.

"You know what?" said Dusty. "Once upon a time I would have gladly tied a paedophile to a bed of nails and subjected the creep to torture with a red hot branding iron. I'm sure you can guess what part of his body would be sizzling under the iron." I shifted uncomfortably in my seat. "Then one day I remembered something Uncle had said to me when I was a kid."

Dusty's godfather, who she respectfully called Uncle, had a quiet way about him – as if he experienced life from within a knowledge base deeper than that of the average person. His connection to nature, to the plants and animals of the land, was the force that guided him. This meant he was detached from the material existence most people, at least most people in western cultures, are strongly connected to. I hesitate to call it spiritual, not wishing to imply a religious aspect. I think it is more intuitive and innate. The indefinable something that guides Uncle had impacted on me so deeply I've never forgotten my one and only meeting with the dignified Aboriginal man. It didn't surprise me that the life lessons he taught Dusty had stayed with her.

"It was when I attacked Lionel, one of Uncle's kids. Lionel pulled my hair. I mean, pulled it hard. It really hurt. I was about ten or eleven at the time. I had a bit of a temper on me in those days."

I raised my eyebrows at her use of 'in those days'. I'd seen Dusty in temper mode on more than one occasion. In fact, the day I met her I observed her in a spectacular display of anger when she'd taken on a drunken youth who was tormenting a defenceless old sheep with a piece of timber. The guy didn't know what hit him when Dusty used her advanced karate skills to disarm him, flip him over and pin him to the ground.

Catching my expression, she laughed. "All right. I still have a temper but, believe it or not, I have a lot more control over it now."

I chose not to challenge her on that. "What did you do to Lionel?"

"I picked up a piece of wood and whacked him over the head with it."

"Ouch! You killed him?"

Dusty shook her head, her serious expression indicating her remorse for her childhood behaviour.

"Luckily he ducked, so he didn't get the full impact. That didn't stop him from screaming and dancing around like a rooster with its head chopped off." She rolled her eyes. "So naturally Uncle came out to see what was happening which is exactly what Lionel wanted."

"I'm guessing Uncle wasn't happy with you."

"That's an understatement. When I told him it was Lionel's fault because he'd hurt me first, you know what he said?"

"What?" Having experienced the quiet wisdom of Uncle myself, I had no doubt he'd handled the angry young Dusty in his own unique way.

"He said: *If you strike back you sink to the same low level as your attacker.* He told me I was no longer the victim. I had become a thug. He was right."

"So you no longer wish pain and suffering on paedophiles?"

"I didn't say that. I wish it and I fantasise about it. I just know it's not a good idea to act on those wishes."

"So you're saying that if a paedophile abuses a young girl, destroys her innocence and probably her life, she becomes a thug if she retaliates and no longer deserves sympathy?"

I couldn't keep the incredulity out of my voice. I was thinking of my sisters. As far as I was concerned, the victim of a paedophile could do whatever she likes without losing one iota of my sympathy.

"I didn't say she wouldn't deserve sympathy. Of course she would."

"What you're saying is that if the person who killed Walker, assuming that's who Ram is, was one of his victims, she had no right to kill him?"

"I understand why she had the desire and the intent but, acting on that makes her a murderer. As a victim I would feel only compassion for her. As a murderer I see her differently."

"If you solve this case and cause one of Walker's victims to be punished, won't you be doing more harm than good?" Seeing some hesitation in Dusty's expression I took the opportunity to hammer home my point. "You can't really believe she deserves to be punished as a murderer, after what he did to her?"

"It does present a moral dilemma." Dusty heaved a sigh. "The thing is, if we let one person get away with murder because we think it is justified, where do we draw the line? Who draws the line? My job is to track down the murderer. It's up to the legal system to judge whether the murder was justifiable and to allow for mitigating circumstances."

"If the law punishes a person, isn't that the same as retaliating?"

"Not really. Punishment by law is decided after due consideration of evidence and circumstances."

I knew she had a point.

CHAPTER 23

"FINE!" IT WAS a declaration Dusty had accepted the truth about the dead monk and was ready to move on.

Jake, who had returned to Cairns a few days earlier, had sent through the altered age progression image of Paul Walker. When Dusty emailed a copy of the new photo to Saya at Sunyarta, he confirmed the person in the image was Ram. Both Dusty and I were disappointed the man we had thought to be a nurturing, gentle monk had turned out to be a vile paedophile.

"This changes everything," continued Dusty. "Walker could have been killed by one of his victims." I noticed she was now referring to him as Walker instead of Ram. "That would explain the kick in the testicles. And disrobing him; she wanted to remove any suggestion that he was really a monk and also strip him of his dignity, the same as he had done to her. And pushing him over the edge of the cliff, like a discarded object. That's what he did to her; treated her like a thing, an object to be used and discarded at will."

Her eyes gleamed at the prospect of being on the trail of the killer. Despite her repugnance for what Walker had done, Dusty was still determined to solve the case.

"There could be other victims," she continued, "but the obvious place to start is with the three girls who outed him."

The thought of what Paul Walker's victims must have suffered gave me a sick feeling in the pit of my stomach. I was reluctant to locate any of them. It didn't seem fair that she, whoever she was, might end up in jail. The law had let her down by acquitting her abuser. Now I was going to help the law to take her freedom away.

Unwilling for that to happen I delayed trying to locate the victims.

Instead, I continued researching Walker. He had, I discovered, grown up in Portsea with one sibling and later took up a teaching post at a primary school in Melbourne.

The school where Paul Walker had worked was understandably loath to talk about him. They had done their best to remove any cyber links connecting the school with Walker. However, on the internet it's always possible to find old files. I found enough to put together a dossier on the dead monk.

He had been popular with fellow staff members and students. Once a week he gave up his lunch break to hold an art class for kids who had talent in that area. Up until the time the three girls made their accusations, there'd been no indication he was anything other than a dedicated teacher who worked hard to help students do well. Somehow, the fact that he'd been able to hide his dark side so completely made him an even more sickening and sinister individual.

Another procrastination strategy was to step up my enquiries re Moose. Dusty had suggested I contact his associates first to 'suss them out'. She would then go and see any who would be willing to talk about Moose, or showed even the merest hint that they might be willing. She suggested I ask them if Moose had mentioned a leather sandal or thong.

"What if Moose took Ram's missing thong as some kind of joke?" she said. "If you ask them about it, they probably won't realise the significance of it and won't see any harm in talking about it." She crossed her fingers for luck and held them up for me to see. "Someone out there might know what Moose did with Ram's sandal."

I had previously contacted the list of associates supplied to us by Jake but to no avail. The usual response from Moose's friends was that they had nothing to say except to declare Moose was a 'good bloke'. That probably just meant he was no worse a criminal than any of them. His neighbours described him as 'a bit rough but otherwise okay'. I extended my research and found a couple of his ex-girlfriends. One refused to speak with me and the other one's only complaint about Moose was that he was 'a bit tight with his money'. No-one remembered Moose joking or boasting about acquiring a single leather thong. It occurred to me that most of these people probably bought marijuana from Moose and didn't want to risk upsetting him.

When I reported my disappointing results to Dusty, she was philosophical. Although she hadn't dismissed him as a suspect, her interest in Moose was not as strong now that she was focusing on the sexual abuse victims. Consequently, she was not quite so tolerant when I admitted I'd not yet had a chance to trace any of the girls who had accused Walker. Dusty saw through my lame excuse and fixed me with a piercing look.

"We do need to interview them, Sean."

"They were only kids when Walker…" I didn't want to bring pictures into my mind by finishing the sentence.

"I understand why you're not enthusiastic about finding the girls. Don't forget, until I solve the case we don't know for sure if the killer was one of Walker's victims. Finding them might mean establishing their innocence." Appreciating my uncertainty, Dusty took pity on me.

"Come on. Let's take a break."

She slung her bag over her shoulder and picked up her phone. "We'll go to Alexandra Village and see what they have to say about Walker."

After parking the car in one of the back streets, we set out on foot through the town to the other end of Port Douglas. The buzz of diners in the cafes followed us as we walked along Macrossan Street. Queues of people waited at the Gelati Bar. Children pointed excitedly to the menu on the back wall urging their parents to buy the flavour they wanted.

We continued on to the end of Macrossan Street, turned left into Wharf Street and soon reached our destination. The retirement village was set back from the road nestled behind an impressive cluster of tropical vegetation dominated by tall palms. Dusty peered at a label on one of the palms at the entrance.

"Don't ask me to read its Latin name but it's commonly known as Alexandra Palm. So now we know how Alexandra Village got its name."

"Now, that's what I call good detective work."

Dusty responded to my teasing with a mock scowl.

A surprise awaited us inside. Coming towards us as we opened the door in all her bejewelled glory, wearing a magnificent silver turban that glistened in the light, was Carmen Miranda.

"Daa…rlings," she drawled. "You have come to dance? It is too late. My class, it is finished."

Dusty laughed. "Do you hold dance classes for the residents?"

"Residents. Staff." Carmen waved an arm in elegant dismissal of her obvious popularity. "They all love to dance with Carmen. It is the exercise very good, isn't it?" She started toward the door. "I go now. I must fetch Sylvia and Eric."

I recalled her mentioning those names before. Rocky had suggested she might be referring to a couple of dogs that were boarding with her.

"Are they the dogs you're looking after?"

Carmen looked up at me. "Dogs?" Confusion registered on her face but cleared almost immediately. "Oooh the *leetle* doggies! They are no more with me. I have only the birds, my pretty birds." She made a flying motion with her hand. "You will come to my home one day? We will drink the wine together."

As was expected of me, I held the door open for Carmen. She swept out with a regal flourish. Strange that Rocky didn't know about her birds. Maybe they were a recent addition to Carmen's household.

At the reception desk, Dusty stated our business and we were directed to the manager's office. We passed a common area where elderly residents were seated in a semicircle lifting hand weights in unison under the guidance of a young female instructor.

The manager, a plump woman in her mid fifties, greeted us with a friendly smile, introducing herself as Myrtle Hoskins.

"We were all devastated when we heard about what happened to Ram," she said, her face arranged to express appropriate sorrow. "He was the loveliest man. Such a beautiful reading voice." A sigh of resignation. "We'll do anything we can to help you find the person who took his life. Not that it'll bring the poor man back but…" She trailed off with a helpless gesture, blinking behind her glasses.

When Dusty fished for any hint of animosity toward the monk, Ms Hoskins was aghast at the mere suggestion of such a thing.

"Ram was loved and respected by everyone; residents and staff alike. He was gentle, patient and generous with his time. You never got the sense he was doing us a favour; it was more like he saw it as a duty, a duty he enjoyed."

"Clearly, Ram had no enemies here," said Dusty as we stepped back out into the warm air.

CHAPTER 24

O N OUR WALK back to the car, we heard the distant sound of someone strumming a guitar. The music became louder as we drew nearer, but was abruptly replaced by raised voices coming from a simple weatherboard house set back from the road behind unfenced lawns and surrounded by palms. Just before the steps leading up to the verandah, a sign proclaiming *The Clink Theatre* disabused me of the notion that the building was someone's home. On the verandah with his back to us was the owner of one of the voices: Rocky.

"There's no need to do this." Although I couldn't see the female speaker, I could hear the distress in her voice.

Rocky cajoled her. "Beth. It's for the best."

Dusty touched my arm lightly and whispered. "Beth? The ex-fiancé?"

"I need the job, Rocky." Beth beseeched him. "You're not being fair."

"You'll be fine, Beth. I'll give you an awesome reference and make sure other employers know what a fantastic chef you are. Actually, a friend of mine needs a chef for his new cafe."

Dusty and I started to move on. Lingering any longer would look like we were spying on them.

"Oh. Rocky!" This was uttered with a mixture of frustration and resignation.

A few moments later, a flash of bright pink passed us. A young woman with shoulder length wavy hair, wearing shorts and a pink top marched ahead of us. She seemed oblivious that she'd bumped me accidentally as she passed and strode on to eventually stop in front of a parked car in the next block.

"Designer clothes," observed Dusty.

Funny how women can instantly pick that sort of thing. What I'd noticed was that this was the same girl who'd been having a tense discussion with Rocky outside the Cafe last week.

Leaning her body up against the passenger side of the car with her back to the footpath, the woman buried her head in her folded arms. Dusty slowed her pace.

"See if you can work your magic, Sean O'Kelly."

"Magic?"

"You have a knack for calming out-of-control women."

Was she thinking of my meeting with Kellie Edwards in the Sanctuary car park or of the times I had helped her through her own angry tantrums? Either way, I wished she hadn't placed the burden of expectation on me.

As it turned out, my so-called magic skills were not needed. Dusty managed on her own when we drew level with the distraught woman.

"Beth?" Hearing her name spoken in an unfamiliar voice caused her to spin round in surprise. She stared at Dusty, quickly brushing away remnants of tears from her cheeks. Her chocolate brown eyes, crinkly black hair and strong facial features were a striking combination. In fact, the strength in her face was such that tears seemed incongruous.

"Who are you?" A musical voice. Her tone was curious but not unfriendly.

"My name's Dusty Kent."

"Oh, yes. Rocky mentioned you."

Dusty introduced me and reached into her bag for the police sketch of Walker.

"Do you know this man?"

Beth studied the photo. After a few minutes she nodded.

"It's Ram. He looked better in real life though. This makes him look a bit older than he was." She handed the photo back to Dusty. "He had a kind face."

"You were seen talking with Ram just before he died." A puzzled look crossed Beth's face. Dusty prompted her memory. "I'm talking about the last time he came into town; the day before his death." Recollection now gleamed in Beth's eyes, quickly followed by a flash of sadness.

"I remember."

"What were you talking about?"

"Nothing. Just passing the time of day." Seeing Dusty's curiosity, Beth explained. "Ram was kind to me one day; just after Rocky and I broke up." She looked back toward the Clink Theatre from where the strains of Rocky's guitar could be heard again. A blush crept up her neck and tinged her cheeks.

"I was at the monastery and went into the garden for some quiet time. Instead, I got all worked up and started crying." A rueful smile crossed her face. "Rocky had just broken off our engagement. I took it pretty hard. It was my own fault though. I should never have pressed Rocky about getting engaged. I knew he wasn't ready for a commitment." Her eyes rolled upward in a self deprecating gesture. "So there I was bawling my eyes out when Ram came across me and sorta calmed me down. He just sat silently on the other end of the bench. That's all he did, but I felt his empathy." Beth laughed self-consciously. "It seems whenever I get in a tizz over Rocky, someone nice comes along to make me feel better." Her smile included both of us. "After that, whenever I saw Ram in town I always stopped to speak to him."

"Did he mention anything out of the ordinary when you were talking to him in the street that day? Did he seem worried about anything?"

"No. He never really said much."

"Did anyone else speak to him while you were with him?"

Beth ran her fingers through her hair. Her eyes drifted to the left as she tried to recall her meeting with the monk.

"No." A thoughtful expression crossed her face. "Something a bit odd did happen though."

"While you were talking to Ram?"

"Yes. I noticed Kellie Edwards walking towards us. She was glaring at Ram, as if she was mad at him. I thought maybe she was riled up about something and was sort of looking through Ram, not really looking at him. Later I found out she blamed Ram for her son's death. That's so unfair. Her son took his own life. How can anyone stop another person from doing that?"

"Did she say anything to Ram?"

"No. But if looks could kill…"

"What about Ram? Did he say anything or acknowledge her?"

"No. I'm not sure he even noticed. He was always so… I dunno, sort of focused in the moment. He didn't really get distracted by anything else, if you know what I mean."

"Yep, I know what you mean." Dusty jerked her head back in the direction of the Theatre. "Were you and Rocky rehearsing for a performance?"

The music had stopped. Looking back, we saw Rocky walking in the opposite direction with his guitar slung casually over his shoulder. Beth watched Rocky's retreating back for a few moments before answering Dusty's question.

"Rocky's rehearsing. I'm just helping out with the costumes; I'm good with that sort of thing. Rocky's doing the music for one of the other plays in the same show. Funny really, cos the play he's working on is so… Well, it's about a cross-dressing football player and Rocky is such a…such a man."

Beth laughed when she saw the puzzled expression on my face. "He's so straight. That's what I'm trying to say. Not that cross-dressers are necessarily gay; I don't mean that. It's just that Rocky doesn't seem comfortable with alternative gender stuff. Like, he freaked out when Arabella was here for a festival. Rocky's Cafe did the catering for a lunch where Arabella was guest of honour and he deliberately avoided her. People were coming up to her all day long but Rocky wouldn't go near her."

"Arabella?" Dusty looked mystified. Before Beth could respond, her expression cleared. "Oh, *Arabella*! I know who you mean." Throwing a glance in my direction, she added, "But you'd better explain to the Irishman."

Beth grinned at me. "Have you heard of Arabella? She's a famous

Australian performer."

I had to admit my ignorance. "Don't know the name. Is she a cross-dresser?"

Beth shook her head. I could feel Dusty's eyes on me. Was I about to fail some sort of test? Had I already failed by not recognising an Australian icon?

"Arabella's a beautiful, sexy woman." Dusty shared a conspiratorial smile with Beth.

"Arabella's transgender." Beth decided to let me in on the secret. "Some men don't get that she's not a male anymore. They feel threatened."

I didn't really get it either. Dusty relieved my discomfort by changing the subject.

"If you don't mind my asking, Beth, what happened between you and Rocky today?"

Pain flashed in Beth's eyes. She chased it away with a wry smile.

"He dumped me again. Dumped me as his chef this time. He thinks it would be better for me if I wasn't around him so much."

"Because you're not over him yet?" Beth nodded. "Very noble of him." I thought I detected a flicker of sarcasm in Dusty's tone.

"He's right," said Beth. "It's just that I feel like such an idiot for not being able to let go. I never met anyone like Rocky before. He's different from most men; strong but gentle. And..." She paused, searching for the right words. "You know how it usually is with a man." She looked at Dusty. "They don't really get women. It wasn't like that with Rocky. He understood me."

She heaved a sigh, pushed herself away from the car and retrieved her keys from the pocket of her shorts.

Before Beth drove off, Dusty took her contact details and asked her to get in touch if she remembered anything more about her meeting with Ram.

"Now I wonder why Kellie didn't mention she'd seen Ram the day before he died." Dusty watched Beth's car disappearing into the distance thoughtfully. "I need to have another chat with the angry vet."

CHAPTER 25

INSTEAD OF RETURNING to the car, Dusty beckoned me back toward the Clink Theatre.

"I want to introduce you to someone."

Mystified, I followed her down the path and up the steps to the verandah of the Theatre where she gestured at a poster in the window.

A shapely woman in a body-hugging glittering white dress with an elaborate feathery cape draped over her shoulders looked to be in full song with her arms flung forward and head thrust back. For a split second I thought I was looking at Rocky's neighbour but quickly realised my mistake. This beautiful blonde woman was not Carmen.

"Meet Arabella," said Dusty. "You wouldn't believe she used to be a man, would you?"

My mouth dropped open. I shook my head vigorously.

"How…? I mean…" I was flummoxed. "How did she… how did he become a woman?"

"She had a sex change operation when she was in her mid twenties. Back in the eighties, I think."

"In the 1980s?" I had heard of people having sex change operations. I didn't realise it was happening way back then. Looking at the picture of the very feminine Arabella, I found it impossible to imagine her as a man. "She looks so…"

Dusty smiled her understanding. "I know. As well as the operation, she would have had hormone treatment that gave her all the female attributes girls develop during puberty. Eventually she emerged as a woman, with the characteristics and emotions of any other woman."

Dusty admired the poster for a moment longer. "She's gorgeous. A bit old for Rocky though. I don't know what he was afraid of. Some men just can't handle that sort of thing, especially men brought up in country areas, I think. Somehow or other they see gender change as a threat to their masculinity."

I thought I detected a hint of triumph in the laugh that followed, as if Dusty was relishing the idea of this male weakness. It might have just been my fancy but I felt obliged to mount some sort of defence.

"Rocky seems comfortable in his own skin. I can't see him feeling threatened."

Dusty gave me one of those piercing looks of hers – a look that seems to probe right inside to uncover hidden disquiet.

"I could say the same about you, Sean. You seem confident with your masculinity and comfortable with yourself. You don't mind being a bit of a computer geek and you don't see the need to play muscle games to prove you're a man." She paused. "But would you be at ease meeting a transgender woman?"

I had to lower my eyes. I'd never had a problem with other men who were gay. A man who has turned into a woman is different. I couldn't put my finger on just why it bothered me though. I suppose a psychiatrist would tell me I felt threatened in some way.

Dusty reassured me. "No need to be embarrassed. Transgender is probably outside your comfort zone. After all, we don't get to meet many people like that so we don't have the opportunity to become accustomed to them. Actually, I think you would cope well enough if you met Arabella."

I appreciated her vote of confidence, but I wasn't sure I'd pass that particular test.

When I suggested it was time to go, Dusty didn't seem to hear me. She was staring at the poster of Arabella as though she'd spotted some tiny detail in the picture that fascinated her.

"Do me a favour, Sean," she said. "On the other side of the road, diagonally opposite, is a silver Toyota." I realised she had been staring at what she could see reflected in the glass of the poster case, not a detail in the picture. "Can you just take a stroll past the car and check the registration number?"

She was thinking of the mysterious stalker of course.

"Okay." Humouring her was probably the best option.

"I have a feeling it'll be the same rego number we made a note of the other day," she said as I turned to go.

She was right. Dusty's lips set in a determined line when I told her.

"That does it! This time I'm going to corner her."

I followed her as she marched across the road. We positioned ourselves a short distance from the car behind a thick clump of bushes where a couple of large rocks served as seats.

"Look!" I pointed down at the footpath where the name *Ellen* had been chalked in elegant white script. "I saw that on the footpath one night just after we arrived here."

"How odd," said Dusty. "It's beautifully done. Someone declaring his love. Maybe it's unrequited love and he's too shy to make his feelings known." A far-away look came into her eyes. Her voice took on a theatrical tone. "So he writes her name on the footpath, hoping she will see it and understand who it is."

"And then what?"

"And then true love will bloom." Dusty laughed. "Maybe I'm getting a bit carried away." She grabbed my arm. "It's her," she hissed.

"Ellen?"

"Don't be daft. Look! It's the driver of the car."

The woman who was casually crossing the road carrying a take away coffee container had short dark hair and large gold hoops in her ears. She looked to me to be a perfectly ordinary and innocent woman going about her usual business.

"Are you sure? You haven't really had a good look at her before."

"I'm sure. I recognise the hair style. Besides, she's wearing the same earrings."

Dusty waited until the woman had zapped her car to unlock it. Then she darted out like a cat springing on prey. Dusty was beside the woman before she had a chance to open the car door. I remained on the footpath within hearing distance.

A startled expression crossed the woman's face when she saw Dusty but she recovered her poise almost immediately.

"Want to tell me why you've been following me around?"

Innocent indignation crossed the other woman's face. She looked askance at Dusty.

"I beg your pardon." Her voice had the confident tone of authority.

I stepped back, intuitively distancing myself from what was looking like evolving into an embarrassing mistake on Dusty's part.

"You've been following me around in this car for the past few days. I want to know why." Dusty leant on the driver side door, glaring at the woman.

"Please step aside. I'd like to get into my car." This was said with cool disdain, implying Dusty was nothing more than an inconvenient pest. I considered retreating behind the bushes.

However, Dusty was sure of her ground and not easily intimidated. "I will. As soon as you answer my question. Why have you been following me around?"

"I have not been following you." It was an emphatic response delivered through clenched teeth. Dusty was not fooled. She had that tell-tale gleam in her eye. The woman was lying.

I breathed a sigh of relief and abandoned the idea of hiding in the bushes. A passing car slowed down. The driver turned his head to observe the two women. Since they were not really in danger of being hit in the wide street, he was probably being curious rather than careful. I stepped forward and waved him on.

Dusty locked eyes with the other woman until she eventually capitulated.

"Okay. I'll come clean." The woman gestured toward the footpath and they both joined me.

"You're Dusty Kent. You're a celebrity." Dusty's scornful look indicated she expected a better explanation. "My name's Louisa Penrose."

Dusty folded her arms across her chest. "And?"

"I'm a journo too." She handed Dusty her business card. "I was trying to pluck up courage to ask you for an interview."

"If you don't have the courage to approach people, you shouldn't be a journalist."

"I don't usually have a problem. But you're famous and you don't do many interviews. You've been quoted as saying you prefer your books to speak for you."

"Correct."

"I don't blame you. Your books and your investigative work into cold cases are second to none."

She'd struck the right chord with sincerity in her tone. I saw Dusty's body relax. She wasn't immune to flattery. However, that didn't mean she was going to let Louisa Penrose off the hook.

"None of this explains why your details are under restricted access." The look in Louisa's large brown eyes reflected surprise combined with alarm.

Dusty waved an introductory hand toward me. "Meet my maze master, Sean O'Kelly." I reached out and shook hands with the self-proclaimed journalist. "He's an IT professional; an expert in his field. He wanders around cyber space dredging up information I might not otherwise be able to access." Now I fancied the alarm in Louisa's eyes had deepened. Dusty added a tongue-in-cheek disclaimer. "Nothing illegal, of course." I did my best to keep a straight face. "I asked him to dig up information about you." Louisa Penrose's body stiffened. "When he tried to research your car using your registration number, he drew a blank."

The look of relief that briefly shadowed Louisa's face when she heard the last sentence made me wonder whether she'd been afraid I might have discovered something else.

"Oh." Louisa now looked relaxed. "It's not my car. I borrowed it from a friend. I don't know why the details aren't available." She walked around to the driver's side door of the car. "Please accept my apologies for causing you worry. I never meant you any harm." Her hand paused momentarily with the door half open. She looked across the top of the vehicle at Dusty. "About that interview?" This was followed by a smile; quite a sweet smile that erased the authoritarian persona and seemed to take years off her.

Dusty didn't answer but obtained the name of the motel where Louisa was staying.

"Louisa Penrose is hiding something," she said as we strolled back to where we'd parked the car. "She just handed me a pack of lies. Does she think I'm stupid or something?" Dusty rolled her eyes in disgust. "See what you can find out about her, Mr Maze Master."

CHAPTER 26

LOUISA PENROSE'S WEBSITE was informative because of its lack of information. Although it showcased samples of articles apparently written by her, mostly relating to crime, it was very basic. Her contact page listed the same details as those on the business card she'd given to Dusty. Same mobile number and email address but no physical address. I couldn't read anything into that. Lots of people keep the contact details on their websites to a minimum. Yet I heard warning bells.

By this time, Dusty had gone to Cairns to spend a couple of days with Jake. She planned to break the news to him about Ram's true identity. Apart from that, I doubted they would be spending a lot of time discussing the case.

The loneliness I experienced when Dusty left took me by surprise. I kept busy putting together the backgrounds and establishing the whereabouts of the girls who had accused Paul Walker of sexual assault. Abbie Kowalski. Kimberley Grey. Lena Patterson.

I drew a blank with Lena but found a couple of social media sites for Abbie and Kimberley. Unfortunately, they yielded little information. Their profile photos had been removed and it looked like many of their posts had been deleted. It was almost as if the girls were deliberately trying to hide.

I had some luck when I checked the social media sites for Kimberley's sister, Savanna. There I found a photo of the sisters together when Kimberley was a teenager. Both girls had long hair pulled back in a ponytail. While Savannah, who looked like a timid little thing, had brown hair and wore glasses, Kimberley was a green-eyed blonde.

Although I hadn't yet been able to locate the women, I had managed to piece together some background material.

Abbie Kowalski was the daughter of Polish migrants who had arrived in Australia in 1981. The following year they had a son and in 1984 Abbie was born. Abbie and her brother David grew up in Melbourne and had no other siblings.

Lena Patterson was an only child who was born in Victoria and grew up in Melbourne.

Kimberly Grey's family had moved to Melbourne from Perth when Kimberley was a toddler. Her brother Lyell was a year younger and sister Savannah five years her junior.

When Dusty returned, her shining eyes and buoyant spirits evidence enough of her feelings for Jake, I told her about Louisa's website.

"Show me." She leant over my shoulder to peer at the computer screen. "Hm. Interesting." Dusty pulled up a chair next to me. "Let me have a closer look." I swivelled the laptop around to give her a better view.

"I think your warning bells are right. Her bio is minimal. Nothing really concrete there that people could check out. She doesn't seem to have had any articles published in major newspapers or on any of the usual news blogs." Dusty thoughtfully perused the site again. "She's not making any real effort to promote herself. A freelance journalist should be showcasing her best work, promoting her skills."

Dusty had articulated what I hadn't been able to identify.

"Right. I see what you mean. It was the same the other day when she met you. She should have promoted herself more to you in order to convince you to grant her an interview."

"Yep. It's not as if she's new to the game. According to this website she's been a journo for six years. Which means she should have more credits to her name. Look at this! In the personal interests section, it says she's a songwriter. I bet you anything that's the closest she comes to being a writer. Journalist, my foot!" Dusty laughed at her use of the colloquialism. "My nan used to say that if she didn't believe what someone had told her."

I nodded to indicate I was familiar with the expression. "Right. Why would she set up a false identity with a phony website and organise fake business cards?"

"Exactly. There must be something behind this charade. I bet it's connected to the case." Dusty pushed the laptop back to me. "Who is Louisa Penrose? See if you can answer that question for me, Mr Maze Master."

CHAPTER 27

D ESPITE MY BEST efforts, the question remained unanswered the next day when Dusty hired a guide with a four wheel drive to access the area where Moose Mulligan had had his plantation. Although it was abundant with plants, we could see no pot growing on his property.

"Surely he could do something else with this land," said Dusty. "Something productive."

"Probably given up. Decided the whole world is against him so doesn't see any point in trying."

"Yep. You could be right."

We left the site of Mulligan's now defunct marijuana empire to tour the National Park next to it. The Park was verdant with magnificent rainforest and carried a deceptive aura of peace and tranquillity. Dusty laughed at my discomfort when the guide warned us of various potential threats. Apparently, danger lurked at every corner. I was used to hearing warnings about snakes and spiders, always an unseen peril in the Australian wilderness, but a new and unexpected threat here in the rainforest was a vicious plant. Those deadly stinging plants were not necessarily hiding deep in the forest; some grew close to the pathways.

"They look innocent and beautiful," said the tour guide. "Don't let that fool you. They use their beauty to lure you toward them, to make you touch them."

"Like the sirens in Homer's Odyssey," suggested Dusty.

The guide, a rugged man in his fifties whose passion for the natural environment was more evident than any knowledge of Greek mythology, barely acknowledged the interruption.

"The last thing you want to do is touch one of those innocent-looking plants. If it doesn't kill you, the agony from a single touch will send you as mad as a cut snake. The pain can stay with you for months or years."

Thankfully, we exited the rainforest without injury of any kind.

When we returned to Port Douglas, we were heading toward Rocky's Cafe when Dusty seized my arm and whispered in my ear.

"Look who's going into the Post Office."

I looked up just in time to see Kellie Edwards, a take away coffee container in one hand, hurrying up the steps of the Australia Post building opposite.

As we crossed the road, I pointed to a red car parked at the kerb with the familiar image of paw footprints on the rear window. "That's Kellie's car."

"Good. Let's wait for her here."

We sat on the edge of a stone support shaded by the Post Office verandah.

Dusty looked at me with a mischievous grin. "We'll be a nice surprise for her."

Kellie returned to her car a few minutes later. When she saw us, her face didn't exactly express pleasure.

Dusty feigned delighted surprise. "Kellie! Fancy seeing you here. Actually, I've been meaning to contact you."

Kellie dropped her now empty coffee container into a kerbside bin and pressed the button on her remote key to release her car lock with a sharp click. She stood uncertainly on the footpath, undecided whether to go straight to her car or to advance toward us. Unable to make a choice, she remained where she was.

"Haven't got much time – have to get back to the clinic." She was laying down an escape route in case the ensuing conversation with Dusty turned out to be uncomfortable. "I hope you're going to tell me you know what really happened to my son."

A positive response to that might have brought her over to us but Dusty would not resort to any sort of trickery which could give Kellie false hope.

"Not exactly." Dusty stood up. "However, I promise you I will do my utmost to find out exactly how your son died." She paused, fixing Kellie with a steady gaze. "No matter what."

Throwing Dusty a sharp look, Kellie took a step in our direction. "What do you mean? No matter what."

"I mean even if I find that you took matters into your own hands."

"Took matters into my…" Kellie looked around furtively lest anyone be listening, moved closer to us and lowered her voice. "What are you suggesting?"

"Lies make me suspicious. You lied to me, Kellie."

"I did no such thing." Despite this denial, I noticed some hesitation in her voice. She averted her eyes. Dusty picked up on this immediately. I knew she'd planned on asking Kellie about glaring at Ram while he was talking to Beth in the street. Sensing Kellie was thinking of something else, Dusty waited. Silence might loosen the other woman's tongue.

After a few moments of biting her lower lip and staring down at her feet, Kellie spoke, her voice quavering.

"I wanted to be in the place where he'd died. I wanted to feel…I dunno…feel his spirit, I suppose."

"So you lied about where you were on the anniversary of Josh's death, the morning Ram died. You *were* at the Sanctuary. What time were you there?"

Kellie heaved a sigh. "Around five-thirty or just after that."

"Why so early?"

"I always go for my jog early in the morning."

"Is the Sanctuary on your normal jogging route?"

Kellie shook her head, eyes downcast.

"What did you do when you got to Sunyarta?"

"Nothing." Kellie fidgeted with the bundle of keys in her hand. "It didn't feel right. I thought I'd go into the grounds, to sit in the gardens and see if I could feel Josh's presence. But…I dunno…being there just made me feel unsettled. I had this strange feeling."

Interested, Dusty inclined her head. "Like a chill down your spine. That sort of feeling?"

"Yes, like that. I wanted to feel peace but it was the opposite. I went back home."

"Why didn't you tell me this when I asked you where you were on the morning of the murder?"

Kellie looked toward her car as if considering escape. However, she accepted the inevitable and answered Dusty's question.

"Because you were already treating me like a suspect. If you found out I'd been there, you were bound to jump to the wrong conclusion. Besides, as far as I was concerned, it was my private business and had nothing to do with the monk's murder."

"Unfortunately, privacy goes out the window during a murder investigation. When someone is being secretive, it tends to look more like the person is attempting to hide their guilt." Dusty raised a placatory hand before Kellie had a chance to protest. "For now, I'll give you the benefit of the doubt. However, there's something else you haven't told me."

Kellie ran her fingers through her hair and straightened her body as though ready to defend herself. Dusty continued.

"I believe you saw Ram in Macrossan Street the day before he died." Kellie shook her head and began to protest. Dusty cut her off. "You walked past while he was talking to Beth Pomeroy and gave Ram a venomous look."

Kellie frowned. "I don't remember doing that."

"You know what?" said Dusty when Kellie had driven away. "If that had been Kellie on trial in a courtroom, the prosecution would have been scathing."

Dusty took a deep breath, arranged her face in an authoritarian expression and spoke in a stentorian voice. "You don't remember? Don't remember! Ms Edwards, you expect us to accept an excuse much used by guilty people seeking to avoid incriminating themselves with a truthful answer? And you stretch the realms of credibility even further by asking the jury to believe it was mere coincidence you were on the scene when the man you hated and blamed for your son's death was murdered?"

CHAPTER 28

I WAS MAKING no further progress in tracking down Abbie, Kimberley and Lena when it occurred to me that if one of the girls did murder the monk, it was possible she lived in the area. She might have seen Walker when he was in town one day, recognised him and decided to get her revenge. Grey and Patterson were fairly common names but I guessed there wouldn't be many entries for Kowalski in the local phone book so I started with Abbie. I guessed correctly. In fact, not a single entry for Kowalski.

However, the electoral roll was more helpful. To my surprise, I found a D. Kowalski living in Mossman. Could this be Abbie's brother? I went back to social media. I hadn't checked for David Kowalski previously but now I found his Facebook page which yielded more information than his sister's had. It was difficult to see what he looked like from his profile picture which showed him underwater in full snorkelling gear. His website didn't feature many posts. Most of the recent ones were photos of beaches and rainforests and action shots of David kite surfing and abseiling. The caption under one read: *Mossman Gorge.*

I couldn't wait to share the news with Dusty. It was only just after seven on Saturday morning, but I knew she was likely to be out of bed, perhaps getting ready to go for a swim. I tapped on her door with my usual special knock, two slow knocks followed by a hand slap. Dusty answered the door in a knee-length white T-shirt, her dishevelled hair looking like a wild mop of auburn frizz. Covering her mouth with her hand she stifled a yawn, waved me inside and gestured at the coffee pot.

"Make yourself a cup." She sank into an armchair. "I'm not ready for anything yet."

The espresso machine was soon bubbling, sending out a tempting coffee aroma. I poured myself a cup of the steaming liquid and sat down opposite Dusty.

"Is this an emergency or do you have something exciting to report?" She poked at her hair with her fingertips, making it look even more dishevelled.

"I have something exciting to report."

Dusty's eyes widened in surprise to be replaced by a gleam of anticipation as I told her what I'd discovered.

"Fantastic work, Mr Maze Master! Let's head off to Mossman right now. Being Saturday morning, there's a good chance David Kowalski won't be working. We can catch him at home and surprise him. That way, he's more likely to unintentionally let information slip." Dusty jumped up and headed for her bedroom. "It won't take me long to get changed. Meet me downstairs at the car."

My stomach was telling me I should have waited until after breakfast to give Dusty the news.

"Don't worry. I haven't forgotten about food." She threw me the keys to her FJ Holden. "You can have a big breakfast in Mossman." Dusty laughed at the expression on my face which was probably one of relief.

She joined me in the car park a short time later dressed in a lime green T-shirt, turquoise shorts and thongs. "This is a significant development in the case, Sean. If this guy is Abbie's brother, he should be able to give us an address for his sister and hopefully she will know where Kimberley and Lena are."

It was an easy drive to Mossman. We encountered little traffic, arriving just after eight o'clock. Our first stop was a cafe. My large plate of sausages with scrambled eggs and smashed avocado on toast had my undivided attention.

Dusty wanted to make breakfast a quick meal. With the promise of a sunny Saturday, she was concerned David Kowalski might head down to the beach before we got to his house. Rather than lingering over coffee at the table, she ordered a take-away cappuccino.

"Since you're driving, I can enjoy this on the way." She threw me a cheeky grin as she picked up the container of hot coffee. "Just be careful going over bumps. You don't want to be responsible for spilling my precious first cappuccino of the day."

As it turned out, it wasn't my driving that would cause her to spill her coffee. I was a short distance behind Dusty and saw the incident unfold.

She had just stepped out of the cafe and started toward the car when a tall man in his mid thirties whose tousled snowy hair gave him a Nordic appearance collided with her, knocking her cappuccino out of her hand. He had exchanged a few words of greeting to someone walking past and his head was still turned in the opposite direction. As a result, he didn't see Dusty. Her container of coffee flew out of her hand into the air. The top, which she'd already loosened in anticipation of sipping the cappuccino, flew off in a different direction. When the hot coffee poured out of the container, Dusty stepped back quickly to avoid being splashed.

Nordic stared at Dusty, momentarily taken aback. Given a little more time, he might have gotten around to apologising but Dusty, suddenly robbed of the coffee she had been looking forward to, reacted swiftly and vehemently.

"Why don't you look where you're going!"

Her reaction seemed to cause him further surprise. He looked down at the coffee-stained footpath as if trying to take in what had just happened.

"Look what you've done to my cappuccino. I didn't even get to taste it." Dusty threw her arms in the air. "Not even one single sip!"

Nordic's blue eyes went from the spilt coffee to Dusty, sweeping over her as if seeing her for the first time. The corners of his lips curved in a half smile. Amusement brightened his eyes. He seemed to find Dusty's anger entertaining. I held my breath, knowing this was a sure fire way to ignite the flames.

Dusty stared up at him, arms akimbo, nostrils flaring. He was roughly the same height as me but Dusty was in no way intimidated. Knowing she could fling him to the ground with one quick karate movement no doubt gave her confidence.

"Well? The least you can do is say sorry!" Her green eyes glared at him.

Nordic looked down at her as if she were a performing dolphin, a crooked smile on his face. When he finally spoke, his words threw Dusty off guard.

"What are you doing tonight? I'll buy you another coffee and dinner to go with it."

It was Dusty's turn to be taken aback. However, she ignored his question and took a few steps toward the car.

"Cool car, by the way." He'd struck the right note. Dusty was proud of her car which had belonged to her late father. I could see her animosity was beginning to wane.

"You don't see many of these around." Nordic stepped closer to the FJ, running his hand gently over the bonnet. "Been well looked after too."

Dusty melted. "Sorry I flew off the handle."

"No way." He protested emphatically. "It was my fault." He proffered his hand. "I'm Skee." Dusty shook his hand and introduced herself.

"At least let me buy you another coffee." Skee gestured at the cafe.

Dusty laughingly declined his offer, telling him she had an appointment to keep. I took that as my cue and stepped forward to join them.

"G'day mate," said Skee, shaking my hand firmly when Dusty introduced us.

Now that friendly relations had been established, Dusty took the opportunity of gleaning some local knowledge. She started by asking for directions to get to the address we had for the man we were hoping was Abbie's brother. Her car was fitted with a navigator, but Dusty was paving the way to try to get more information from Skee.

"It's just around the corner." He obligingly told us how to get there.

Dusty then asked if he knew David Kowalski. In a small town like Mossman, the two men could easily be acquainted.

Skee shrugged. "Everybody knows everybody around here."

As if to prove the point he nodded and smiled at a passer-by. When Dusty started asking him about David Kowalski, the friendly relations seemed to cool.

"Why do you want to know about him? Are you with the police?"

Dusty explained she was a journalist and wanted to get in touch with Abbie Kowalski who was possibly related to David.

Skee's brow furrowed. "Good luck with that." He stepped back onto the footpath. "Gotta go. See ya." He hurried away before we could respond.

Dusty looked after him thoughtfully. "I wonder why he assumed the police might want to talk to David. Maybe Abbie's brother is a bit of a larrikin."

CHAPTER 29

Although David Kowalski's home was not far, we decided to take the car rather than leave it parked in the street.

"Someone might take a liking to the hub caps," Dusty joked as she opened the passenger door.

"Or your number plate." Dusty's eyes widened in horror at this suggestion. The car's number plate, STAR77, reflected her superstitious side. STAR is for lucky star and seven is a lucky number.

When we arrived at our destination, I pulled up outside a blue weatherboard cottage raised from the ground and surrounded by palms and other tropical vegetation. Like many homes in the area, it was unfenced, giving it a welcoming look.

Just as we reached the steps leading to the front entrance, the door opened. A woman in her early to mid thirties stepped out. Her long fair hair was pulled back from her face and held firm by an orange headband. Seeing us, she smiled a greeting and left the door open before running down the stairs, a large bag swinging from her shoulder. Dusty called after her.

"Does David Kowalski live here?"

"Kovalski," she said as she descended the steps. "Spelt with a 'w', pronounced with a 'v'. Go on in. He's in the kitchen." She continued her hurried exit.

Despite the invitation and the open door, Dusty was hesitant to walk in unannounced. She tapped lightly on the door and called out as she stepped inside.

"In here."

Before I could place what was familiar about the voice that answered, we entered the dining area and came face to face with the fair-haired Nordic we had encountered in the street. He was sitting on a stool, an elbow resting on the breakfast bar and a mug in one hand. I could smell freshly brewed coffee. He greeted us with a cheeky grin and a mischievous gleam in his eyes.

"Fancy seeing me here, eh?" Skee was obviously pleased with our reaction at unexpectedly seeing him again.

Dusty was not in the mood for jokes. "Why didn't you tell me you share with David?"

"I don't." Skee was still smirking.

"Whatever." A note of impatience had entered Dusty's voice. She didn't want to be distracted by a smart alec. "Where's David? I'd like to talk to him."

Skee placed his mug on the breakfast bar and, without getting off the stool, bent at the waist in a mock bow.

"At your service." He laughed; enjoying the irritation he was causing Dusty. "Also known as Skee as in Kowal*ski*."

He used the same pronunciation as his blonde housemate and emphasised the last syllable. Dusty didn't join in the laughter.

"Have a seat, why don't you?" Skee gestured toward a table near the window. "Now is my chance to offer you a coffee. No cappuccino maker but plenty of hot coffee in the pot." He held the coffee plunger aloft.

Dusty shook her head, her expression making it clear she wanted to get down to business.

"Suit yourselves," Skee said when I also shook my head at the coffee pot.

"Anyway, you've just missed Abbie." His tone was less jocular now.

"That was Abbie?" Dusty glanced back in the direction of the front door. "Your sister?"

"Yeah! That was Abbs." A note of defiance in his voice suggested he had alerted Abbie to make herself scarce before we arrived. "She's gone off to meet her boyfriend."

Dusty's brow furrowed. "You knew I wanted to speak to her."

He shrugged. "What do you want with my sister?" A serious expression now clouded his face as though he'd guessed Dusty wanted to talk to Abbie about her past.

Dusty reached into her bag, drew out the photo of the younger Paul Walker and laid it flat on the table.

"Do you know this man?" She pushed it toward David. Although he'd remained on the stool, he was not far from the table. When he looked down at the picture in front of him, his face darkened, his eyes narrowed and his jaw clenched. He glanced involuntarily in the direction of the front door as though wanting to make sure his sister had left.

"Paul Walker." With a sneer of disgust, he flicked the photo with enough force to send it across the table. It sailed over the edge onto the floor. "Look. I don't want to be rude, but I think you'd better go. My sister's got on with her life. She doesn't need all this thrown in her face again. She certainly won't be interested in rehashing it for the sake of some magazine article or whatever it is you're writing."

I bent down and retrieved the photo which had landed face down on the wooden floorboards.

"I'm not writing a magazine article. I'm an investigative journalist. I'm investigating…"

David interrupted. "Has that bastard done it again?" His face hardened. His fingers closed into tight fists.

"Paul Walker is dead." Dusty studied his face as she spoke.

"Dead? Good! Bloody good riddance. Vile piece of scum."

"He was murdered."

"Even better." A grim smile of satisfaction. "Finally got what he deserved. Abbs'll be relieved to know he's dead. Mostly because it means he won't be able to hurt anyone else. I don't want you bothering Abbs with this crap. She's doing okay these days. Let her be." Then a thought occurred to him. He looked at Dusty. Before he could ask the question, she answered it.

"Yes. Walker was living in this area. In Port Douglas to be exact."

"Holy shit! He would have ended up dead a lot sooner if I'd run into him."

He seemed so genuine. I felt sure he was speaking the truth. Unless he was a very good actor.

"Is that right?" Dusty eyed him with suspicion.

"Could you blame me? After what he did to my sister."

"You would have killed him as payback for what he did to Abbie?"

David glared at Dusty, determination shining in his eyes. "Yes! No, actually, I would've kept him alive and tortured him for days."

"David, where were you on Wednesday February 19th between four-thirty and six in the morning?"

"I wasn't murdering that maggot if that's what you mean. Unfortunately!"

Dusty put her head to one side and waited.

"Five months ago?" said David when he realised Dusty wanted an answer. "You're asking me to remember where I was early in the morning five months ago?" Dusty nodded. "Hell! I dunno. Probably still asleep or getting ready for work."

"You start work early?"

"Yeah. Most days. Usually on the job by seven. That way I'm not working in the heat of the day. I'm an electrician."

"Paul Walker was a monk at Sunyarta Sanctuary in Port Douglas."

David shook his head in disbelief. "A monk? What a sneaking, sleazy hypocrite!" He clamped his lips shut as if he was in danger of saying something he shouldn't – probably a string of graphic expletives. "You're not telling me he was the monk who was murdered."

Dusty nodded. "So where were you that morning?"

"Well, if we're talking about the day the monk was killed, I can tell you exactly where I was. I was working in Port as it happens. That day, I started work at seven. Left here around six-thirty."

Something as unusual as murder, let alone the murder of a monk, was bound to stand out, especially in an area consisting mostly of small towns. However, Dusty didn't take that as a given.

"How is it you're able to be so precise about your movements that day?"

"Because when I heard about the monk's murder, I realised I'd been working on a house in Port the day it had happened. So that day kinda stuck in my head." Picking up on Dusty's scrutiny, he added. "Because he was a monk and because a murder had happened in this area, not because I knew he was Walker. I didn't."

"So you often do jobs in Port Douglas?"

"Sometimes. I work for a big company in Cairns. They send me all over the place."

"To be more precise," said Dusty. "What were you doing early that morning before you started work?"

David shrugged. "Obviously, I was climbing out of bed and getting ready. Where else would I be at that hour of the day?"

"Can anyone verify that?"

David grinned, a little of his earlier playfulness returning. "Since you're the one playing detective, I'll leave it up to you to try to prove I wasn't here."

I could see Dusty didn't appreciate being accused of 'playing detective'. She ignored the remark, smiled sweetly and aimed a barb at David which erased the grin from his face.

"That's okay. Actually, I'm more interested in where your sister was that morning."

David scowled. "My sister had nothing to do with Walker's murder."

Dusty, apparently satisfied with his reaction, gathered up her bag ready to leave.

"He seems a pretty straightforward sort of guy," I said as we walked out to the car later.

Dusty nodded. "Except he's keeping something back. Possibly to protect his sister. Is it something significant to the case or something unimportant he thinks might look bad for Abbie? Or something that might look bad for him?"

I'd judged David to be someone incapable of duplicity; however, I knew Dusty was a master at picking up on the subtle clues people gave out without realising it. She would, by hook or by crook, find out what it was he was hiding.

CHAPTER 30

"TO ANSWER YOUR question…" Dusty was standing in front of the windows of her apartment, gazing out at the clear blue sky. I didn't recall asking a question. She turned to face me, laughing at my baffled expression. "When we walked up to Sunyarta the first time, you asked me about my mother's case."

I had held back from reminding Dusty about it because I felt more restrained than usual about enquiring into her private life. For one thing, since Jake arrived on the scene, I wasn't sure if I could expect the same closeness Dusty and I had once shared. Did she still see me as her 'good friend'?

To hide my uneasiness, I responded flippantly. "Right. I believe you like, promised to tell me over a gin and tonic."

Dusty walked over to the bar, propped herself up on a stool and responded with her dazzling smile. "You're the barman."

I mixed two tall tumblers of gin and tonic with twists of lemon decoratively arranged along the rims. Thinking that the faux barman-with-customer situation might make it easier for Dusty to talk, I remained behind the bar.

"To be honest with you, Sean, I didn't want to talk about my mother's case because…" Her chest heaved under the weight of a deep sigh. "Because I have to talk about her as a dead person." Her shoulders slumped. She stared at the drink in front of her.

The last time we'd worked together a police informant had taken Senior Sergeant Ken Nagle to a bush site near Claigan, the country town where Dusty was born, claiming it to be the place where Anna Kent was buried.

"They found…" I hesitated, not wanting to use the word 'body'.

"They found someone buried at the site?"

She nodded. "Last year. Not long after we left Darwin." Her eyes met mine in an agonised expression. "They use the term remains. They call her 'the remains' or 'the body'." The terminology was understandable especially as the authorities had not yet identified the person who had been buried. If it was Dusty's mother as was likely, she had been there for more than thirty years.

"It hurts when I hear Mum spoken about like that." Her face tensed as she fought to keep back the tears.

Dusty had once told me that, although living with the loss of her mother and the awful strain of not knowing, the one thing she took comfort from was the hope her mother was alive somewhere. A part of her must have known it was a forlorn hope. Nevertheless, she had clung to it.

Ice cubes clinked against glass as she raised her drink to her lips. When she had taken a sip, Dutsy lowered the glass and gave me a half-embarrassed smile to indicate she'd recovered her composure. She seemed to be about to say something else but, apparently changing her mind, lowered her eyes. I allowed a few moments to pass before continuing our conversation.

"Does Ken have any suspects? What about the informant who took him to the burial site?"

"His name's Dave Turner."

"Right. So this Dave Turner could be the murderer. He'd have to be the prime suspect, wouldn't he?"

"Unfortunately, Dave Turner's alibi is rock solid." Dusty explained that Turner had been interviewed during the original investigation and his alibi, that he was working on a job two hours' drive from Claigan where Dusty's mother was last seen, had been thoroughly checked.

"Right. So how did Turner know about the burial site?"

"He says he was taken there by a friend of his. The friend didn't say anything about anyone being buried there. He just said it was sacred ground."

"That could mean anything. Why assume it was a burial site?"

"Apparently the friend let something slip when they were having a few beers together that made Turner suspicious. So Turner asked him if he had anything to do with my mother's disappearance. The guy didn't answer, just looked at Turner. A look that sent chills down his spine. Not long after that, Turner's friend took him to the burial site and swore him to secrecy. The guy told him it could become his sacred place too. Turner took that as a threat."

"Sounds a bit suss to me. If Turner's telling the truth; if he knows who the murderer is, why can't he tell Ken? If he's like, about to die, he doesn't have much to lose. Right?"

"Wrong. He's afraid for his family. The murderer, this so-called friend of his, kept threatening Turner over the years. When he got married, the friend reminded him of the sacred place. Turner knew that meant his wife could end up there. The same thing happened when his daughter was born. He told Ken he'd be willing to give evidence and name the man if the man was dead. Because of his diagnosis, Turner knew he had no real chance of outliving the guy. He decided the least he could do was to let me know where my mother was."

"So Turner's friend must be Jimmy, the guy who was driving the orange Datsun and spoke to your mother that day?"

"It's probable, but we don't know for sure. Turner denied it was Jimmy. The trouble is none of the men Turner knew at the time was called Jimmy, or Jim, or James or even Jeremy."

"Right. Not as easy as it sounds."

"It's a complication, that's all. Ken will get there in the end. I'm sure of it." She raised her glass. "To success for Ken's investigation." Our glasses clinked.

Dusty sipped her drink thoughtfully. When she spoke, her tone of voice indicated a change of subject.

"I've got my fingers crossed that I get results from the ads."

I had not been able to locate Paul Walker's family. Walker being a fairly common name meant the possibilities were too many for me to sift through quickly. Instead, Dusty had taken half page advertisements in several Australian newspapers asking for relatives of Paul

Walker and anyone else who might have information about him to contact her. The ad mentioned that a monk murdered in Port Douglas had been identified as Walker. Dusty had been hesitant to include this but eventually decided it was necessary in order to underscore the seriousness and urgency of her request.

"If we find his next of kin, we'll be able to get a DNA analysis done and prove beyond doubt the dead monk is Paul Walker."

"Are you still hoping he's not Walker?"

A wistful smile spread across her face. "Maybe I'm doing an incy-wincy bit of wishful thinking. In reality, I don't think there's any doubt. Still it's good to have certainty. That's not the only reason for locating Walker's family members. They can give me more background information which might help with the case. Besides, his parents are probably still living and they have a right to know their son is dead."

"They might not care."

"I had considered that. In fact, it's possible anyone who knew Walker would prefer to forget him so I'm not expecting an overwhelming response to the ads."

CHAPTER 31

DAVID HAD PROMISED to ask his sister to call Dusty. When he warned her that Abbie was unlikely to be willing to help, Dusty told him she had the backing of the police and the more cooperation she got the less likely it was the police would come knocking on their door. This seemed to convince him. Dusty was confident Abbie would call her eventually. She was right.

When Abbie rang, Dusty arranged to meet her in Anzac Park at the northern end of Macrossan Street.

"I hope you don't mind meeting here." Abbie gestured at our surroundings.

We were sitting, facing the water, on a bench under a magnificent old fig tree. Today Abbie's blonde hair was swept back from her face with a sky-blue headband that highlighted the blue of her eyes.

"Being near nature is kinda healing." Her rueful smile hinted at her vulnerability.

"I understand," said Dusty. "I wish I didn't have to put you through this."

"I guess if it wasn't you, it'd be the police. Again! I had enough of police interviews when I first reported what happened. I understand why they have to give me the third degree but..." She looked up at the overhanging green branches of the fig tree's immense canopy which provided a shady oasis.

Dusty liked me to be present when she interviewed witnesses and suspects because she valued my observations. On this occasion I was not entirely comfortable. I felt a male presence might be intimidating for Abbie. However, when I asked her if she would like me to leave and come back later, Abbie said she was happy for me to stay. All the same, I put a little distance between us by positioning myself at the other end of the bench. Having worked with Dusty on several cases now I'd become quite good at being a background prop.

Dusty took out her voice recorder, holding it up to show Abbie who nodded her agreement to the taping of the conversation.

"I'm afraid I might have to repeat some of the questions you've already been asked by the police." Abbie nodded her understanding. "Please don't think I doubt your testimony, Abbie, but I need to ask you this. How did you know the person who assaulted you was Walker?"

Abbie looked at the ground, shifted in her seat and crossed her legs at the ankles.

"I believe the assault took place at a school camp. You said it was dark and you woke up to find Walker in your bed. I have to ask, Abbie, so please don't take it the wrong way. Since it was dark, is there a chance you might have been mistaken?"

Abbie's eyes glistened. She looked down at her hands.

"It was his voice," she said softly. Then she repeated it in a stronger, defiant tone as though Dusty might contradict her. "It was his voice. I recognised the voice."

"Was there anything else?" Dusty's tone was gentle.

"What he said."

"Which was?"

Abbie swallowed and struggled to compose herself before continuing.

"He said: *Just call me Paul.* That's what Mr Walker used to say to us. That's why…" She shook her head. "It was awful."

Dusty picked up on her half finished sentence.

"That's why what?"

Abbie averted her eyes. "Nothing. I don't even want to talk about it."

"That's precisely what he warned you against at the time, wasn't it? He told you not to say anything. Threatened you. Is that right?"

Abbie nodded. "He said no-one would believe me if I said anything."

"Did he ever touch you again?"

Abbie pulled her shoulder bag up to her chest and folded her arms to hug it to her body. "Why are you putting me through this again?" She squeezed her bag tighter. After a few minutes, she relaxed her grip on the bag, glancing apologetically at Dusty. "I'm sorry. I know you have to ask questions."

"It's all right, Abbie." Dusty reached for her own spacious bag. "We're probably not allowed to do this in the park." She pulled out something wrapped in newspaper. "But what the hell!" She un-wrapped three bottles of vodka based drinks and handed them round. We each unscrewed the tops on the bottles and drank.

When she saw Abbie was more relaxed, Dusty continued.

"Paul Walker taught you in primary school. That's when the as-sault occurred. Correct? When you were in primary school?"

"Yes." Abbie lowered her eyelids.

"When you were older you decided to speak out about what he'd done?"

Abbie inclined her head. "I was seventeen. By this time I was in high school."

"Did something happen at that time to prompt you to speak out?"

"I was talking to Kim, Kimberley Grey. We lived in the same street so knew each other quite well. Her younger sister, Savanna, was in Mr Walker's class by this time. Kim told me Savanna kept saying how nice Mr Walker was."

"Kimberley was worried about her sister?"

"Yes, because Savanna was going on a Year Six camp, the same one Kim and I went on. That's when I realised Kim must have been molested as well. It was a weird moment. We just looked at each other. We didn't have to say a word." Abbie raised her bottle to her lips and gulped down more of the vodka mix. "All that time I thought I was the only one."

"Yes. He probably said you were special, something like that – made you think he'd chosen you as his special one."

Abbie nodded. "He said it was to be our secret. If my parents found out, I'd get into big trouble." Her cheeks tinged with pink.

Dusty placed a reassuring hand on her arm. "Nothing to be ashamed about. You were just a kid and the victim of a master manipulator. People like that know how to exploit and control children."

"I know. It's just when I look back it's all so obvious. I can't understand why I was so scared of his threats. I should have told my parents." Her mouth twisted. "I know. You can't put a wise head on young shoulders. I know that. Still…"

"You still beat yourself up. I understand. You mustn't though, Abbie." Dusty placed her half empty bottle on the ground in front of her. "So Kimberley had been assaulted by Walker at the same holiday camp?"

"Yes. She'd also found out about Lee, Lena Patterson. Another victim. I should have known really. Lee had been so full of beans and always ready for an adventure. She was one of the smart kids. But after that camp she was a different person: moody and quiet and she kept pretty much to herself. She wasn't one of the clever kids anymore – she struggled to pass her subjects. It was odd really, I'd always thought of Lee as tough, one of the toughest kids in school – a real tomboy. Strange that she seemed to have been the one most traumatised by what happened."

"Were there other victims of Paul Walker? Apart from you three girls."

"No. Mr Walker… I mean…" Abbie hesitated, absently twisting the strap of her bag. I saw Dusty lean forward as though something in Abbie's voice had alerted her to a point of interest. Or was it a lie she'd spotted?

"That man must have hurt others," Abbie mumbled. "But no-one else came forward."

CHAPTER 32

"IT MUST HAVE taken courage for you three girls to speak out."

"We didn't want to. That's for sure. But we knew we had to. Thinking about little Savanna being a victim made us realise our silence meant he had had the opportunity to abuse other girls." Abbie grimaced in disgust. "It was a horrible thought."

"So that's when you went to a lawyer?"

"Yes. The lawyer said it was the sort of crime that was hard to prove. She pointed out the difficulties and how some people would not believe us and some would hate us. She warned us it would change our lives. After she'd done her best to point out how bad the consequences could be, she asked us if we still wanted to go ahead. We all said yes. All three of us hated the very thought of speaking out; of telling other people, making it public. But we didn't have any other choice."

"Then when it came to giving evidence, Lena found it too traumatic?"

"She was okay at first; just as determined as me and Kim. Then at the last moment, she backed out. Her testimony was to be the final one, but after seeing how upset Kim and I were on the stand, she just got scared. We didn't blame her. We were surprised cos we thought she was tough, but we totally understood and respected her decision. It wasn't easy telling every detail of what happened to us in front of strangers and being grilled by lawyers. Actually it was horrible. They made it seem like we were liars."

A shadow flickered across Abbie's face.

"As I understand it, the defence team claimed you and Kimberley had colluded to try to get money by way of compensation. They suggested one of you had found out about the payout Paul Walker received from his wife's life insurance when she died the year before."

"We didn't even know about the money."

"The other issue was Walker had an alibi for the time of Kimberley's assault. What was the set up at the camp? Weren't you sleeping in a dormitory style situation with other girls in beds close by?"

"Most of the time. Some of us volunteered to help with cleaning and preparing meals and that sort of thing. As a reward, we were given the privilege of sleeping one night in a yurt on our own. They had four Mongolian yurt tents, small ones, around the camp fire. The yurts were separate from the cabins where everyone else was sleeping."

"So each night the yurt tents were occupied by four different girls?"

"They alternated; girls one night, boys the next. All the accommodation was split gender."

"Did you have adult supervision?"

"Yes. Team leaders were on duty all night. They walked around the grounds, around the cabins and the yurt area and kept the fire stoked."

"Paul Walker was one of the team leaders?"

"He was."

"It does seem strange Walker was seen at the other end of the campsite at the time Kimberley claimed he was in her tent."

Abbie turned sharply to glare at Dusty. "Claim? Are you implying Kim was lying?" Dropping her empty bottle on the seat, she stood up quickly and faced Dusty, hands on hips. "After all we went through the worst thing, the very worst thing you can do, the worst thing anyone can do, is call us liars." Her chest heaved.

"I'm sorry, Abbie. Bad choice of word. I don't believe for one minute any of you were lying. Not for a single second." Abbie's tense body relaxed as Dusty continued. "Please don't think I doubt your word, Abbie."

Gratified by Dusty's response, Abbie's eyes glistened as she began to explain. "Kim realised she must have got the time wrong. It was the middle of the night and she was in a state of shock. The yurts didn't have clocks and we weren't allowed to have mobile phones at the camp. Kim's watch was one of those ones with marks for the hours instead of numbers. It would have been easy to misread the time. Besides, Kim didn't really know how long she was curled up in her bed crying before she checked the time."

"After all you girls went through, Paul Walker got off scot free." Dusty shook her head sadly. "It's so wrong."

Abbie opened her mouth as if to speak, then closed it again, sitting down heavily as though drained of energy. Dusty cast a sympathetic look at her.

"Abbie, I'm sorry to rake all this up. I wouldn't do it if I didn't think it was absolutely necessary."

"I understand." Abbie sighed and leant back against the back of the seat.

"After the court case," Dusty continued, "you were quoted in the local newspaper as having said: *That twisted maggot will pay for what he did.*"

Abbie nodded. "All those years when I'd kept what happened buried. I didn't feel anger – just shame and a deep hurt. The anger flared up when the court case brought everything to the surface. As far as I was concerned, he'd deliberately exploited our innocence and our respect for him as a teacher. He'd just used us, like we weren't even human beings. Like we were just things without feelings. In the court, he made us out to be liars. I was livid!"

"So when you moved here and you saw Walker in the street one day in Port Douglas, you saw a way to 'make that twisted maggot pay'?" Dusty's tone was sympathetic. "I wouldn't blame you at all for wanting to get your revenge." She looked across at me. "I think Sean would have been tempted to help you."

Abbie's indignant retort came before I had a chance to respond. "I didn't! I had no idea Mr Walker was living at the monastery. Besides…" Abbie stopped abruptly.

I had the impression she'd been about to say something she would regret. Dusty leant forward, her eyes gleaming.

"Besides," Abbie continued quickly. "How would I have even

known he was in Queensland? I didn't know." I watched her toes curl under in her thongs. "Neither did David." Abbie rubbed her hands along her forearms, as though to wipe away goose bumps. "The first we knew about it was when you told David the other day."

"Fair enough, Abbie. By the way, where were you the morning Walker was murdered? Specifically between four-thirty and six o'clock. Sorry, but I have to ask."

Abbie nodded. "David said you'd ask me. He could've told you where I was. It's just that he's protective. I don't mean over protective, he's just always ready to defend me if necessary." The thought of her brother brought a bright smile to her face. "I was at David's place. I stay there a lot. Other times I stay with my boyfriend. That morning I got up early and had breakfast with David around six o'clock."

Dusty eyed her thoughtfully for a moment before asking her next question.

"Were you in Port Douglas the morning Paul Walker was murdered?"

"No." I noticed a slight hesitation before she answered. Dusty must have noticed something too because she leant forward, the pupils of her green eyes dilated and fixed on Abbie.

"David was in Port that morning. Were you with him?"

Abbie folded her arms across the front of her body. "I had nothing to do with the murder. Neither did David."

Dusty leant back. The expression on her face reminded me of a feline licking her lips after a satisfying meal. She made an abrupt change of subject.

"Do you know where I might find Kimberley and Lena?"

"I kept in contact with Kim off and on, but we sorta lost touch. I don't know where she is now." Abbie's voice was tinged with regret. "Lee dropped out of school not long after the court case. I heard she went to America. She always said she'd leave Australia when she got the money." In response to Dusty's raised eyebrows, Abbie explained. "Lee had money coming to her from some sort of family trust when she turned eighteen."

Abbie reached into her bag, took out her phone and began tapping on the icons until she found what she wanted.

"This was taken of us together on the first morning of the court case." She held up her phone to show Dusty. "I like to remember us as we were then. That's me in the middle. Kim's on the left, Lee on the right."

Dusty studied the photo. "Hm. There's something familiar about Lee. Does she have brothers or sisters?"

"No. She's an only child."

"I wonder why she looks familiar. Maybe she reminds me of someone."

"Someone famous maybe." Abbie laughed. "We were always trying to find resemblances between ourselves and movie stars."

"That could be it. She must remind me of someone I've seen in a movie," said Dusty, holding the phone toward me.

I bent forward to look at the picture of the three teenagers. The girls were standing close together arm in arm, all smiling at the camera, happy smiles of anticipation. Lena's brown eyes, large and round, were accentuated by her cropped fair hair. In contrast to Lena's gamine appearance, Kimberley with her long blonde hair and fair skin was a feminine beauty.

"I didn't really stay in contact with Lee. I think she felt a bit awkward with us because she hadn't gone ahead and given evidence."

Back when the photo was taken, the girls must have had such hopes Walker would be convicted. Abbie might have read my thoughts.

"We were so happy. After all we'd gone through and all the work our lawyer had put in, the day of the court case had finally arrived."

"Shame the case didn't turn out the way you'd hoped," I said.

Abbie sighed and flashed me a quick, sad smile. "It is what it is. I didn't take the law into my own hands and kill the monk."

Dusty eyed Abbie thoughtfully, as though contemplating challenging her. However, she let the moment pass and handed the phone back.

"I'm surprised the three of you don't keep in touch on social media."

A bitter smile darkened Abbie's expression. "We copped heaps of abuse because a lot of people thought we were lying about Mr

Walker. I cut myself off from social media completely for a long time. I still don't use it much."

"What a pity you all lost touch," said Dusty.

Abbie's eyes lingered over the photo before she clicked it off the screen and put her phone back in her bag. "I know, but we weren't close friends at school. The main thing connecting us was what happened at the holiday camp."

"Not something you wanted to talk about or remember?"

"Exactly. I feel bad about Lee though. Kim and I didn't want her to feel guilty. We should have tried harder to convince her of that. I thought…I thought she might have…died."

Dusty understood what she meant. "You mean you thought she might have taken her own life?"

"Yes." A soft answer, barely audible. "Her parents didn't believe what she said about being molested so Lee turned her back on them. To have gone through all she went through and then her own parents didn't believe her. It was too much."

Abbie stared out at the water. A paddle steamer was chugging home into the inlet while in the distance a white cruise ship glided along the horizon.

"Lee wrote a song, you know." Abbie paused, still gazing into the distance. "I don't think anyone ever heard the song except me and Kim. I can still see Lee, with her guitar propped up in her lap, strumming and singing in her sweet voice."

Dusty smiled. "Can you remember the song?"

"Just the chorus." With her mind still apparently far away, lulled into nostalgic reverie by the movement of the water, Abbie began to sing softly.

Magic me away.

Vanish me through the atmosphere

Carry me far from here

Beyond this hell of mine.

Take me back to my innocent time.

Magic me away.

CHAPTER 33

AFTER ABBIE LEFT us to meet her boyfriend at a hotel in Macrossan Street, Dusty and I stayed under the fig tree, discussing the case.

"Well, Sean, there goes any hope Ram might have been wrongly accused. There's absolutely no doubt in my mind Abbie is a genuine victim. I felt so bad about putting her through it all again." Dusty heaved a sigh.

I too had been feeling uncomfortable watching Abbie recounting her dreadful experience.

We were silent for a few minutes, gazing out toward the Great Barrier Reef and listening to the rainbow lorikeets and starlings that had gathered in the trees to start their dusk birdsong. Dusty was the first to break the silence.

"Did you notice Abbie's tone of voice when she spoke about Walker? Sometimes she had loathing in her voice. At other times the loathing wasn't there. It was as if she had ambiguous feelings about Walker, maybe even had some affection for him."

"Affection! Are you sure?"

"Hmm. Maybe affection is not exactly what I mean." Dusty ran a hand through her hair and furrowed her brow as she paused to think. "It was as if she'd sort of split Walker in two: the abuser she despised and the teacher she liked."

"Right. Makes sense in a way. Walker was popular with his students. When she was young, Abbie knew him as a teacher and probably liked him."

"Ye…es. That could be it. When she's talking about him, she's subconsciously remembering the teacher she once liked; it comes out in her voice. Crikey! It must really mess up her head."

I was beginning to realise how deeply her teacher's abuse had affected Abbie. I turned to Dusty.

"If Abbie's a genuine victim, it means she's a possible suspect. Right?"

"She certainly had motive and only has her brother to verify her alibi. He'll back her up even if she's lying."

"Do you think she was lying? Did the Dusty Kent lie detector pick up anything?"

"Yep. She lied about not being in Port Douglas on the morning of the murder. And I kept getting the feeling there was something she wanted to tell me but couldn't bring herself to do so."

"I thought that too. You said David was hiding something. Maybe Abbie knows what it is and thought she should tell you. Torn between doing the right thing and loyalty to her brother."

"Possible. She was keen to let me know David had nothing to do with the murder. Why did she find it necessary to include her brother in her denials?"

"You mean she protested too much on his behalf?"

"You got it." Dusty pointed a finger of approval at me. "Methinks the lady doth protest too much."

"I understand why David feels protective toward his sister," I said. "But would he commit murder to avenge what had been done to her so many years ago? If it had just happened I could understand him attacking her abuser in a fit of anger but…"

Dusty held up her hand. "I know what you're saying. But think about it, Sean. His anger on her behalf might have been simmering below the surface all these years. Then one day he comes across Ram, recognises him, sees him walking around free. That could have brought David's anger charging to the surface like a sudden surge of electricity." She looked at me with a twinkle in her eye. "After all, he is an electrician."

"Very funny."

Dusty executed a mock bow from the waist before becoming serious again. "I think we need to have another talk with David

Kowalski."

Once again I put myself in David's place. If it had been my sister who'd been molested, would I carry the anger with me through the years? Would the sight of the perpetrator years later trigger a violent reaction? The answer came quickly. Yes! But would I actually murder the pervert? Not an easy question to answer. The sticking point in relation to David Kowalski was that I didn't think he would have the skills to hide his guilt from someone as astute as Dusty.

"David seemed genuinely surprised when you told him about Walker's murder."

"He did. I believed him at the time. But…"

"The Dusty Kent lie detector is not infallible."

"You got it."

Dusty gazed at the water where the setting sun had created warm orange streaks on the surface. She picked up her bag.

"Let's grab a bite to eat before the tourists fill up all the restaurants."

We gathered up the empty vodka-mix bottles and dumped them in the bin. "By the way," said Dusty as we checked for oncoming traffic before crossing the street, "I want to go back to Sunyarta tomorrow."

CHAPTER 34

AT SUNYARTA, DUSTY asked to speak with the monk who had sighted Ram's body on the rocky ledge and raised the alarm.

A young monk, whose Asian features suggested he might have Burmese ancestry, appeared in the doorway. Saya beckoned him in and introduced him as Ashin Jag. When Dusty asked him to tell her how he came to discover Ram's body he bowed his shaven head. The sadness in his eyes when he looked up suggested the murder had troubled him. He sat upright with his hands resting in his lap. Dusty studied him intently as he answered her questions.

"Why did you go to look for Ram that morning?"

"He did not come for breakfast." Jag spoke quietly. "Ashin Ram usually sits next to me. On this day, his seat remained empty all through our morning meal."

"Did you immediately assume something was wrong?"

"We eat only two meals each day. One in the morning, one in the afternoon. The morning meal breaks a long fast. It is unusual for a monk to miss this meal unless he is sick. Also…"

The young monk hesitated. His eyes went to Saya.

Saya encouraged him. "Speak."

"Also what?" Dusty prompted. "Anything you can tell me might help us to find out what happened to Ram."

"When he came back from the town the day before, he was not at peace with himself."

"Do you know why?"

"No. But I became troubled when he was not at breakfast."

"So you went to Ram's meditation place?"

"I went first to see if he was still sleeping. After that, I went to the meditation platform. He was not there. I walked around."

"Why? Why didn't you just come back when you saw Ram wasn't there?"

Jag blinked and inclined his head as though considering this.

"Yes," he said after a few minutes, as if acknowledging the rationale behind Dusty's question. "I do not know why."

"How did you come to see the body?"

"While walking around the platform, I saw a flash of yellow out of the corner of my eye. Naturally, this yellow of our robes is familiar to me. It caught my attention." I recalled Dusty saying Ram's yellow robe had been tossed over the cliff and became snagged on a bush. "I went closer to the edge and looked down. On seeing the body of our brother I went straight away to the office where I found our venerable Saya." Ashin Jag brought his hands together in the prayer position and bowed his head toward Saya.

"Did you see Ram's thongs next to the platform?" Dusty asked as the young monk straightened.

"I saw only one."

Dusty locked eyes with him. "Did you push Ram over the edge of the cliff, Jag?"

His impassive features flickered briefly before settling again. "I could not do that."

Saya offered further explanation. "It is against our teachings to harm another being."

When Jag had gone, Dusty recounted to Saya all we had learned about the monk he knew as Ashin Ram. He maintained his serene expression throughout, showing neither surprise nor distaste. When Dusty had finished, he sat quietly with his head bowed. I had the impression he was waiting for her words and the images they had conjured up to leave the room. When he spoke, his voice was calm, his manner composed.

"I do not know who Ashin Ram was before he came to us but I know he was a good monk. From the first day he came to Sunyarta he was exemplary in his monastic pursuit. His commitment to our teachings was absolute." Saya had deftly negated any accusations

Dusty might have made against Ram. He'd also caused me to reconsider my suspicions about him. "I do not mean to fault your investigation." Saya lifted a hand slightly in a gesture of apology. "But I believe you have not yet arrived at the truth of Ashin Ram."

It was not surprising that someone who had a close association with the dead monk would be unable to accept what he'd done. Dusty and I had been reluctant to do so too even though we hadn't actually met the man. If Saya had sat in on the interview with Abbie, he would have been unable to deny 'the truth of Ashin Ram'. Dusty chose not to debate the issue with him. Instead, she took the opportunity to follow up on something we had previously discussed: possible reasons for a monk to strike at the time that he did.

"Saya, do you remember anything out of the ordinary happening here at Sunyarta in the months leading up to Ram's death? Anything that might have upset one of the other monks?"

"I do not think so." He paused to consider the question further and eventually shook his head.

When Dusty asked him if any of the monks had recently entered the Sanctuary he told us Jag, who had been there for five years, was the most recent arrival.

We politely took our leave after receiving permission to walk around and talk to the other monks.

"I haven't ruled out the possibility one of the monks here is a psycho," Dusty said to me as we walked along the path away from Saya's office.

"What about Jag?"

Dusty shook her head. "I don't think he's a psycho."

"But you were using the Dusty Kent lie detector on that innocent young monk, weren't you?" Her grin was enough to tell me I was right. "So? What did your lie detector tell you about the prime suspect who found the body?"

Suspecting me of mockery, Dusty flashed me a sideways glance then, when she realised I was not being flippant, shook her head.

"Nothing."

The monks we talked to as we strolled through the grounds were engaged in various activities: arranging flowers, making bread, picking vegetables in the garden, preparing food in the kitchen, sweeping and cleaning around the buildings. Dusty observed them, pausing occasionally to speak briefly to some. Each one accepted her interruption to their work with a smile and willingly answered her questions.

"Did you identify any psychos lurking among the yellow robes?" Now I was being flippant.

Dusty rolled her eyes. "Stop taking the Mickey!" She laughed and matched my teasing mood. "The Dusty Kent psycho detector was off duty today."

"Now ain't that a savage shame." That earned me a playful punch in the arm.

At the exit, Dusty turned to look back and cast her eye over the buildings, a thoughtful expression on her face.

"Are they exactly what they seem? Or are we just seeing the smooth surface – like looking at their lovely gardens without seeing the dirt and compost and writhing worms underneath? What lies behind Saya's unflappable exterior?" She looked at me for confirmation, her brow furrowed. "I'm too suspicious, aren't I?"

"That's one of your strengths. You wouldn't be so good at catching murderers if you didn't forage right down to the bottom layers."

Dusty gripped my arm but not in response to my insightful comment. She was staring up into a tree. I followed her gaze. A black bird was perched in one of the high branches, almost camouflaged by leaves.

"I told you!" she hissed.

"How long do crows usually hang around to warn of evil?"

Dusty shrugged. "A few days."

I pointed out it had been three weeks since she first spotted the crow at the Sanctuary. She acknowledged my point but remained troubled, unable to shake the conviction the crow was a messenger of death.

Back at the car, we paused to admire the view.

"I was thinking about what Saya said." Dusty was staring out at the ocean in the distance. "He's no fool yet he's convinced Ram was a good person. He might be right, you know. What if Ram left Walker the abuser behind when he entered the Sanctuary and became Ram the good monk?"

Dusty tapped the screen of her phone, bringing up the photo of Ram's painting of a coffin in a tree trunk. "This could symbolise a metaphorical death; the death of Paul Walker."

"Are you saying he locked himself away in a monastery as a way of stopping himself from hurting young girls again?"

"It's possible. The trauma of being openly accused and having to defend himself in court could have been a turning point for him so he resolved not to offend again. I went to a website about paedophilia." Dusty screwed up her face in disgust. "It was more about treatment and prevention so not too gross. Apparently, paedophiles are driven by urges they find virtually impossible to control. According to this website, therapy can help them curb their sick impulses." She swallowed. It was a repugnant subject to talk about. "Walker might have had therapy after he was caught and decided the only way to be sure he wouldn't reoffend was to remove himself from temptation. As far as we know he abused only females, so a monastery would hold no temptations for him. He didn't own a mobile phone so had no access to online child pornography."

I started to feel marginally less hostile toward Walker. If Dusty's theory was correct, at least he'd tried to stop himself from abusing. But had he succeeded?

"If he was genuine about not wanting to re-offend why did he start going out into the community? Did he find it too difficult to give up his so-called urges?"

"There's no evidence he attempted anything improper while he was in town. Volunteering might have been his way of doing penance for his past actions."

"So we're back to his past; to his past victims?"

"I think so. Unless sinister secrets lurk below the serene surface of Sunyarta."

CHAPTER 35

"COME ON. TIME for another talk with David Kowalski," said Dusty one morning.

"Another drive to Mossman?" I enjoyed taking Dusty's car out on the open road.

"Nope." She grinned at me. "He's right here in Port Douglas."

"You want to check their stories? David and Abbie's?"

Dusty shook her head. "I'm thinking of something else. What if he saw the monk one day and recognised him?"

"Right. You're seriously considering David as a suspect?"

"If Abbie was your sister and you came face to face with her rapist, what would you do?"

In my mind's eye I could see the familiar, happy faces of my sisters and felt the anger rising in me. I might be 'sort of a computer geek' but I was a man. What would I do if someone abused one of my sisters? I considered this before answering Dusty.

"I think I would have gone for his throat and tried to throttle him. I couldn't have just let him walk away. You don't really think about the consequences when someone close to you has been hurt."

"Exactly!"

"Just the same, I don't think I would have carried out a premeditated murder. I might have wanted to, but I doubt I'd have gone through with it."

"What if you had also been the victim? Your anger and need for revenge would have been even stronger."

"David?"

"So far we've assumed Walker only abused girls. But what if that was not the case?"

David was working at a business premises in the process of being refitted. The work vans parked outside were the only clues work was being carried out there until we stood in the open doorway. The sounds of machinery, hammering, men's voices and a booming radio greeted us.

"Smoko!" Dusty called, standing on the doorstep with a container of coffee and a meat pie she'd bought on the way.

"Bribery," she'd explained to me. "He agreed to talk during his smoko if I supplied the snack."

A lull in the buzz of conversations inside followed Dusty's announcement. David's answering voice yelled, "Room at the end!"

We stepped onto the protective matting into the dark interior of the hallway. Paint smells and a dusty haze greeted us. In one room two workmen were hammering while another was using a sanding machine. One of the hammerers looked up as we passed, grinned and jerked his hammer toward the end of the hall. David was working alone in the 'room at the end' where electrical wiring emerged from various holes in the wall. Dressed in work boots and long shorts well equipped with pockets containing various tools, he was on a ladder guiding a length of wiring along the top of the wall where it met the exposed ceiling.

"Smells good," he said over his shoulder as he descended the ladder. When he stepped onto the floor and turned around, I saw the front of his T-shirt bore the slogan *Ladies Love Tradies*. Either this was the T-shirt he reserved for days when special visitors were on site, or David's tastes were more refined than most other tradesmen.

Dusty gave him the coffee, standing well back and holding it out with one arm extended.

"Hey! No need to be so cautious. I'm not going to knock this one to the ground."

Dusty grinned and handed him the paper bag containing the pie. David gestured to the window sill which jutted out from the wall enough for us to lean on and use as a stool seat. Finding the sill too high, Dusty turned a large spool of electrical wiring upright and sat down on it.

"Righto," said David, crossing his feet at the ankles and reaching into the paper bag. "You've kept your end of the bargain. What did you want to ask me?"

His unguarded manner might have been due to the fact that Dusty had assured him beforehand she would not interrogate him about his sister. He obviously felt confident about handling any other queries.

Dusty looked up at him. "I wanted to ask about your school days."

David dismissed his school days with a derisive snort. "School wasn't my favourite time." Dusty's interest was piqued. "Sitting at a desk all day, writing things down," continued David. "It just wasn't my thing. English was the worst." He looked at Dusty with a rueful smile. "You would have been one of those kids English teachers love. I wasn't." He stared down at his feet. "Reading was a nightmare. I couldn't figure out how to stop the letters from jumping around all the time. The teachers just scoffed at me when I tried to explain what was happening – thought I was making up excuses."

I remembered a kid at my primary school who complained about letters jumping around on the page. During reading time he would stare at his book with beads of perspiration glistening on his forehead. When the teacher asked him to read aloud, he just looked at her with tears in his eyes. Reading was easy for me so I didn't understand his problem and, like any other heartless brat, I dismissed him as 'one of the dumb kids'. I subsequently learned he'd been diagnosed as dyslexic, a condition I didn't understand until later in life. Remembering this child gave me a glimpse of what school might have been like for David Kowalski. I realised his vulnerability could have made him a target for the likes of Paul Walker.

"I suppose you were bullied as well," said Dusty. "Because of your unusual surname."

"Yeah. A bit. But I gave as good as I got in the school yard. Hearing my name mispronounced all the bloody time during roll call and presentations – that was what annoyed me."

Dusty's empathy for the young David was not about to distract her. She took aim with an unexpected question. "Were you one of

Paul Walker's students?"

David lowered the pie he was about to put in his mouth. "Why do you want to know?"

"Were you?"

His eyes narrowed. "Bloody hell! Are you suggesting…?" He scrunched the paper bag into a ball and threw it angrily to the floor. I quickly reached across to steady his container of coffee which he'd placed on the window ledge between us.

"That scum didn't touch me. If he'd tried, he would've come off second best. I can tell you that."

Such a strong denial was either true or he wanted to believe it was.

Dusty eyed David pensively for a moment before signalling surrender with a raised hand. "I had to ask, David. I'll be writing a book about this case when I've solved it. My readers will want to know I've covered all angles."

That was true but I suspected part of the reason for posing the question was to unsettle David and consequently weaken his resistance to the question she was about to ask him.

"Well, you can tell your readers that if I'd known about my sister at the time, I would've…" He broke off, pressing his lips together in a hard line.

David seemed to have lost his appetite for the pie. He placed it on the window sill, picked up the coffee container, popped the plastic lid and gulped down some of the hot coffee.

"Which leads me to my next question." Dusty offered David an apologetic smile. "Don't take this as an accusation. It's just one of those things I have to ask."

David finished his coffee, tossed the empty container into a plastic bucket in the corner of the room and looked at Dusty warily, his brow wrinkled in a deep frown.

"No-one would blame you if you wanted to punish Walker for what he did to your sister. As you say, if you'd known what Walker was doing at the time you'd have acted." Dusty paused then went in for the kill. "Did you have anything to do with the death of the monk known as Ram?" She watched David's reaction intently. The look on her face told me she had switched on the Dusty Kent lie detector.

David maintained eye contact and answered tersely. "No. Neither did my sister. Tell your readers that."

I would once have seen his ability to look Dusty in the eye and answer her question directly as an indication he was telling the truth. However, on a previous occasion Dusty had informed me that the ability to hold eye contact during questioning is often a skill developed by liars. Did that apply to David? Dusty might enlighten me later.

CHAPTER 36

"WE CAN CROSS Lena Patterson off our list of suspects," Dusty said a few days later.

My research on Lena had been time consuming. Knowing she would have turned nineteen in 2003 had given me a starting point. I was able to confirm, using my 'highly trained IT skills' to navigate some secret corners of cyber space, that Lena Patterson had flown to Thailand that year and later to the United States.

I then tried all sorts of internet searches, using her name, variations of her name and whatever background details I had, to find her in America. It was not a fruitful search, made more difficult by the fact that Patterson is a fairly common name. However, in the end I satisfied myself Lena had not returned to Australia and that was all we really needed to know.

Initially, Kimberley Grey was also dismissed as a suspect. I had established that the Grey family had returned to live in Western Australia several years ago. But I subsequently discovered both Kimberley and her brother Lyell had come back to the east coast. Lyell was working as a fashion designer in Melbourne while Kimberley had moved to Sydney and was now working in the skin care section at a large department store in the city centre.

Dusty had telephoned Kimberley, introduced herself and explained she was investigating the murder of Paul Walker. Kimberley had understandably been cool but answered Dusty's questions politely, saying she had had no idea Paul Walker was a monk or that he was living in Queensland. At first, Kimberley seemed to have a solid alibi. She worked Monday to Friday so could not have been in Port Douglas on the day of the murder which was a Wednesday.

However, after checking the airline schedules, Dusty found the route from Sydney to Cairns was well serviced with daily flights and decided to delve further.

"What if Kimberley did know Paul Walker was in Port Douglas? What if she found out somehow and decided to get her revenge for what he'd done to her? She might have asked someone to cover for her on the Wednesday, sign her in or whatever they do in big stores. She could have flown to Queensland after work on Tuesday, stayed in Port Douglas that night, and flown back to Sydney on Wednesday morning. After murdering Walker."

Dusty called the department store using her celebrity status to be put through to a senior executive who was happy to oblige by personally checking Kimberley's work records.

"Kimberley didn't have anyone covering for her," said Dusty when she finished the call. A smirk of satisfaction and the gleam in her eye warned me of more to come. "On Wednesday February 19, Kimberley Grey was not at work. She'd called in sick."

"Right. So she lied. Not a good look."

Dusty grinned. "Especially when it's Dusty Kent she's lied to."

"It was months ago though. She might have simply forgotten she had had a sickie."

"Exactly what she'll say if I call her and confront her. Which I won't, because I'm not going to waste my time. I have what I need: the indisputable fact that she was not at work on the day of Walker's death and therefore had the opportunity to kill him. She only had the one day off sick so if she did come to Port Douglas, it was by plane. What we'll do is check to see if she took a flight to Cairns on the Tuesday."

"You mean what *I'll* do."

"Yes, Mr Maze Master. *You* will go sneaking into those dark pockets of cyber space using your hacking skills to check the passenger lists of flights from Sydney to Cairns. Oh, excuse me, did I say hacking? I meant highly developed IT skills."

I acknowledged her teasing with a nod. Using 'highly developed IT skills' as a euphemism for 'hacking' was a standing joke between us. Technically, hacking is what I do to get the information for Dusty but all I do is gain unauthorised access. I don't spread viruses or attack websites. I'm really just spying.

This morning we had returned to the same cafe we had breakfasted at when we first arrived in Port Douglas. I had not yet had a chance to complete my latest spying assignment. Instead of coconut juice, this time Dusty had opted for tea. She stirred the tea leaves round in the pot thoughtfully.

"If Kellie's telling the truth about what time she was at Sunyarta on the morning of the murder, and if Moose is telling the truth about the time he was there..." She paused and looked at me as though waiting for me to finish her sentence. Unfortunately, I failed to understand the significance of what she was saying. Dusty spelled it out for me. "There must have been someone else there that morning. Moose glimpsed someone in the shadows at around five o'clock; it couldn't have been Kellie since she wasn't there until closer to six."

"Right. Moose and truth? They don't seem to go together."

Dusty laughed. "I agree. If he's telling the truth, who was the other person? It could have been any one of the other possible suspects: Kimberley, Abbie or David."

"Or a rogue monk at Sunyarta," I suggested.

"Yes. There's still that possible snake in the grass to keep in mind." Dusty closed the lid of the teapot.

"You haven't forgotten Ram's missing thong?"

Dusty looked at me quizzically.

"That's the one aspect of the murder scene that doesn't fit with one of Walker's victims being the killer." I was still hoping the murderer wasn't one of the girls. "Isn't a psychopathic monk more likely to take a trophy? Surely, Walker's victims would be just as loathe to keep anything belonging to him as Kellie Edwards would be."

I saw Dusty's acceptance of my point reflected in her eyes.

"I agree. However, it's possible the missing thong will be explained by something we don't yet know."

Dusty cradled her cup of tea in both hands and inclined her head slightly toward a table off to the right. "They're having a long holiday. They were here the first day we came. Remember?"

I glanced over at the table she indicated and saw the elderly English couple. 'Ducks' had his head down, working his way through a large plate of bacon, eggs and sausages. His wife's eyes met mine. She flashed me a smile, apparently remembering our brief exchange on the beach the other morning.

"There's someone else hiding in the grass." Dusty had returned to our conversation. I gave her an enquiring look.

"Louisa Penrose. Where does she fit into all this?"

"You think she might be involved in the murder in some way?"

"There's something odd about the woman." She paused to sip her tea. "What if she's also one of Paul Walker's victims? As Abbie said, there must have been other girls he abused, girls who didn't come forward. What if Louisa Penrose is one of them?"

"Why follow you? If she killed Walker, isn't she putting herself at risk of being found out?"

"It wouldn't be the first time a murderer has tried to get close to an investigation or even to be part of it. And what about her initials? Is it just coincidence they are the same as Lena Patterson's initials? I think I'd like another chat with that so-called journalist. Let's shake her up and see what rattles."

After breakfast we drove to the motel where Louisa Penrose was staying.

"Keep an eye in the rear vision mirror for a silver Toyota," said Dusty.

If Louisa was following us, she was doing a better job of remaining out of sight than previously. In fact, since the day Dusty had confronted her, we hadn't seen Louisa or her car. We probably shouldn't have been surprised therefore, when we arrived at the motel, to discover Louisa Penrose had checked out.

"Nincompoop!" Dusty slapped the side of her head with the heel of her hand as we walked back to the car after speaking with the motel receptionist. "I can't help thinking that woman has a strong connection to this case and I've just let her slip through my fingers."

Dusty called Louisa's number several times and left messages but did not get any response.

"Why not ask Jake to track her down?" I suggested.

"I'll do that if necessary but…"

I took the hint. "I'll do some more digging and see what I can find out."

The frustration of letting a possible suspect get away was eased somewhat when Dusty had a piece of luck with her advertisement asking anyone knowing Paul Walker to get in touch. In fact, she received several calls. Most of them were nuisance calls or people who knew a different Paul Walker. This particular response came by way of a surprise visitor.

CHAPTER 37

THE VISITOR ARRIVED two days later just as Dusty and I were heading to the Marina to catch a catamaran out to the Great Barrier Reef.

By now we'd been in Port Douglas for almost a month. If I didn't know better I'd suspect Dusty of deliberately drawing the case out in order to keep spending time with Jake. Although he'd gone back to Cairns, he travelled up to Port whenever he could and, when not together, they communicated regularly. I'd never seen Dusty so light hearted. To her credit, she didn't allow her emotions to interfere with her work ethic or dilute her strong focus on the case.

On this particular day, I had spent a long night checking airline flights to see if Kimberley had flown to Port Douglas. With various airlines flying the route several times a day, it was a tedious exercise. To make matters worse, after doing all that work, I discovered it is possible, although illegal, to travel on a domestic flight under a false name.

"Serious?" said Dusty when I told her. "I never knew that. So we still have no idea whether Kimberley flew to Port Douglas or not."

"Right. I could have saved myself a lot of work if I'd checked about travelling under a false name first."

"Not really, Mr Maze Master. I would still have asked you to check in the hope she'd booked a flight in her real name which would have given us absolute proof. Anyway, I think I'd better fly down to Sydney to interview Kimberley Grey."

Then she took pity on me and suggested a day out on the ocean would 'recharge our batteries'.

We had bounced down the stairs, both of us feeling a sense of freedom at the thought of being out on the water for the rest of the day with laptops and mobile phones locked away in the safe. Dusty was wearing a turquoise sarong over her bikini, hair piled up on her head and, as the tour included snorkelling, she was devoid of jewellery.

Hearing Dusty's name mentioned as we passed the front desk, we paused. The charming receptionist was explaining to an elderly lady that she was unable to give out guest details. She offered to pass a message on to Ms Kent. Dusty interrupted them to address the visitor.

"Are you looking for me? I'm Dusty Kent."

The woman who turned toward us was in her late seventies with short grey hair neatly styled. Kindness etched her lined face but sadness clouded her eyes.

"I'm so sorry, dear," she said in a soft voice. "I should have called you first."

Dusty put her head to one side, offering the woman a tentative smile. "Do I know you?"

"No, but..." She glanced toward the receptionist who was now absorbed in something on her computer screen, politely affecting disinterest in our conversation. "My name's Joyce Walker. I'm Paul Walker's mother."

Dusty took her arm and steered her gently away from the desk area.

"I know I should have called first, dear." Dusty waved her apology aside. "It's just that I've waited so long. As soon as I read your piece in the paper I booked a flight."

Dusty was immediately solicitous. She harboured tender feelings for elderly women, no doubt because of her close relationship with the grandmother who took over her mother's role. "You've come straight here from Cairns Airport? You must be ready for a nice cup of tea."

The coach trip from Cairns added an extra hour or more to travel time.

"Oh, they looked after us well on the plane, dear. Don't worry about me."

Dusty shepherded Mrs Walker up to her apartment. Upstairs, I made an excuse to go to my own apartment after a look from Dusty that was both an apology for the aborted catamaran trip and a request to cancel our booking. When I returned, both women were seated at the table on the balcony, each with a steaming cup of tea.

"You've got a lovely accent," said Joyce Walker, when Dusty introduced me.

"He's from the Emerald Isle, Mrs Walker. I'm doing my best to Aussify him."

"Oooh, don't you go doing that. He's just fine as he is." I took a liking to Walker's mother and sat down next to her. "Please call me Joyce."

"Okay, Joyce it is then. So you're Paul Walker's mother?"

I expected Joyce's face to darken with the burden of being the parent of a paedophile when she heard her son's name. I saw only sadness.

"Yes, dear, I am. I cannot tell you how it made me feel when I read your advertisement. I've waited so long for news of Paul. Then to find out that…to find out what happened to him. It was a dreadful shock. At first I didn't believe it. But the details you included in your advertisement about his art, his date of birth, and how long he'd been living here, that sort of thing… To think he'd been living here all those years and I didn't know."

"The police can do a DNA test to be absolutely certain." Dusty reached out and touched Joyce's hand in sympathy. "I'll put you in touch with the Queensland police later. They can give you more details." Dusty explained how she came to be investigating the murder, choosing her words carefully when she came to the part about Paul Walker's past.

"At the moment I'm investigating people, well, women actually…I mean…"

"It's all right, dear. I know what you mean." Joyce's eyes moistened. She rummaged in her handbag and drew out a letter. "I wanted to…" She stared down at the letter before continuing. "My son wrote this. It's an awful letter but… He wrote it years ago. I've waited so long. Now it's too late." Her hand tightened around the letter, crumpling the paper. "It's his confession, you see. He gives details about that night at the school camp. Not graphic details, you understand, but enough to make it absolutely clear what he did to those three girls and where the blame lies."

"It's not too late, Joyce. It can still be helpful to the girls: Abbie, Kimberley and Lena. To know he confessed will mean a lot to them."

"Yes, it might help the girls a little. I'm grateful for that. I'm just so sorry for Paul. It's too late for him."

She held the letter up as though it represented her son, her hand shaking slightly. "He never wanted to be the way he was, you know." Her eyes met Dusty's. "It was his uncle. I blame myself. You see, his uncle had train sets. Puff, that's what we called him when he was a little boy, loved trains so we let him stay with his uncle a lot. We never knew. My husband and I never knew what was going on. I know not all children who are abused become abusers themselves but for some it is a trigger. That's what happened to my son. Before that, he was a lovely boy."

Dusty and I exchanged glances. If either of us had been clinging to any last hope Ram had not been a paedophile, it had now been completely extinguished. Dusty waited patiently for Joyce to continue, understanding how difficult it must be for a mother to admit such an awful truth about her own flesh and blood.

"He wrote this letter as a sort of reparation." The look on Dusty's face revealed her unwillingness to accept that. Seeing this, Joyce shook her head.

"I don't mean he was trying to make amends to the girls. Despite his despicable inclinations he at least knew he could never undo the damage he'd done to those innocent girls or make up for it in any way."

Dusty arched her eyebrows. What did she mean by reparation then? Joyce continued.

"I mean reparation to his brother." I recalled from my research Paul Walker had one sibling: an older brother called Colin. "He was always jealous of his brother. There was only a year between them, you see. At first, it was just normal sibling rivalry. Later, we found out his uncle had done his best to inflame that jealousy."

Dusty frowned and considered this for a moment. "You mean the uncle was afraid he'd confide in his brother and so did what he could to drive a wedge between the boys?"

Joyce Walker sighed and nodded. "Children are so vulnerable, aren't they? Especially vulnerable to manipulation by adults." She started to unfold the letter. "I've hung on to this letter all these years. I knew it would mean so much to Paul. If only he could have read it."

Joyce had apparently mixed up the names of her sons. My mother used to do that sometimes with my sisters. Dusty's face was a cloud of confusion. "Paul? Didn't Paul write the letter?"

The rustling of paper ceased. Joyce jerked her head up and stared at Dusty.

"Paul? Oh no, dear. Not Paul. Colin wrote this letter; his brother." She passed it across the table to Dusty. "I hoped Paul could use it in some way to clear his name. I know he was acquitted but most people still believed he was guilty. He lost his job, his reputation and it all happened not long after his wife died while he was still grieving. It was so unfair; utterly cruel."

Dusty laid the letter flat on the table and positioned it so that I could also see it.

"Colin was a teacher too, you know." Joyce's eyes were fixed on her tea cup. She shook her head slightly, perhaps to express regret for the circumstances that formed the character of her eldest son.

The letter was a confession written by Colin Walker, evidenced by his address at the top and his signature at the bottom which had been witnessed by a third party. He confessed to the sexual abuse of Kimberley Grey, Abbie Kowalski and Lena Patterson.

Paul's brother detailed how he sneaked into the school camp that evening. He stated that he'd deliberately impersonated his brother. He was angry at Paul for not being able to see what the uncle was doing to him when they were kids just as he was angry at his parents for not protecting him. As an adult, he realised his enmity was irrational. Sadly, by then, hatred had already infected him. He confessed to being pleased his brother had been accused and disgraced. Later he regretted it but didn't have the courage to come forward.

"He wrote it not long before he died." Joyce spoke softly. "He'd been arrested and charged with sexual abuse of a minor but took his own life before he could stand trial. He even had the letter witnessed by a Justice of the Peace, to make sure it was taken seriously. Of course, the witness had no idea he planned to commit suicide."

Dusty and I were both too emotional to speak. Joyce on the other hand needed to talk.

"Paul was never like that; like his brother – could never be. He was a sweet boy. Luckily his uncle never touched him. If he had, I think Paul would have reacted very differently to Colin. I think he would have retreated, shut himself away from everyone."

"Just like he did when his brother betrayed him?" Dusty refilled Joyce's cup from the pot on the table.

Joyce nodded. "He just disappeared. Broke off all ties, even with us. It hurt his father and me deeply, even though we knew he would have done that for our sake more than his own. He knew being the parents of a son who was thought to be a paedophile would make us targets of people's hatred. He wanted to spare us that as much as possible by disappearing. That's the way Paul was." She lowered her eyelids. "We would rather have had him in our lives. Besides, we never for a moment believed any of the accusations against Paul." Joyce smiled through her tears, dabbing her eyes dry with a tissue. "If the girls had been able to see his face that night, they might have realised it wasn't Paul."

"So the brothers didn't look alike?"

"You could pick a family resemblance but their features were not identical. The main difference was their eyes. Paul had a condition called heterochromia which means his eyes were not the same colour. He had one blue eye and one brown eye. Colin's eyes were both blue." Joyce sighed.

It hadn't been clear from the photo I'd found of Paul Walker that he had different coloured eyes.

"Did Paul know his brother had set him up?"

"Not at first, but he worked it out. He didn't tell us but he did write to Colin, asking him to come forward. We found the letter among Colin's things. In the letter he said he knew it was Colin when he heard the girls in court saying they recognised his voice. Colin and Paul sounded identical when they spoke, and when they laughed. The girls didn't know Colin. They probably didn't even know their teacher had a brother so naturally they believed it was Paul's voice." Joyce stared at the steam swirling from the hot tea in her cup. "In one way, I'm surprised Colin kept Paul's letter. In another way, I think he knew deep down that one day he would come forward and clear his brother's name. Maybe he even hoped someone would find the letter and thus force him to confess."

Joyce sank back into her chair. She looked like she'd completed an emotional marathon.

"Joyce. May I take a copy of this letter? I'd like to include it, parts of it, in the book I'm writing about my investigation into your son's death."

"Oh yes, dear. I'd like that. I want people to know the truth about Paul. He was an artist, you know. An accomplished artist. He would have been happy spending his life painting but it takes a long time for an artist to get established. In the meantime there's no money coming in. So he became a teacher. He liked the idea of having regular holidays when he could devote himself to painting."

"Sean and I saw some of Paul's paintings at Sunyarta Sanctuary where he'd been living. I have pictures of them on my phone but I think it would be much nicer for you to view them for the first time in real life. We'll take you there after lunch."

A short time later, after establishing that Joyce had plenty of time before her flight back to Melbourne which wasn't until the evening, Dusty insisted on taking her to lunch at Rocky's Cafe.

CHAPTER 38

W HEN WE ARRIVED, Rocky was sitting out the front of the cafe strumming his guitar. Dusty seemed absorbed in the melody he was playing. Finishing the tune with a final accented note. Rocky smiled at us, his guitar still resting against his chest, fingers dangling over the strings.

"Does this mean business is quiet?" said Dusty.

"It's the calm before the storm. Another ten or fifteen minutes and the place'll be jumping."

"This is Joyce." Dusty gestured to Ram's mother but didn't elaborate on the introduction. "She's just here for the day. I couldn't let her leave Port Douglas without experiencing the one and only Rocky's cafe."

Rocky beamed proudly.

"This cafe has the most interesting wallpaper I've seen," I said.

Her curiosity piqued, Joyce wandered into the cafe.

"How's your investigation going?" Rocky rested his guitar in an upright position on the ground next to his chair.

"Very well indeed." Dusty beamed. "I think I'm on the edge of a breakthrough."

"Good." Rocky nodded approvingly. "I heard the monk who was murdered was a pedo."

I looked around quickly, relieved to see Joyce was now down at the other end of the cafe well out of earshot and absorbed in the messages on the wall.

Dusty was cautious in her response. "He had been charged with sexual offences but he was acquitted."

I knew Dusty was exercising considerable self control to refrain from defending Ram. Although she might have been disappointed the bush telegraph had inevitably spread this news, she would not attempt to correct the misinformation just yet. It could give her an advantage and might be a useful surprise to spring on a suspect.

"It's a shame." Rocky glanced up in the direction of Sunyarta. "People will think the other monks are the same and turn against them. That's not fair; they're good people. They've done so much for Port. The hill for a start; no trees up there at all until they started the monastery. It was just a barren bump on the horizon. Look at it now; it's so green."

Dusty nodded. "Yep, what they've done up there is impressive."

Rocky picked up his guitar and ushered us into the cafe where I joined Joyce at the wall.

"Interesting reading?"

Rocky had told me on a previous occasion that he'd asked local people to write a word or short phrase about Port or their lives, or just anything at all, on slips of paper. The result was a collection of intriguing random messages that he'd pasted on the wall: *Crossin' Macrossan. Pitchfork Betty. Grandma died today. Cane cutters can!*

"Yes." Joyce answered my question with a smile. "Although, to tell you the truth I haven't taken it all in. My mind has been else-where."

"Perfectly understandable." As I turned to guide her to the table Rocky had selected for us, one of the notes on the wall caught my eye. I hadn't noticed it before. Now it stood out like a neon light. *Ellen.* It was written in the same distinctive script I had seen on the footpath.

I asked Rocky about it. "Yeah, sometimes Ellen is written in sev-eral places around town. Not sure what that's all about. Bit of a mystery."

Lunch was another excellent meal; local reef fish accompanied by fresh salads to which yellow hibiscus petals and basil had been added. All served by the smiling, obliging Nathan.

Apart from a couple of locals who recognised Dusty and offered us friendly waves, most of the clientele were tourists. Snippets of animated conversation about experiences diving off the Great Barrier

Reef and touring the rainforests filtered through to my ears. The tourists were waxing lyrical about 'crystal clear creeks, breathtaking scenery, gorgeous butterflies and beautiful birds'. I must have missed all the beauty while I was focusing on avoiding dangerous flora and fauna.

While we were waiting for our coffees at the end of the meal, Dusty excused herself to make a call.

"I've just spoken to Detective Sergeant Jake Feilberg," she told Joyce when she returned. "He's arranged for a driver to take you to Cairns when you're ready. He'll meet you there and answer any questions you have about your son's death and take a sample from you for DNA comparison. But before that, we'll drive you up to the Sanctuary."

On the drive to Sunyarta, Joyce revealed that allegations made against Colin Walker had been hushed up by various schools where he'd worked for fear the truth would harm the school's reputation.

"What?" Dusty and I were both horrified. Was I being naive in assuming schools would put the welfare of their students as their number one priority?

"I know," said Joyce. "It's hard to believe, isn't it? He was my son but I would never have wanted his crimes covered up. I knew nothing about any of this. I only started to put the pieces together after Colin died."

At Sunyarta, we introduced Joyce to Saya. He accepted the news that Ram had not been an abuser after all with a dismissive wave of the hand indicating he had known all along. He invited Joyce to view her son's paintings, ushering us into the office but discreetly remaining just outside the door.

Dusty pointed to the picture with the coffin. "I thought this one symbolised his confession. Obviously I was wrong."

Overcome with emotion, Joyce stared at the painting in silence. She remained quiet and still for so long that Dusty and I made to tactfully leave the room. We were at the door when Joyce turned, her eyes glistening, and called us back.

"It's the Egyptian story of the god Osiris." She dabbed at her eyes with a tissue. "Ancient history is one of my areas of interest." Joyce turned back to the painting. "This is the ancient tamarisk tree. In its trunk is the coffin of Osiris. He was murdered by his younger brother Seth who was jealous of Osiris's popularity. Seth tricked Osiris into lying in the coffin then slammed the lid shut, locked it and threw it into the River Nile. The coffin was carried down the river and eventually became lodged in a great tamarisk tree which grew around it. Osiris died inside the coffin. He was eventually rescued and brought back to life but was never the same again and could no longer live his former life."

"So the painting represents Colin's betrayal of Paul. Colin being Seth and Paul being Osiris."

Joyce nodded. "That's what I think. One aspect of Osiris is worshipped as the Ram God."

"Serious? So that's why he chose Ram as his monk name."

Joyce smiled at the painting, the affectionate smile of a mother looking at the achievement of a much loved son. "Not that he would have seen himself as a god. He was too humble for that." She paused to study the painting further. "I think it represents his pain. Being an abuser was so against the person he was; he couldn't bear the thought of people believing that of him. He wanted to somehow tell the world who he really was."

Joyce raised a hand to the painting and caressed it gently. "He wrote to us you know, after he left; a handwritten note. He understood that seeing his handwriting would be more personal than an email, especially as it would be the last communication he would send." Joyce's voice trembled. She paused briefly to recover her composure. "He wanted us to know he was okay, that he loved us but that it would be better for everyone if he went away."

"Did the postmark give any indication of where he was when he sent the letter?" The detective in Dusty was never far from the surface.

"He posted it from the airport." Joyce's tone might have reflected the sad finality she must have felt when she received that last letter from her beloved son. "We had no idea where he went."

After that, we left Joyce to wait in the car while she spoke privately with Saya.

"I wonder why Saya didn't mention the different coloured eyes when we asked him to describe Ram." Dusty paused before almost immediately answering her own question. "I suppose Ram's eyes just became commonplace after a while so they didn't stand out in his memory."

When Joyce joined us around thirty minutes later, I was struck by the change in her. She seemed at peace; it's the only way I can describe it.

Back in town, we waved goodbye to Joyce as the unmarked police car pulled away from the kerb on its way to take her to Cairns.

"You know what? I've got a better idea."

Sometimes Dusty does that. Her mind seems to be always active with several ideas even when she is doing other things. She'll suddenly comment on one of those ideas as if she'd been having a conversation with me.

"Better idea about what?"

"Kimberley. Instead of flying down to see her, I think I'll invite her to Port Douglas for an all expenses paid holiday. She should be able to get a few days off. I'll book her into Four Mile Resort. It'll make the invitation too tempting to pass up. Maybe I should add a little bit of intrigue – tell her there's someone up here who's been asking about her."

Noticing the look on my face, she said, "What? It's true in a way. Abbie would love to catch up with her old school friend."

The mischievous glint in her eye gave away her hidden agenda. No doubt Dusty planned to use that moment of surprise when the two friends were reunited to catch them off guard and possibly cause them to let something incriminating slip.

CHAPTER 39

IN THE FOLLOWING days, Dusty and I saw little of each other.

At one point Dusty popped in to see how I was going. To her triumphant satisfaction, I had discovered the testimonials on Louisa Penrose's website were false and in all likelihood the so-called journalist was not using her real name. Although I'd been able to find birth records on the Queensland Registry for a Louisa Penrose who would now be thirty-one, roughly the age of Dusty's stalker, I had been unable to confirm the existence of an Australian journalist by that name.

"Just as I thought," said Dusty when I told her. "She's borrowed someone else's name to hide her true identity. Now why would she need to do that?"

"She doesn't want the brilliant Dusty Kent to know who she is."

"Exactly. I'll ask Jake if he can find out anything about her."

On another occasion when Dusty came in to check on me, she experienced a light-bulb moment and became very excited.

"Arabella!" she yelled. "Arabella!" I had no idea what she meant. "I have a crazy idea. I need your magic skills to confirm it."

After that, I was kept busy with cyber research. I also needed to spend quite a bit of time on the phone to various people and organisations in Melbourne.

By Monday morning my research was finished. After listening to my report, Dusty picked up her shoulder bag and headed for the door. "Come on, Mr Maze Master, you deserve a nice big Italian lunch."

Once in the town centre, we parked the car in a side lane and walked along Macrossan Street toward Rocky's Cafe, enjoying the warm tropical air.

"I just need to check something with Carmen," said Dusty as we drew level with the quaint cottage belonging to Rocky's neighbour. "I have a feeling she's an early riser. She might have seen something on the morning of the murder."

Carmen, wearing a magenta turban and a dress of matching colour that hugged her body and fell to her ankles, stood in the doorway fare-welling a couple of guests. It wasn't until the elderly couple escaped Carmen's effusive hugs and turned around that I recognised the English octogenarians Dusty and I had seen at Four Mile Beach from time to time.

The woman looked up at me, beaming in recognition. "Hello, love."

"Aha. You have come." Carmen extended a bejewelled arm toward us. "You must meet my very good friends. They go quickly to catch the bus." She eased herself between the couple, wrapping her arms around their shoulders. "I am introducing you to my dear, dear friend, Sylvia and her most dashing husband, Eric."

The mysterious Sylvia and Eric! Remembering how we'd conjectured they might be pet dogs or caged birds made it hard for me to keep a straight face.

Eric nodded as if in agreement with Carmen's assessment of him as 'most dashing', straightening his body slightly.

Sylvia dazzled us with her smile. "Isn't Port Douglas beautiful? It's our favourite place in all of Australia. Our favourite place in the world, really." She turned to her husband. "Isn't it, ducks?"

"Yes." Despite the shortness of his reply, her husband's shining eyes and radiant expression confirmed his enthusiasm for Port Douglas.

"We can't stop," said Sylvia, with an apologetic glance at Dusty and me. "We mustn't be late for the shuttle."

As on the first occasion I'd seen them, I felt a desire to help them. "I can drive you if you like."

Sylvia looked up at me, beaming her appreciation. "We're only going along Macrossan Street. Our bags are already at the coach pick-up. Thank you anyway, ducks."

As I watched them make their way along the path, I felt a childish flush of pleasure at being elevated from 'love' to 'ducks'. On impulse, I strode forward and caught up with them.

"I'll walk with you."

Dusty called after me. "Meet you at Rocky's in five minutes."

Rocky's Cafe had become a regular drop-in place for us since we'd arrived in Port. Not only was the food excellent but so was the coffee and Rocky did his best to supply us with local knowledge and answer any questions we had about the area and its people. We'd also discovered Nathan was 'a walking plantopedia' – to use Rocky's words. Our smiling waiter would point at plants through the window of the cafe and effortlessly reel off the names of each one. He even knew their correct botanical names. Whenever Dusty saw a plant that interested her, she would snap a photo of it and later ask Nathan what it was called.

That's what she was doing when I joined her at the cafe after escorting Sylvia and Eric to the coach.

"*Cyrtostachys renda*," Nathan said, smiling triumphantly and pointing at the photo on Dusty's phone of one of the pink-trunked palms we'd first seen near Sunyarta and had since noticed in several places around Port Douglas.

When I sat down, Dusty grinned at me as if I'd passed some sort of secret test.

"Common name is lipstick palm." Nathan was proudly showing off his knowledge. "Lots of palms here: Alexandra palm, fan palm, African oil palm. And ferns: basket fern, tree fern, bird's nest fern…"

Fearing Nathan was about to name all the ferns he knew, possibly all the plants he knew, Dusty interrupted.

"You know a lot about plants, Nathan." He grinned and nodded. "You're observant, too."

"Observant, yes. I observe plants carefully. I look at the leaves and the flowers. Then I know what plant it is."

Dusty looked at Nathan thoughtfully, as though seeing him in a new light.

"The monastery has lots of plants, doesn't it?" she said.

Nathan nodded his head vigorously. "Heaps and heaps. Every day I go to the hill to see the plants."

"Every day? Is it just plants you notice?"

He inclined his head, as though not fully understanding what Dusty meant. "I like plants."

Dusty rephrased her question. "When you go to the monastery to observe the plants, do you see people you know there?"

Nathan giggled. "I know lots of people. They wave to me."

"Did you know Josh, the vet's son?"

Nathan's face clouded over.

"Did you ever see him when you went to the monastery?"

"One time. I saw Josh one time. I waved to him but he didn't see me."

"What was Josh doing the day you saw him?"

Nathan shrugged. "Just sitting." He put his head to one side in an effort to remember more. "Looking at a book."

"Maybe he'd found a secret place in the gardens where he could read without being interrupted."

Gratified Dusty understood, Nathan's eyes shone with pleasure. A customer at another table called him and he hurried away to fulfil his duties. Dusty turned to me.

"That was nice, what you did. Walking with Carmen's friends to the bus stop."

So I had unwittingly passed a test and been awarded brownie points. I was pleased if a trifle embarrassed.

"They're from Berkshire in England. Migrated to Australia almost fifty years ago. A really nice couple. But quite different from their friend Carmen."

"Yep. And I bet they don't know Carmen is a secret marijuana smoker."

"A secret marijuana smoker?" Dusty quickly put a warning finger to her lips. In my surprise I'd raised my voice.

"When I popped in to see Carmen, I detected a distinctive aroma wafting through her house." Dusty raised her eyebrows knowingly.

"Right. Maybe she takes it for medicinal purposes. Was she able to give you any information about the morning of the murder?"

Dusty tapped her nose and grinned mischievously. "A very important piece of information; which I'll tell you about later. Carmen has also agreed to host a little get-together, or fiesta as she calls it, on Wednesday afternoon in honour of Ram."

Before I could explore that revelation further, Rocky emerged from the kitchen and joined us at our table.

"Great to see you both again. How's the case going?"

"We're getting close to wrapping it up." Dusty couldn't keep the excitement out of her voice.

Rocky nodded. "Jake mentioned that when I spoke to him this morning."

Dusty's brow furrowed. "He did?" She seemed disconcerted. "What did he tell you?"

Mindful of the people sitting at nearby tables, Dusty had lowered her voice and indicated, with a warning look, that Rocky should do the same.

Rocky obliged, speaking in almost a whisper. "He said the police were swooping on properties, including Moose Mulligan's, in search of a shoe."

"Did he also tell you the police found a partial shoe print at the scene of Ram's murder and made a copy of it?"

Dusty turned to me. "Did you know a shoe print can be just as distinctive as a fingerprint? Police can make a mould of a shoe print found at the scene of a murder and match it to the shoe worn by the killer."

"Didn't they search for the shoe at Mulligan's house during the original investigation?" I also kept my voice low.

"Being the sort of bloke who knows a lot about police forensics from his experience with the law and from watching crime shows on TV, Moose is smart enough to know he should dispose of all the clothing he wore during a murder including his shoes. But he's also the sort of guy who's tight with his money. Rather than destroying the clothes he would be more inclined to hide it all somewhere until the heat died down." Dusty was in a state of heightened excitement as she usually was when she was closing in on the murderer. "This is a Cinderella search with a twist; when we find the shoe to match the print, we've found the murderer."

Dusty closed her fist and brought her right elbow down in a gesture of victory. Then a serious look crossed her face. "I know you guys go way back as friends, Rocky, but Jake shouldn't really have told you about the searches."

Rocky's tiger's eye bracelet slid along his wrist as he raised his hand, palm up, to show he understood Dusty's concern. "Don't be mad at Jake for telling me," he said with a smile that must have charmed many women. "If it makes you feel any better, he swore me to secrecy."

Dusty seemed appeased, whether because of Rocky's smile or his explanation, I wasn't sure.

CHAPTER 40

O N THE DAY of the fiesta, while Dusty and Carmen were greeting and mingling, I was at a desk at the front of the room setting things up on the computer. We were in what Carmen called her rooftop lounge which had floor to ceiling glass doors leading out to a wide balcony overlooking Macrossan Street. Being a mild day, the doors were open. Abbie and David had already wandered out onto the balcony with their drinks. The balcony was where the 'pretty birds' visited Carmen daily. Rumba and Samba were not pets or caged birds but two wild sunbirds, stunning in appearance with bright yellow feathers on their bellies and a band of iridescent blue on their throats.

Carmen's wide screen television on the wall to my left was to be the centre piece of the event. When the get-together, began I would start a slide show with images of Ram on the TV screen, the first one being the age progression photo. During the evening, other images of Paul Walker, sent to us by his mother, would scroll across the screen. Dusty wanted the people attending to go away with a full and true picture of who Ram really was.

"He's been misrepresented and maligned for far too long," she had said. "It's time to set the record straight."

I was sure the book she would later write to document this case would also go a long way towards doing that. The injustice which had been done to Paul Walker had incensed Dusty. She would do anything she possibly could to ensure the world knew he had never been an abuser of young girls. I wondered how the women who had accused him would react when they found out.

As far as Carmen and the guests were concerned, the fiesta was being held to thank those who had been helpful to Dusty during her investigation. Dusty and I were the only people who knew about her hidden agenda to honour Ram, not only with a visual display but also by revealing who murdered him.

Beth and Nathan had been invited as guests but also as paid catering staff. They were at the back of the room setting up a table of finger food which they would bring around on trays during the afternoon. A smiling Nathan appeared eager to start serving. Her fashion sense on display, Beth looked stunning in a simple grey cocktail dress. From time to time, she cast surreptitious glances at Rocky who was deep in conversation with Kellie near the drinks area. A long table adorned with an embroidered red tablecloth had been placed near the door and laid out with glasses, bottles of chilled wine and a jug of iced water for guests to serve themselves.

The striking differences between Moose and Carmen, who were chatting together, made the pair look almost comical. Moose with his prominent tattoos and black T-shirt, shorts and well-worn thongs contrasted starkly with the diminutive Carmen in her magnificent gold turban, elaborate white and gold dress with puffed sleeves and multiple strings of chunky faux pearls.

"Where do you think she gets her pot from?" Dusty had said when I commented that they seemed unlikely companions. I was still having trouble seeing Carmen as a marijuana smoker. On the other hand, given that she believed herself to be the real Carmen Miranda, I probably shouldn't be surprised by anything she did.

A movement caught my eye. I looked up to see Saya and Jag, both resplendent in their yellow robes, hesitating in the open doorway. Dusty hurried over to welcome them.

Saya had been reluctant at first to accept Dusty's invitation. However, she had been persuasive, suggesting his presence at the get-together would be an important first step in repairing the reputation of Sunyarta. Since the murder, gossip and misinformation had caused many in Port Douglas to become suspicious of the monks and the Sanctuary.

After settling the monks in two of Carmen's plush red armchairs,

Dusty clapped her hands for attention.

"Not everyone is here yet. But I think we'll make a start."

Dusty glanced over at Carmen. A wide grin spread across the older woman's face. Flinging her arms high in the air as though playing a pair of castanets, she twirled her way to the front of the room. Rocky, who had agreed to provide the music for her, picked up his guitar which had been resting against the back wall. He made his way to the front, sat on a chair a short distance behind Carmen and began strumming a lively Latin American tune. Rocky seemed to be able to turn his hand at any type of music. Carmen treated us to a dazzling samba routine. She danced with the vibrant energy of a twenty-year-old, hands flowing, body swaying and occasionally lifting the bottom of her flamenco style skirt. All the while, she smiled broadly and rolled her eyes in the way of the real Carmen Miranda.

The performance brought Abbie and David in from the balcony to join those in the room who were gaping in admiration as Carmen moved with energetic grace through her dance routine on the section of the floor she had claimed as her stage. Saya and Jag looked on in mild appreciation.

At the end of the dance, which lasted less than two minutes, everyone in the room applauded enthusiastically. Moose placed his fingers in his mouth to produce a loud whistle.

"You've still got what it takes, mate," he called.

Carmen, grinning and barely out of breath, bowed and directed the audience's attention to her guitarist.

As our performers left the stage, Dusty stepped up to start the proceedings. With the vivid colour and dynamic animation of the performance suddenly over, she looked at first a lonely figure in her icy blue short-sleeved dress. She was wearing the turquoise flecked opal pendant I'd seen her admiring one day in the window of a jewellery shop. I wondered if Jake had bought it for her. As Dusty stood silently waiting for her audience to settle, I couldn't help comparing her wild, fiery beauty to Ingrid's fresh and glowing style of loveliness.

I had no time to ponder further. At that moment Dusty signalled for me to start the slide show with a slight inclination of her head. I began with the aged photograph of Ram which would stay on the screen for a prolonged period of time.

Dusty had only just finished introducing everyone when another guest arrived; an attractive blonde in a sleeveless black dress which accentuated her smooth white skin. Long hair parted in the middle bounced forward onto her shoulders. She looked around tentatively. Although several years older now, I recognised our latest guest from her photo. I'd almost forgotten Dusty had arranged a private car to bring Kimberley from Cairns airport direct to Carmen's house.

The room fell silent. Heads turned toward the new arrival. Carmen made to go and greet her but Dusty stopped her. I knew Dusty wanted to observe what effect the entrance of her surprise guest would have.

For a split second I viewed those in the room as though they formed a tableau. Moose squinted. Kellie frowned. Saya looked thoughtful. Nathan and Beth smiled. Abbie had her head to one side, an expression of curiosity on her face. David stared as much in appreciation for the woman he was looking at as in surprise. Rocky's expression was difficult to fathom: a mixture of puzzlement and wariness.

Abbie's curiosity turned to astonishment. She gasped.

"Kim?"

Kimberley smiled at her school friend, rushing to embrace her with a cry of "Abbs!"

The tableau was broken. Murmured conversations began.

Dusty gave the two friends a few moments to greet each other before clapping her hands once again for attention. She introduced Kimberley to the others in the room before resuming her speech.

"One of the reasons I invited you all here today was to thank you for making Sean and me welcome during our stay in Port Douglas. Some of you have come forth with information to help with our investigation. Some of you have even tolerated being my suspects." She turned and gestured to the image of Ram on the screen behind her. "I came here to find the person who murdered this man."

CHAPTER 41

DUSTY PAUSED AND looked around the room before continuing.
"The police's first suspect was Mr Moose Mulligan." A grunt
of disgust from Moose. "He believed Ram was the person who told
the police about his secret plantation of pot. A snitch."

"The scum was even worse than that, wasn't he?" Moose pointed
at the image of Ram on the television screen, a look of smug satisfaction on his face that his low opinion of Ram had been vindicated.

"Yeah," agreed David. "Wouldn't put anything past that twisted
termite."

I was glad Joyce Walker wasn't present. She had returned to Melbourne and would be updated on the progress of the case by Dusty
later. Joyce and her husband planned a longer visit to Port at a later
date to attend a special memorial for Ram.

"At first," said Dusty, holding up her hand for silence, "I didn't
know about Ram's background. I looked around for someone who
might have had a motive to kill this man who appeared to be no more
than a gentle monk living a quiet life. I wondered if it could have been
one of the other monks at the monastery. What if one of them was
mentally deranged?" I saw Jag give Saya a sidelong glance. Saya did
not seem to notice; his eyes were fixed on the image of Ram. "In fact,
the possibility of one of the monks being a murderer was first raised by
Joshua Edwards's mother."

Kellie looked at Dusty in anticipation of her theory being confirmed. However, her expression changed to surprise at Dusty's next
words.

"Josh wasn't killed by the same person who murdered Ram."

Before Kellie could react, the door opened. In walked Jake. I wasn't surprised to see him, but I was startled to see the woman by his side.

Dusty paused. Astonishment scrolled across her face followed quickly by consternation. Was her reaction a result of Louisa Penrose's reappearance or was it because she wondered if Jake and Louisa had come as a couple? The sheepish look on Jake's face suggested he might have something to confess. I hoped he would not be so cruel as to take up with a new woman and, without telling Dusty, bring her along here. On the other hand, Louisa Penrose might not be a new woman, but the woman behind the scenes that Dusty did not know about.

Dusty recovered her poise quickly. "Before I continue, allow me to introduce Detective Sergeant Jake Feilberg."

Jake, who was carrying what looked like an evidence bag, gave the room a friendly wave before turning to Louisa. "This is Louisa Penrose."

To Dusty he added, "I believe you know Louisa?"

Dusty nodded curtly before turning to me with raised eyebrows. I was just as perplexed as she. It seemed Louisa Penrose hadn't been using a false name, after all. But was she really a journalist? Did Jake know she'd been following Dusty around? What was her relationship with Jake?

Nathan hurried over and escorted the new arrivals to the drinks table. He took the bag from Jake and, in response to a gesture from Dusty, carried it to the front of the room and placed it on the table next to me. Jake cast a glance back at Dusty and mouthed a message which I think was 'Talk later'.

"As I was saying," said Dusty, "Josh was not killed by the person who murdered Ram." She looked over at Carmen who was curled up on a two-seater sofa near where Saya and Jag were sitting. "Our kind hostess is a good friend of Kellie's and was close to her son, Josh." Carmen's teeth flashed in a broad smile. "Carmen, you took something to Josh while he was staying at Sunyarta, didn't you?"

All eyes in the room were trained on Carmen. The suggestion that she might be somehow involved in Josh's death had taken everyone unawares, including me. Dusty had said nothing to me about Carmen being involved in Josh's death. I couldn't believe this charismatic eccentric would do anything malicious.

"Me?" Carmen sat up, looking genuinely confused.

"You did take something up to the monastery for Josh not long before he died, didn't you?"

"No. I take nothing." Carmen's answer was emphatic.

"Did Josh ever give you a package for safekeeping?"

Carmen started to shake her head then stopped abruptly, realisation in her eyes.

"Sí. Sí. Sí! I remember. So sorry. I forget before."

I was sure Carmen was sincere. She was nearly ninety and smoked marijuana; both those things can affect memory.

"Now I remember," she said. "I keep the book for him then I take it to the Sunyarta."

"A book?" Dusty seemed mystified.

"Sí. It is a red book."

"Did he tell you why he wanted you to keep the book?"

"He say his mother not like this book. She might find it in his room. He want to keep it to read again one day."

Kellie frowned. "Josh was an adult. I had no say over what books he read."

Dusty ignored her. "What was the title of the book, Carmen?"

Carmen's brow furrowed. "I do not remember. I think it is not a nice story. Josh, he say the book has much violence. Me, I think it is just a book. I do not think it is wrong for him to read it."

Dusty nodded. "Actually, the title's not important. It's the format I'm interested in. Was it a hardcover edition, Carmen?"

"Hardcover?"

"Was the cover of the book soft like thick paper, or hard like cardboard?"

"Sí. The cover it is hard. It is a strong book. He give me the book. He put it on the high shelf in the cupboard in the hall. He ask me if it will be safe there. I tell him yes it is a safe place. He is happy. Keep my book safe for me, Carmen, he say to me. So I keep his book safe."

Kellie, who seemed to realise the significance of Dusty's question, buried her head in her hands.

"When did he give you the book, Carmen?"

"Long time ago." She paused in an effort to remember. "Maybe two years."

Dusty nodded as if this fitted in with what she had been thinking. "About the time he came off the drugs."

Kellie shook her head in disbelief.

Dusty continued. "Then one day he sent you a message asking you to take it to the monastery?"

"Sí, sí. What can I do? I take the book to the Sunyarta and put it where he say."

"Where?"

"In the rocks; some big rocks. He tell me it is not nice for the monks to see the book. They do not like violence. So I must hide it and he will take it from the rocks."

Dusty looked around the room. "It wouldn't be difficult to conceal a stash of heroin in the hardcover spine of a book. Josh must have hidden it there and left it with Carmen as an emergency supply; in case he found it too difficult to stay clean. Then one day while he was at the monastery, he felt he needed it and sent a message to Carmen."

As the realisation of what she had unwittingly done sank in, an expression of chagrin clouded Carmen's face. "He lie to me. I believe him. I am sorry."

Kellie turned to Carmen and screamed at her. "Why did you do it? Why? You killed him!"

A series of expressions patterned Carmen's face: bewilderment, shock, shame, remorse. She seemed to crumple in on herself, like a balloon deflating.

Rocky, who had been talking to Jake and Louisa, quickly crossed the room to stand by Carmen.

"Don't blame Carmen. She didn't know."

Dusty's nostrils flared, an angry flush rose in her cheeks. She marched across the room and stood in front of Kellie, glaring at her. "Don't dump your guilt on Carmen!" She spoke through gritted teeth.

"The only person responsible for Josh's death was Josh."

"No!" Kellie turned her fury on Dusty, lunging at her with clenched fists.

Dusty's karate training was instinctive, her reaction fast. Her open hands flashed out to block Kellie, then she bent her elbows to protect her face and immobilised Kellie by somehow locking the other woman's right arm around her body. Dusty was positioned to flip Kellie onto the floor but the fight went out of Josh's mother as quickly as it had flared up.

Dusty had reacted so quickly Jake had taken just a few steps toward them and I was only half out of my seat before it was over.

"It's all right, guys," said Dusty, still holding Kellie in position. "We're all good here."

Kellie's body slumped. Dusty lowered her onto a nearby sofa. Beth hurried over with a shot of brandy in a crystal tumbler, urging Kellie to swallow it.

"My beautiful boy. It's all wrong." Kellie gulped the brandy and handed the empty glass back to Beth.

I couldn't help wondering about Kellie's outburst. Was it triggered by grief that her son had caused his own death or remorse that her accusation against the monks had been unfounded? Or was it something else?

CHAPTER 42

BETH SAT DOWN next to Kellie, receiving a nod of thanks from Dusty as she straightened up and made her way back to the front of the room.

"Both Kellie and Moose had a motive to kill Ram. They both admit to being on the hill around the time he was murdered. Each of them had the physical capability to bash him over the head with a rock and push him over the edge of the cliff."

Kellie was too emotionally spent to protest. Moose let his feelings be known with a vulgar expletive. Dusty's stern look reprimanded him.

"Moose told me he'd briefly glimpsed the shadow of someone else on the hill that morning between four-thirty and five. That person wasn't Kellie because she was there later – around five-thirty. I deduced that it must have been the murderer Moose had glimpsed. Kellie had an uneasy feeling, perhaps a sense of evil, when she was there. I think Ram was already dead by this time. That was what Kellie was sensing: the recent violent death of a fellow human being.

"If I took those two people at their word, a third person had been there at the same time as Moose. This unknown person had killed Ram before Kellie arrived. Since no-one else in the town had a motive to kill Ram, I needed to seriously consider the possibility he was murdered by one of his fellow monks." Dusty glanced apologetically at Saya. "Then my investigation took a dramatic turn."

I hit the appropriate button to move the slide forward to reveal a younger picture of Paul Walker.

"I discovered Ram's real name was Paul Walker." Dusty gestured at the screen. "I learned he was a teacher who had been accused of abusing three young girls in his classroom. Now the possibility of other suspects opened up. When I found out one of those abuse victims, Abbie Kowalski, was living in this area, alarm bells rang. It was too much of a coincidence. I had to investigate the possibility she knew Walker was living in Port Douglas and had exacted her revenge on him. When I sensed Abbie had lied to me about being in Port the morning of the murder, she went to the top of the list of suspects."

"So she lied. Big deal!" David folded his arms across his chest and grimaced defiantly. "She wasn't there when the so-called monk was murdered. That's all that matters."

Dusty didn't seem to notice the interruption. "When I interviewed Abbie, I sensed she was holding something back. I was determined to find out what it was. I listened to the recording of the interview several times and noticed Abbie seemed ambivalent about her abuser. Sometimes she spoke of him almost with affection while at other times with the tone of abhorrence you would expect. Eventually, I worked it out. That's when I knew Abbie had no reason to murder Paul Walker."

Abbie jerked her head up quickly, a startled expression on her face, alarm in her eyes.

"No reason!" snapped Kimberley, her chin jutting out. "After what that man did to her, did to all of us."

"That low life deserved to be topped." Moose snarled.

"Damn right!" David placed a comforting arm around his sister's shoulders.

Dusty ignored the protests. "Abbie had no reason to kill Paul Walker because he did not assault her."

Abbie lowered her eyes and stared at the floor.

"Are you calling Abbie a liar?" demanded Kimberley.

"What are you talking about?" David glared at Dusty. "If you'd seen the state she was in during the court case…"

"I have no doubt Abbie's distress was genuine. She had suffered terribly as a young girl when she'd been abused. Like Kimberley and Lena, she had to relive that ordeal in a court of law in order to make her abuser accountable for his actions."

David frowned in confusion. Kimberley opened her mouth to speak. Dusty stopped her with a raised hand.

"I'm not suggesting Abbie hadn't been assaulted. However, Paul Walker was not her abuser."

Silence. Saya was nodding his head. David was looking at his sister. Abbie's eyes remained averted.

"Eventually I realised Abbie knew something which I found out only recently." Dusty turned to Abbie, addressing her in a tone that brooked no argument. "Abbie. The time has come for you to tell the truth."

Tears rolled down Abbie's cheeks. She looked apologetically at her brother and Kimberly in turn.

"Abbs?" David looked bewildered.

Abbie's voice was almost a whisper. "It wasn't Mr Walker."

Once again Dusty held up her hand for silence. Abbie took a few moments to compose herself before continuing.

"I didn't know until later. A few years after the court case." Her pleading eyes met Kimberly's. "It wasn't Mr Walker, Kim. It was his brother."

"His brother?" From the astonishment in Kimberly's voice it was clear she didn't know Paul Walker had a brother.

Dusty interrupted to recount her meeting with Joyce Walker before turning back to Abbie. "How did you find out about Ram's brother?"

"I met him one day at a school where I was working as an after care co-ordinator. I'd been sent there by an agency, because the regular co-ordinator was ill. I didn't see him at first cos I had my back to him when I heard him speaking to another staff member." Abbie shook her head and covered her ears.

"It was Mr Walker's voice. My heart started pumping. When I spun around to face him, he was looking straight at me. At first I thought it was Mr Walker. During the seconds I was staring at him, I realised it wasn't. He looked like Mr Walker but different somehow and his eyes were different. I was confused and just stood frozen to the spot. He was leering at me. The other staff had left the room by this time. It was just the two of us. He said: *You thought it was my brother that night, didn't you? Your precious teacher.* That horrible man stood there watching me as I struggled to realise what he meant. When he saw from my expression that I understood, he just gloated at me. I swear if I'd had a gun in my hand at that moment I would've killed him."

"It wasn't Mr Walker?" Kimberley was struggling to accept what her friend was saying.

"Bloody hell!" said David, horror etched in his expression.

It occurred to me that if David had killed Ram he must be in a storm of guilt right now.

David looked accusingly at his sister. "You didn't tell me!"

Abbie stared at the floor. "I'm sorry. I just felt so bad about accusing Mr Walker. I was so sure it was him that night. Then to find out I was wrong..." She shook her head helplessly. "After meeting Colin Walker, I was in a terrible state for a long time. I didn't know what to do. In the end I just sort of locked it all away in my mind."

"You didn't tell the truth to me," said Dusty, "because you felt guilty about not speaking out to clear Paul Walker's name."

Abbie nodded. "I should have told you. I just didn't want to go through it all again. I'd managed to come to terms with what had happened and get on with my life."

Dusty reassured her. "Don't beat yourself up too much, Abbie. Most of us in your position would have done the same."

Dusty turned her attention to David. "Although Abbie knew Paul Walker was not her abuser, her brother did not. He remained on my list of suspects. David was also in Port that morning, although he claims he didn't get there until after the time of the murder. Did David kill Ram in revenge for what had happened to his sister?"

"No!" An anguished protest from Abbie. She touched her brother's arm affectionately. "I was with him that morning."

Stony-faced, David stared silently at Dusty.

CHAPTER 43

Dusty continued. "Then yet another suspect emerged. I discovered one of the other sexual abuse victims had the opportunity to commit the murder. Kimberley Grey lived in Sydney but the day Ram was killed, she was not at work. She lied to me about that. So my suspicions deepened."

Kimberley shook her head. "I didn't lie. I completely forgot. It wasn't until after I spoke to you that I remembered. I didn't fly to Port Douglas and murder anybody on my day off. I had a really bad migraine. I get them a lot. I usually dose myself up to make sure I can still go to work. I hate taking time off. But this one hit me hard. The painkillers I took on Tuesday evening knocked me out and I overslept on Wednesday. When I did wake up, I was still groggy. I knew I wasn't going to get to work on time so I decided it would be better to take a sick day. That's all there was to it."

"Unfortunately, I only have your word for that."

Kimberley threw her arms in the air. "Oh! Come on!"

Somehow, her protest did not seem strong enough. What was preventing her from expressing a more forceful denial?

Unperturbed, Dusty continued. "In my quest for a selection of suspects, I also considered the other young girl who'd been abused, Lena Patterson. She was apparently living overseas and had been doing so since she was nineteen. But..." Dusty paused for dramatic effect. Kimberley and Abbie looked at each other then turned to Dusty expectantly. "I had a suspicion Lena had come back to Australia. Although my techie maze master hadn't been able to find any record of Lena returning to the country, I couldn't shake the feeling she was actually here in Port Douglas."

Abbie looked around as though searching for her school friend. Her eyes rested for a moment on Beth.

"I wondered if Lena had changed her name and her appearance. She could have done that for the perfectly understandable reason of leaving her past behind. When Abbie showed me a photo of Lena as a teenager, I was immediately reminded of someone but couldn't put my finger on who it was. Later, I imagined her as she might be now only with dark hair. Then I added a pair of gold hoop earrings." Louisa Penrose fingered one of her earrings and glanced nervously at Jake. "The image I conjured up reminded me of a woman who'd been following me around, whose name I subsequently discovered was Louisa Penrose. Surely, her initials being the same as Lena Patterson's couldn't be a coincidence. Had Lena returned to Australia under the name of Louisa Penrose? Had she found out Walker was living here in Port Douglas and decided to get her revenge for what he'd done to her?"

Louisa gaped at Dusty in astonished disbelief. Kimberley and Abbie were both staring at Louisa. Jake tried to get Dusty's attention with a wave of his hand. She appeared not to notice.

"I was attracted to this theory…"

"I'm not Lena Patterson," cried Louisa.

"Then one day in Macrossan Street I saw something that confirmed my theory…"

"Dus," called Jake, starting to walk towards Dusty. She stopped him with a look. Dusty's green eyes are very expressive. She often uses them to issue commands. In this instance they commanded Jake to be quiet and let her finish what she wanted to say.

Dusty continued, barely missing a beat. "Confirmed my theory Lena was in Port Douglas."

"You mean this lady really is Lena?" said Abbie.

Dusty shook her head. Jake relaxed and stepped back.

"Where is Lee?" Abbie looked over at Beth again.

"Let's ask someone who's close to her." Dusty looked across the room to where Jake, Rocky and Louisa were standing. "Rocky, you're close to Lena, aren't you?" Rocky's face drained of colour. "You wanted to avenge Lena, didn't you? You wanted Paul Walker to pay for what he'd done, what everyone thought he'd done."

Nathan was looking at Rocky with a puzzled expression on his face.

"It wasn't me," protested Rocky.

"It wasn't Rocky," agreed Nathan.

"I know," said Dusty. "I know it wasn't you, Rocky. I know it was Lena. You both knew Paul Walker well, didn't you? You recognised him the day you rescued him from Moose. Isn't that right?"

Rocky shook his head. His eyes seemed to be glistening.

"The other day," said Dusty, "you mentioned Jake had told you the police were going to search Moose's house looking for a shoe that would match the print of a shoe left at the murder scene."

"Holy crap!" Moose glared at Jake.

A hint of a smile played around Dusty's lips when she heard Moose's reaction but she quickly became serious again. "During that phone call Jake also revealed the police planned to search the premises of everyone the monk had contact with in the twenty four hours before he died, which included your place. Jake said he wanted to re-assure you he didn't consider you a suspect. He explained I had suggested the extra search warrants in the interests of being thorough for the readers of my book."

Rocky looked across at Jake who was staring steadfastly at Carmen's shiny floorboards.

The expression on Dusty's face as she continued was one of sadness. "That wasn't strictly true, Rocky. You see, the police didn't issue any search warrants at all. Jake got a warrant to place hidden cameras in a residence. In one residence only. Yours, Rocky." Dusty paused. I had the impression of a cat reluctant to pounce on a mouse it had grown to like. "Those cameras, which had already been installed before Jake called you, recorded what you did a short time after he told you the police were going to search your premises."

Rocky looked like a young boy who had cheated in an exam only to be caught out by the school principal.

"You took a particular pair of shoes from your wardrobe. Later that day, under the cover of darkness, you took that pair of shoes and put them in a plastic bag. You then drove to the golf course just out of town and threw them into one of the lakes on the course."

Dusty moved closer to where I was sitting.

"What you didn't know was that one of Jake's officers followed you that night." Dusty reached for the evidence bag Nathan had placed on my table and opened it. "And retrieved these shoes." Dusty took a grubby pair of men's sneakers from the evidence bag and held them up.

CHAPTER 44

ROCKY'S FACE COULD not hide the emotions seething under the surface. Dusty reached into the bag again and took out the mould police had made from a shoe print. She placed one of the shoes on the mould and moved closer to Rocky.

"It's a perfect fit, Rocky."

Rocky shook his head vigorously. "I didn't kill anyone."

"I know." Dusty's voice revealed her sorrow at what she needed to do. "But you must take responsibility for what you and Lena did."

"You mean Lena and Rocky murdered the monk?" said Kimberley. "What's going on? Where is Lena?"

Dusty held up her hand for silence. "When it occurred to me Rocky might have been involved in Ram's murder I went to see Carmen. I asked her to tell me anything she could remember about the morning of the murder. Carmen said that at around four-thirty she heard Rocky's bicycle – one of its wheels has a slight squeak when it first starts to turn. She thought someone might have stolen the bicycle. Later, when she was dressed for the day, she saw Rocky's bicycle in its usual place at the front of the cafe and concluded she must have been mistaken. I knew she was not. Using his bicycle, Rocky would have got up to the monastery quickly, quietly and without being seen then back in time to do the morning preparations and open the cafe at seven o'clock."

"All right, I was there," admitted Rocky. "I'm sorry I lied." By way of apology, he flashed his winning smile although I fancied it was not as natural as it usually was. "I just went for an early morning bike ride and ended up on the hill. That's all."

"You don't know how much I'd like to believe that, Rocky. But if your shoe print was next to Ram's meditation platform, it means you were right next to him. Of course, it is possible you went to speak with him. The problem is, shoe prints can also be taken from fabric. What if I told you forensic evidence proves this is the same shoe that was used to kick Ram in the groin."

Rocky's face blanched.

"So let me put it to you again. You recognised Paul Walker when you spoke with him the day he had the run-in with Moose, didn't you?"

Rocky lowered himself slowly into a chair.

Jake ran a hand through his hair, looking at his friend as though trying to unravel a complex puzzle. He spoke to Rocky in a tone that was firm but tinged with regret. "It's over, mate. Just tell us what happened."

Rocky buried his head in his hands then looked up and stared at the television screen as he spoke. "I recognised him straight away. Recognised his voice first. Then his eyes; one blue, one green. Who else has eyes like that? I said to him. 'You're Paul Walker, aren't you?'"

"What did he say?" asked Dusty.

"*I was once.* That's what he said." Rocky bit his lower lip. "He was so calm. That made me angry. How could he sit there and calmly admit to being the monster who abused his students? I asked him if he remembered Lena Patterson. He just hung his head. So I said: 'Do you remember what you did to her?'"

Kimberley gasped.

"What did he say?" asked Abbie, leaning forward in anticipation.

"He just said: *I am Ram.* But the look on his face was pure guilt. Then he got up and left. I was flabbergasted. He didn't even try to apologise. I was so angry I was shaking. How could he be so arrogant? What a bloody hypocrite; living up there in the monastery like some holier-than-thou pillar of the community."

Dusty went over to Rocky and put a comforting hand on his arm. "I understand your anger, Rocky. I'm very, very sorry about what happened to Lena. No one could blame her for wanting her abuser dead. I don't think Lena ever planned to harm Walker. She'd buried the trauma of what happened to her and got on with her life until a chance meeting with a monk. When she met Ram here in Port Douglas and heard her teacher's voice again, the trauma of the experience and deep sense of guilt at having let down her friends when she found she didn't have the courage to give evidence in court came rushing to the surface. She was gripped by a kind of madness which triggered her decision to kill."

"Where is Lena?" Kimberley sounded frustrated.

"Has she already gone back to America?" said Abbie.

"I will tell you exactly where Lena is in just a moment. You see," continued Dusty, "before Lena went to the United States, she spent a short time living on the streets in Melbourne. She was close to a young man who died of a drug overdose and was buried in a pauper's grave. He was living under an assumed name because he didn't want his family to find him and discover what he'd become. No one knew who he was except Lena but he'd sworn her to secrecy. Even after he died, she kept his secret. Later, she took his name, his real name, probably as a way of honouring him."

"*She* took *his* name? How does that work?" Kimberley was not the only one in the room who was confused.

CHAPTER 45

"WHEN SHE HAD a sex change operation," said Dusty, "Lena became Angelo Rocco Tibaldi. Better known as Rocky."

"Bugger me dead!" Moose expressed his surprise in typical style.

Abbie and Kimberley were staring at Rocky open-mouthed. I knew they were looking for any traces of the girl they once knew. Just as I had done. But Rocky's masculinity was dominant and the manliness of his facial features disguised the resemblance to the girl he'd once been. It was a stroke of luck that Dusty had picked up on it.

Dusty glanced over at Beth who seemed to be in a state of shock. "Beth thought Rocky avoided Arabella when she came to Port Douglas because he couldn't handle 'gender stuff'. Actually, Rocky was afraid Arabella would somehow be able to tell that he too had undergone sex re-assignment."

"I didn't know it was his brother." Rocky looked up at Dusty, despair in his face, regret in his voice. "Why didn't he tell me it wasn't him?"

Dusty sighed. "Because he knew you wouldn't believe him. Since the court case, he'd gone through life with people not believing him until he finally relinquished his claim on the truth."

Jake, his face impassive in the way of trained police officers, led Rocky to the door where two constables were waiting to take him into custody. Standing in the doorway watching them leave, Jake's shoulders slumped. When Rocky had arrived in Port Douglas using his old school friend's name, Jake had had no reason to doubt him. Lena had known the real Rocky well enough to be able to minimise any differences when she took over his name and his persona after her operation. If Jake had noticed any difference between this Rocky and the real Rocky he would have put it down to the changes brought about by maturity.

When Jake turned and faced the room, I saw the strain in his face only momentarily; he was quick to pull himself together and return to where Louisa Penrose was standing.

Dusty first became suspicious of Rocky when he said he hadn't been in Port Douglas at the time Four Mile Resort was built.

"He corrected himself and explained that he meant he was only a child at the time and couldn't remember the event," Dusty told me. "His explanation was perfectly plausible but I filed it away. The other thing I noticed that day was his use of the word 'buddy'. I know men in Australia sometimes use that word but I associate it more with America. When we were looking for Lena, who'd gone to the United States, I wondered if Rocky had ever been there."

Those two seemingly insignificant things had opened Dusty's mind to the possibility that Rocky could be hiding something. When she saw him strumming his guitar outside the cafe the day we took Joyce there, a mental image of Lena playing her guitar as described by Abbie, flashed before her eyes. It was not the tune which had so absorbed her attention that day as I had supposed, but Rocky's features. She realised Lena's young face, when Abbie showed her the photo of the three girls, had reminded her of Rocky, not a film star as she had thought at the time. At first she thought he was somehow related to Lena; maybe a half brother or a cousin.

On her instructions, I had thoroughly researched Angelo Tibaldi. When I eventually worked out he had been living on the streets in Melbourne under an assumed name and died of a drug overdose, we knew Rocky was not who he said he was. During one of my many phone calls to Melbourne in search of the truth I learned Tibaldi had been close to a teenager called Lena.

That's when Dusty had yelled 'Arabella' and told me about her 'crazy idea' of Lena undergoing a sex change.

The pieces fell into place after that. It wasn't too difficult to track Lena Patterson using my 'highly developed' cyber spying skills although it had been risky hacking into some of the websites with confidential medical information. Lena had had 'transgender reassignment surgery' in Thailand before going to the United States as a man. I'd been right flummoxed when I discovered Lena and Rocky were one and the same.

In the silence that followed Rocky's departure, images of Ram's magnificent paintings rolled across the screen. Kimberley and Abbie watched the slides with tears in their eyes. The slide show stopped with the final painting, the one of the coffin in the tamarisk tree, remaining on the screen.

CHAPTER 46

D USTY WAS STANDING next to my table when Jake and Louisa, approached. Jake opened his mouth to speak. Dusty ignored him and looked directly at Louisa.

"Why were you stalking me?"

A soft pink blush tinted Louisa's cheeks.

"Dus," said Jake. "This is Senior Constable Penrose."

"You're a cop?" Dusty looked at Jake, her eyes demanding an explanation.

Jake cleared his throat and rubbed the back of his neck. "Don't blame Louisa, Dus. It was my idea. I wanted you to have some protection while you were on this case. I knew you wouldn't agree to it so I sort of did it without telling you." Seeing Dusty's nostrils flare, he rushed on defensively. "I was worried the killer might come after you."

"You weren't supposed to spot me," said Louisa with a rueful smile. "I'm afraid I stuffed it up. I wasn't good at being an undercover protection officer. I'm so sorry if I caused you any concern."

Dusty looked from one to the other, hands on hips, eyes blazing.

"Protection! Me?" Her scathing glance swept over Louisa from head to foot, dismissing her suitability as a bodyguard. Dusty's next words were fired straight at Jake. "How dare you! You condescending…"

Jake interrupted what might have been a thoroughly entertaining description by putting his hands up in surrender. "I know, I know. I'm an arrogant prick." An expression of chagrin clouded his face. "It wasn't like that though, Dus. I reckon I've been in the police too long; always seeing people at their worst, witnessing violence on a regular basis. After a while, you get into the habit of expecting people to be hurt or murdered. I didn't want anything to happen to you."

I saw Dusty relax and knew Jake had managed to extinguish her fire. She beckoned me to join them. As I stood up she said, "I've got all the protection I need. Why do you think I chose a six foot Irishman for my research assistant?"

Jake seized the opportunity to change the subject. "Louisa did manage to solve one mystery." Dusty gave him a quizzical look. "She begged for a chance to redeem herself. I suggested she might be able to track down Ram's missing thong."

Louisa smiled self-consciously. "I roped in my husband to help. We posed as a tourist couple." She glanced at Dusty. "This time I was wearing a blonde wig and I stayed well out of your way."

Dusty's icy stare challenged her to continue.

Louisa swallowed. "I found out there's been a shoe thief operating in Port Douglas for the past twelve months or so. People taking an early morning dip at Four Mile Beach sometimes returned from their swim to find one of the thongs they'd left on the beach had gone missing. So all I had to do was lie in wait in the early morning. It didn't take long to catch the thief in action."

"So you've arrested a thong thief?" quipped Dusty.

"Not exactly. I found the cache of stolen thongs, including Ram's. They were all piled up in a hollow log."

"A hollow log! What sort of thief are we talking about?"

"A forest kingfisher."

"A kookaburra?"

"Not exactly. The forest kingfisher is a more colourful bird than the laughing kookaburra. It has a blue head and turquoise feathers on its back."

"Turquoise?" A faint smile crossed Dusty's face. "I think I like this thong thief."

Moose interrupted us to give Dusty a vigorous slap on the back. "I had my money on you to prove the police were wrong about me." He shot a scornful look at Jake and turned to go, almost bumping into Saya as he did so.

Saya stepped back deferentially. Moose paused as though undecided whether to pass the monk without speaking or let loose a tirade
of abuse. Before he had a chance to do either, Saya disarmed him.

"You are a good man, Mr Mulligan," he said quietly.

Moose straightened and jerked his head up, temporarily taken
aback. He recovered quickly and growled at Saya. "Me? You got the
wrong bloke, mate. I'm no angel. I've done a lot of rubbish things;
been behind bars for some of them."

Saya inclined his head. "It does not matter. You are a good man."
It was a sight to see this bulky, tattooed, self-declared criminal begin
to melt before my eyes. His stance relaxed. He shifted from one foot
to the other and scratched his clean shaven scalp.

"I am sorry we are on your land," continued Saya.

Now Moose's bravado completely evaporated. He opened his
mouth to respond. The words seemed to stick in his throat. Finally, he
licked his lips and managed a gruff reply. "I reckon I'm gonna do all
right out of the land I've got. I heard on the bush telegraph that
Australia's about to legalise cannabis. Can't wait!" A sarcastic grin
spread across his face. "Got the perfect land to grow it on." As his
embarrassment ebbed away, Moose became more cordial. "It's all
good, mate," he said to Saya. "I might not like the way you people got
the land but I was wrong to blame you. I know that."

He cleared his throat, seemed to be about to say more but stopped
as though afraid he might say something to weaken his tough guy
image. Moose headed toward the door, turning briefly to announce to
no-one in particular, "They'll be paying me to grow pot. How good is
that!" He winked over at Carmen on the other side of the room.

As Moose departed, Nathan bustled over to tell us coffee was
being served on the balcony. Clearly upset about Rocky, he was
unsmiling and solemn-faced but determined to carry out his catering
duties efficiently.

Saya and Jag left soon after Moose, politely declining the offer of
coffee. They needed to get back to Sunyarta. As they were taking their
leave, Dusty told Saya how she feared for his safety after her sightings
of the black crow at the Sanctuary which she took to be a sign of

imminent death.

Saya looked surprised. "Crow? I have not heard this bird at Sunyarta."

"Really? It must be a quiet crow," said Dusty. "I saw it a few times; on the track leading up to Sunyarta and in the big tree near the gate."

"Ah, the big tree. The black bird that sits there visits us regularly. Its colour is like a crow but it is more beautiful, like blue-black. This bird is the spangled drongo."

"Drongo?" Dusty laughed. "I guess I'm the drongo then!" The monks smiled. They all seemed to be sharing a joke I was not privy to. I hate that!

CHAPTER 47

I T WAS NEARING evening when Dusty and I strolled along Macrossan Street down to the water. We sat for a moment's reflection under the ancient tree where we had interviewed Abbie.

Only a few of us had stayed for coffee on Carmen's balcony. David, Abbie and Kimberley decided they needed 'something stronger'. Before they left, Dusty assured them she would not use their real names in the book.

"I'm sure you'd rather get on with your lives without the whole world knowing who you are and where you live," she said.

"We'll raise a glass to you at the pub across the road," said David. "Before we get down to serious business. Abbs and I want to convince Kim to stay."

"You mean, *you* want to convince her," said Abbie, giving her brother a good natured jab in the ribs.

"Well, why not? Plenty of room at my place." David met Kimberley's eye and grinned.

Kimberley's blush and answering smile suggested she was giving the invitation some consideration.

Louisa had excused herself as her husband was waiting to drive her back to Cairns. Jake left soon after to conduct the formal interview of Rocky.

"Let's meet up later," he said to Dusty as he was leaving.

"Of course." I thought I detected a hint of coolness in Dusty's response.

Out on the balcony we saw no sign of Rumba and Samba but I did notice the grand bird bath Carmen had provided for them. In a shaded corner stood an elegant cane peacock chair and on its seat a glass float bowl such as might be used to display water lilies in the foyer of a luxury hotel.

We were a quiet group as we sipped our coffee. Even Carmen's exuberance had been dulled by the events of the afternoon. Her sorrow at discovering she had unwittingly played a role in Josh's death had been compounded by the shock of learning the neighbour she regarded with much affection was a murderer.

"I am sad for Rocky. He was a girl. It is true?" Carmen looked around for confirmation of this startling fact. We all assured her it was true. "That is strange for me to think about but it does not matter. It is murder that is wrong. To kill the monk, that is bad."

Later, her smile returned when Kellie offered her a heartfelt apology for accusing her of being responsible for Josh's death.

"I'm so, so sorry for what I said." Kellie reached out to Carmen, clasping her hand. "You have never been anything other than a good friend. You were not in any way responsible for what happened to Josh."

Kellie turned to Dusty. "I owe you an apology, too. I don't know what came over me, attacking you like that. I think I always feared Josh might have been responsible for his own death but I just couldn't face it."

Dusty graciously accepted Kellie's apology, assuring her no harm had been done.

"What will happen to Rocky's Cafe now?" I asked.

"The cafe, it is mine."

Carmen explained that the terms of the lease with Rocky were such that if he ever gave up the business whether by choice or circumstances the business and the premises would revert back to Carmen. She had wanted to maintain control of the premises and who occupied it. In exchange for agreeing to these conditions, Rocky had taken over the prime position premises at an extremely low rental.

Carmen explained that she would keep the cafe going, beaming across at Beth and Nathan. She had insisted they join us for coffee, waving away their protests about tidying up and washing the glasses.

"I am thinking these two lovely ones will help me."

Beth and Nathan immediately gave their enthusiastic agreement.

"You can change the name to Carmen's Cafe," I suggested.

"That is a good idea you make," agreed Carmen. "Rocky, he call it 'La Cucina di Rocco'. That is false. No?"

"False?" I wasn't sure what she meant.

"Rocco, it is not Rocky's name." She wagged a finger in disapproval. "It is not good to use the name that belongs to someone else."

Dusty and I looked at each other and laughed. Neither of us dared to point out to Carmen the irony of her statement.

The memory brought a smile to my lips now as I gazed out at the Coral Sea.

"I've accepted that my mother is dead." Dusty's eyes followed a catamaran returning from a day out on the Reef. "I know the DNA results will just be a formality."

I didn't know how to respond to those softly spoken words. "Will you go back to Claigan now that we've finished here in Port? To work with Ken on your mother's case?"

Dusty shook her head firmly.

"Ken is one of the best detectives I know. He wants to find out who killed my mother almost as much as I do. Besides, he promised that if it got to the point where he felt they had the guilty person but didn't have enough evidence to make an arrest, he'd call me in as a consultant to help close the case. I'll go to Claigan though; to see Uncle. He doesn't know about the latest development in my mother's case yet."

Even though she had had the dizzy distraction of re-igniting her relationship with Jake, it must have been difficult for her to carry a burden of sadness the whole time we'd been here. She had not allowed it to show or to interfere with her determination to solve Ram's murder. When I acknowledged this, she dismissed it with one of her characteristic cheeky grins.

"You've gotta be tough when you grow up in the bush." By 'bush' she meant her hometown in the far east of Victoria.

"By the way," I said, "how come the police report didn't mention a footprint had been found at Ram's murder scene?"

"Oh, didn't I say?" She affected an air of innocence. "No foot
print was found at the murder scene." She grinned at me. "The
mould was made after the police retrieved Rocky's shoes from the
water. I must have forgotten to mention that to Rocky."

"And to me!"

"Because I know how you love surprises."

I don't have any particular affection for surprises but Dusty insisted I did.

A boisterous group of children raced past us to the water's edge.
Smiling after them, Dusty suggested a walk.

"One thing puzzles me," I said as we strolled along the footpath.
"Why did Rocky come here to the hometown of the real Rocky?
Surely, he risked being exposed as an imposter."

"Not really. When he was Lena, he was close to the real Rocky
and would have learned that Mr and Mrs Tibaldi, the people most
likely to unmask him, had died in a car crash. Lena probably had
enough information about the real Rocky and the people he knew
when he lived in Port Douglas as a child to know there was little risk
of being found out."

"But he could have chosen to live anywhere."

Dusty looked at me thoughtfully. "You have enjoyed a lifetime in
a close and secure family environment so it would be hard for you to
understand the desolation someone might feel without a family. Think
about Lena's situation. By not believing her when she revealed she'd
been the victim of sexual abuse, her family hadn't supported her when
she needed it most. Then Lena suffered the turmoil of a gender
identity crisis. Imagine how dispossessed and alone she must have felt.
It's no wonder she, I mean he, gravitated to a place where he would
find warmth and acceptance in the form of old school friends of the
real Rocky and local people who knew the Tibaldi family."

I was still mulling that over when there on the footpath we saw the
name *Ellen* in familiar calligraphy.

"Now that's a mystery that hasn't been solved," said Dusty, as we
stepped over it.

"These people might know." I pointed to a sign ahead which read *Old Court House* with the subheading *Douglas Shire Historical Society*.

Surrounded by a white picket fence, the Old Court House was a simple timber cottage with verandahs on all sides supported by white posts. Sitting on the front verandah in an old fashioned rocking chair which was moving slowly back and forth was an elderly man, eyes closed.

"Seems a shame to disturb him," whispered Dusty as she pushed open the gate.

As we approached, the chair stopped rocking. The man's eyes opened. He sat up and greeted us amiably.

When we asked the man if he knew who Ellen was, he pointed to a rack of books near the door. "Top shelf. Book with the brown cover."

A grim-faced woman, wearied by a troubled life and aged by hard work stared out from the cover of the book.

"That's Ellen. Ellen Thomson. The woman who brought an end to capital punishment in Queensland."

"Was she an activist?"

"She was hanged."

Dusty frowned. "That's an awful irony if she campaigned against capital punishment."

"She didn't campaign. She and her lover were hanged in 1887 for the murder of Ellen's husband."

"How did she bring about the end to capital punishment in Queensland?"

"They'd never hanged a woman in this state before Ellen Thomson. It was a pretty gruesome hanging. People were so outraged a public campaign against hanging began. As a result, in 1922 Queensland became the first place in the British Commonwealth to end capital punishment."

"So who's writing her name on the footpath?" I asked.

He shrugged. "Never seen him myself. Some say he claims to be a descendant of Ellen's and wants her to have a posthumous pardon."

He jabbed a finger at the cover of the book Dusty was now holding in her hand.

"She was only in her early forties. Had a half a dozen children. Poor woman." He looked at me. "Came from your neck of the woods, she did. She was only a kid when the family came to Australia in 1858."

"Why does her descendant think she should be pardoned?"

"The trial was a joke. She should never have been convicted." The historian shook his head in disgust. "Not only that. On the eve of her execution her lover admitted he was responsible for the murder. He told the authorities Ellen had nothing to do with it, which is what she'd said all along. You know what they did? They went ahead and hanged her anyway."

We could have heard a lot more about the hanging of Ellen Thomson but Dusty interrupted the loquacious Court House historian to buy a copy of the book and we made a hasty retreat.

CHAPTER 48

MY PLANE HAS landed at Melbourne Airport. Along with all the other passengers who've flown down from Cairns, I'm waiting to disembark. People are stretching as they rise from their seats to retrieve their bags from the overhead lockers. My Thunderbird, like Dusty's FJ Holden, was being trucked back. Dusty had taken a flight to Sydney for a brief stopover to meet with an old school friend.

Our last day in Port had been spent on a luxury sailing catamaran. Dusty had rebooked the trip that had been cancelled the day Joyce arrived. "I promised you a relaxing day on the water. I always keep my promises."

I should have told her then about Ingrid. Instead, I told her I was part Australian. Since our last case, I'd managed to do some family research. As well as Irish and English ancestry, my mother's family had Australian genes through my mother's great grandmother.

At my mother's request, I tracked down some distant cousins in Australia. I have connected with them on social media but have not yet organised any face to face meetings. To tell you the truth, I don't see the point; we're all strangers to each other after all. Besides, I'm enjoying the opportunity of being free of family expectations and commitments. Since leaving Ireland, I've discovered I like being a free spirit.

Dusty was delighted when I told her of my family link to Australia.

She had grinned and said, "I'll have to step up my efforts to Aussify you."

I'm hardly aware of my surroundings as I accept the farewell smiles of the flight attendants and leave the plane. Inside the airport, I head towards the arrivals area.

Earlier today, at Cairns Airport, Dusty and I lingered over coffee in the departures lounge while waiting for our respective flights.

"A drongo," I said with a sideways glance at Dusty. "Is that like, someone who gets chased by a cassowary?" I had searched the internet and found out that 'drongo' is Australian slang for a silly person. The spangled drongo acquired the name because it's a bit of an avian comedian.

Dusty laughed, her eyes shining with merriment. "No. Someone who escapes from a cassowary is a smart person." Her expression became serious. "A drongo is someone who tries to recapture the past."

It took me a moment before I realised what she meant.

"You and Jake?"

She inclined her head in agreement. "Yes. Me and Jake. You can't go back." The public address system announced her flight was ready for boarding.

My timing might not have been the best, but that's when I told Dusty about Ingrid. I fancied I saw a fleeting flash of disappointment in her eyes. However, she wished me well with much warmth and expressed a desire to meet Ingrid.

As I emerge into the arrivals hall, I see Ingrid looking captivating in a powder blue woollen jumper and jeans. She is scanning the faces of the people coming through the revolving doors. When our eyes meet, her face lights up.

About the Author

BRIGID GEORGE is the pseudonym of JB Rowley – author of *Whisper My Secret, Mother of Ten* (both Amazon #1 Best Sellers) and the children's series *Trapped in Gondwana*. Why Brigid George? Brigid because that was what JB's father called her. George because that was his first name.

JB Rowley grew up in a small Australian town called Orbost in the state of Victoria. She spent her childhood chasing snakes and lizards down hollow logs, playing Hansel and Gretel in the bush with her brothers, climbing trees, searching the local rubbish tip for books to read and generally behaving like a feral child. To avoid her boisterous brothers she often escaped into the hayshed with a book. Hours and hours of reading from an early age trained her for life as a writer. In primary school her teachers called her 'the one with the Enid Blyton touch'. Her love of reading murder mysteries as an adult has now evolved into a love of writing them.

As a teenager JB had short stories published in one of Australia's national magazines, *New Idea*. Since then she has won several awards for her stories which have also been published in anthologies.

Visit the website of Brigid George.

www.brigidgeorge.com

Visit the website of JB Rowley for more information about her books.

www.whispermysecret.weebly.com

Further information:

While the story of Ellen Thomson is a true story, the idea of writing Ellen as footpath calligraphy was inspired by Arthur Stace who, for almost forty years of his life until he died in 1967, wrote *Eternity* in elegant copperplate on footpaths and walls all around Sydney.

Although the book is set in Port Douglas, the following locations are fictional:

Four Mile Resort

Rocky's Cafe

Alexandra Retirement Village

Sunyarta Sanctuary: You can enjoy spectacular views at the top of the hill in Port Douglas, but you won't see a forest monastery.

Glossary:

Thongs: sandals known in the UK and USA as flip-flops.

Akubra hats: (Akubra is pronounced 'UH – koo – bra') Iconic wide brimmed felt hats made in Australia.

Bathers: a piece of clothing worn for swimming aka bathing suit, swimmers, swimsuit, togs.

Bikie: a member of a gang of motorcyclists.

Bludger: a lazy person who avoids working or doing their fair share of work.

Smoko: a break from work to have a coffee or to smoke a cigarette.

Tradie: a tradesman or tradeswoman such as a plumber or electrician.

Wanker: someone who thinks too much of themselves. Often used in a light-hearted way but can also be used as a derogatory term.

Yellow-bellied dingo: coward.

Measurement conversion

1 inch = 2.54cm

One foot = 30.48cm

One kilometre = 0.62 miles

Review the book

If you have time to post a review after you read the book, that would be enormously helpful. Just one or two lines is all you need to write.

A free gift for you

Go here to enter your details and receive a free booklet. Includes exclusive free story: (a locked room mystery) and exclusive interview with Dusty Kent.

www.brigidgeorge.com/free-booklet.html

Preview Book #5

Tooting Moon

A beautiful Hollywood star drowns in the Indian Ocean. Was it a tragic accident or a wicked murder?

An Agatha Christie style murder mystery set in Australia.

In one of Brigid George's most ingenious mysteries, Dusty Kent must expose a killer of women.

Beautiful Tiri Welsh and her husband Blake Montgomery were iconic Hollywood stars adored by millions around the world. All that changed one dark night in the Indian Ocean, when Tiri drowned under mysterious circumstances. The truth behind her death was never uncovered.

For seventeen years, Tiri's sister fought tirelessly to expose Montgomery as his wife's murderer. Finally, she turns to Dusty Kent

Dusty travels to Broome, Western Australia where the actor now lives aboard his private yacht. She is immediately suspicious of Blake Montgomery, suspecting his urbane charm hides a sinister side. However, to get to the truth, Tiri's is not the only mysterious death Dusty will need to solve.

Dedication

The Dusty Kent series is dedicated to my father, George Rowley; a good man who died too young.

Disguising Demons *is dedicated to my 'pommie parents' Sylvia and Eric Barnes who loved Port Douglas.*

Acknowledgements

My deepest appreciation to crime fiction editor Lisanne Radice who has been generous with her time and caring in her guidance.

BB eBooks has provided spectacular service and impeccable formatting for all of the Dusty Kent books and several of my other books.

Yocla Book Cover Designs provided the sensational cover.

Team Dusty, including Kay Wee and Claudette D'Cruz who travelled to Port Douglas with me to help research the setting – twice!

I am deeply grateful to my beta readers (Anita Marshall, Gael Cresp, Judi Hillyear and Sheila O'Shea) whose invaluable feedback gave the manuscript its final polish.

Douglas Shire Historical Society.

Maria Bianco who generously shared her local knowledge.

Thank you also to the 'informal consultants' who have helped in so many ways. Some have offered information; some have suggested excellent ideas while others have assisted with research and/or acted as my personal assistant.

Friends and family members as well as the Friday Writers and the Writers' Lunch Group continue to provide invaluable feedback and support.

My heartfelt appreciation to all those who have read my other books and made wonderful comments that have validated and encouraged me as a writer.

Made in the USA
Middletown, DE
29 November 2022